DIVIDED WE STAND

William de Berg

ISBN: 978-1-4907-8503-5 (sc)
ISBN: 978-1-4907-8505-9 (hc)
ISBN: 978-1-4907-8504-2 (e)

Library of Congress Control Number: 2017915008

Trafford rev. 10/19/2017

 www.trafford.com

North America & international
toll-free: 1 888 232 4444 (USA & Canada)
fax: 812 355 4082

Where the people fear the government you have tyranny. Where the government fears the people you have liberty.

—John Basil Barnhill, 1914

We will NOT obey orders to impose martial law or a "state of emergency" on a state, or to enter with force into a state, without the express consent and invitation of that state's legislature and governor.

—Oath Keepers website

Enrique Ybarra (USA) Service History

2002 – (Commissioned: Second Lieutenant)

2002 – Fort Benning, GA (Basic Officer Training)

2002–2003 – Fort Hood, TX (First Cavalry Division, Promoted: First Lieutenant)

2003–2004 – Iraq (First Cavalry Division, Ninth Cavalry Regiment)

2005 – Fort Benning, GA (Bradley Leadership Course, Promoted: Captain)

2005–2006 – Fort Hood (First Cavalry Division)

2006–2007 – Tal Afar, Iraq (First Cavalry Division, Third Cavalry Regiment)

2007–2010 – Pentagon, Washington DC (Army Acquisition Command, Promoted: Major)

2010–2011 – Fort Leavenworth, KS (Army General Staff College)

2011–2013 – Kabul, Afghanistan (International Security Assistance Force)

2013–2015 – Fort Hood, TX (Promoted: Lieutenant Colonel)

2015–2016 – Carlisle, PA (Army War College)

2016–2017 – The Hague, NATO Headquarters (Promoted: Colonel)

2017–2019 – Kosovo (Commander, Camp Bondsteel)

2019–2020 – Washington DC, Pentagon (Secretary of the Army)

2020–2021 – Fort Hood, TX (Deputy Commander, Third Corps, Promoted: Brigadier General)

2022–2023 – Fort Riley, KS (Commander, First Infantry Division)

2023–2024 – Fort Hood, TX (Commander, First Cavalry Division, Promoted: Major General)

PART I

CHAPTER 1

The heroin that entered Benito Ybarra's veins was nearing the end of its long journey across thousands of miles and dozens of places. It started out as a latex film on the inside of the bulb of an opium poppy plant, growing under the shadows of an ensemble of brilliant red petals. It was meticulously scraped from the plant and dried to a paste by a woman sweltering in a hijab in the fertile Helmand Valley of Eastern Afghanistan who received less than a dollar per gram from her tribal chief for her backbreaking work. It was then sold by the local khan to smugglers who moved it across Iran to Turkey, where ethnic Albanian gangs formerly of the Kosovo Liberation Army moved it across to a lab south of Tirana, Albania, where the morphine was extracted from the opium and mixed with acetic anhydride to form the heroin. Once refined, the white powder was shipped at night in a fishing trawler to the Calabrian coast near Catanzaro, where it was stored while awaiting transit to its next destination. A few weeks later, the powder was hidden in the gas tank of an automobile transported in a large container ship leaving the port of Reggio—the same ship that had on its prior voyage carried cocaine from the Americas inserted into melons and bananas—and headed for Lagos, Nigeria. There, it was removed from the unloaded car and placed among the personal hygiene items in the luggage of a courier leaving Lagos bound for Houston. Upon his arrival, an independent drug-smuggling operation transported it to San Antonio, where a local hustler started distributing among his friends—one of them being Bennie Ybarra—for over fifty dollars per gram.

Although he had been shooting up on and off for almost ten years, Bennie knew almost nothing about this extraordinary heroin odyssey, nor did he know the details of the heroin's final voyage once it had been mixed with water and dissolved and injected into his veins—the passage through the endothelial cells known as the blood-brain barrier and into the brainstem, limbic system, and hypothalamus, where it entered hundreds of millions of synapses and began interacting with kappa-, delta-, and mu-opioid receptors. He had no idea of the extent to which these receptors in his brain had been desensitized over the years, requiring ever larger amounts of heroin to provide the "fix" needed for him to function but that now, in the new environment of his friend's house, were giving him the full-blown effects of the drug.[1]

As he slowly pressed down on the syringe, gradually easing the dope into his right median cubital vein, all he knew was that the white powder he bought felt damn good—a little more potent but a lot cleaner than the black tar shit coming from Mexico that he usually injected and that turned his veins dark and ugly. It was also more expensive, but the high was worth it. Actually, nowadays it was less about the high and incredible feeling that he felt in the early days of shooting up and more about the relief from the horrible physical and psychic pains of withdrawal—depression and anxiety and physical symptoms that rivaled the worst flu imaginable . . . on steroids.

****

Bennie Ybarra was the last of three brothers born to George and Maria Ybarra. George was a multigenerational San Antonian whose father had worked as a machinist at Kelly Field at the outset

---

1   Tolerance to drugs can be conditioned to a particular environment. In the new environment or with a new method of administration, cues that ordinarily would reduce the effect of the drugs are no longer present, and a much more powerful effect occurs (https://psysci.com/2012/11/06/classical-conditioning-of-drug-tolerance).

of World War II, while Maria's family immigrated to San Antonio from Jalisco when she was in late elementary school. They started dating at Jefferson High School but delayed their marriage until after Vietnam, where George served in the air force as the war was winding down. George was stationed at bases all over the world and eventually made it to chief master sergeant before retiring. Maria had mostly Nahua ancestry and was a very religious woman who was close to her family and mainly looked after the kids while they were growing up. She was delighted when George agreed to settle back in San Antonio.

George was in his late twenties when his first son, Enrique, was born, but he was pushing forty years old and already showing impending signs of diabetes when Bennie was born. Bennie was ten years younger than his oldest brother and six years younger than his other brother, Carlos. Enrique was a star athlete and solid student at Balcones Heights High, whereas Carlos—who everyone called Flaco because he was all skin and bones—was much more gifted academically, showing an early mastery of writing and history. Bennie didn't relate as well to Enrique, given their large age difference and the fact that Enrique seemed to be following in the footsteps of his dad, displaying the same discipline and military bent that George Ybarra prided himself on. Bennie mainly tagged along with Carlos, with whom he shared the same freethinking and rebellious nature, which led to a lot of kidding around as well as more than a few one-sided fights.

The problem with Bennie was the typical "third-child" syndrome among same-sexed offspring, especially when there is a large age gap separating the second and third. Although no parent publicly admits it, the first child is typically taken in by one of the parents—in Enrique's case, by his dad—while the second child often becomes the greater purview of the other parent. In Bennie's eyes, Carlos always seemed to get a pass from Maria, who doted on him despite the clash between her strong Catholic background and his freethinking, even radical views. No one claimed or seemed to notice Bennie as much, and the fact that his parents were already

5

burned out and graying after raising two other teenage boys only compounded the problem.

Everyone said Bennie was funny and smart, even smarter than his two accomplished brothers, but that he was at times too smart for his own good. Bennie breezed through all his elementary and middle school honors classes while barely cracking a book, but the seeds for his later self-destructiveness were being planted even back then. Carlos managed to keep him in check for a while, but after he went off to college at the beginning of Bennie's seventh-grade year, the negative transformation began to take hold. Bennie started to hang out with his friends even late into weeknight hours, his cleverness ensuring he rarely got caught. He started smoking weed, tagging some of the nearby business, and even took part in a little petty shoplifting on occasion. By the end of middle school, Bennie and some of his friends started mixing with a local gang, the MVKs. The MVKs were considered a minor-league gang, like La Treces, the BTKs (Big Time Kings), and countless others throughout the downtown and surrounding San Antonio neighborhoods. They were composed of young teens mostly into drinking and partying and creating minor mayhem, and they might even act as drug runners for one of the larger gangs, but they weren't into guns, mostly just fists and knives.

San Antonio was also a hub for "major league" gangs like the Mexican Mafia, Tango Orejons, and Texas Syndicate, which were involved in much of the drug trafficking in South Texas.[2] Although renowned for its famous tourist attractions, such as the Alamo, Riverwalk, and Spanish missions, San Antonio had been, for decades, a major transit point for drugs—mainly cocaine and black tar heroin—flowing north from Mexico into the rest of the United States. It lay at the intersection of three

---

2   See U.S. Department of Justice, "South Texas High Intensity Drug Trafficking Area: Drug Market Analysis 2011" (2011-R0813-031). See also http://www.breitbart.com/big-government/2016/03/09/loretta-lynch-admits-mexican-border-a-major-shipping-point-for-heroin-and-cocaine   https://en.wikipedia.org/wiki/Los_Zetas.

major interstate highways and was only two and a half hours from Nuevo Laredo, the capital of the violent Zeta cartel. The Zetas, originally composed of Mexican army deserters, had shot and stabbed and beheaded their way into becoming the most powerful cartel in Mexico, arguably in all Latin America.[3] Under the aegis of the Zetas, drugs, human sex workers, illegal immigrants, and various other varieties of nonhuman contraband sneaked across the overstretched Texas–Mexico border. The vast majority of illegal black tar heroin and cocaine arriving in the United States came from Mexico,[4] and a large share of that traffic was transported by Los Zetas and their allies across the Rio Grande in every manner imaginable—from inside gas tanks, tires, wheelchair cushions, even breast implants—before moving along Interstate 35 (the "Narco Highway"), Interstate 10, and other major arteries all coalescing in San Antonio.[5] South Texas politicians acted like the cartels stopped at the border, but everyone knew that the huge drug shipments arriving every day at the border didn't end up disbursed across the urban landscape of America by magic. San Antonio law enforcement agencies would periodically spread a dragnet over the city and arrest a few dozen gang members involved in the drug trade, but they mostly looked the other way as long the drugs flowed through the city while the drug money itself flowed into the San Antonio economy—propping up restaurants, supporting new luxury car dealerships springing up over the northern suburbs,

---

3   https://en.wikipedia.org/wiki/Los_Zetas.

4   http://www.businessinsider.com/us-heroin-coming-from-mexican-cartels.

5   http://www.uncut-reports.com/2013/02/interstate-35-narco-corridor.html; http://www.uncut-reports.com/2014/04/i-35-major-artery-to-nations-drug-trade.html.

and paying for expensive homes in gated developments like the Dominion and Stone Oak.[6]

As he progressed through high school, Bennie could no longer fake it as a student. His grades began to slip on all the late and missing work, and he dropped all but one of his advanced placement courses. George Ybarra was getting more than a little irritated with him, but Bennie would always turn to his mother and manage to eke out her leniency, at least as long he showed up for Mass once in a while and continued to attend his communion classes. Some of his friends in the MVKs, mostly the ones from the broken homes who were doing poorly in school and planning to drop out, started to matriculate to the larger gangs. The Mexican Mafia (La Eme), in particular, appealed to Mexican-American warrior pride, claiming with dubious historicity that South Texans were the first Aztecas and that San Antonio was the site of Aztlan, the mythical Aztec capital before the Aztecs left for Tenochtitlan, the site of present-day Mexico City.[7] Bennie held back, knowing the reputation of the Mexican Mafia, which one supposedly joined and left by the same route—*la muerta*. One night, while cruising through the West Side with a friend who had already begun the process of joining up with La Eme, Bennie was startled when his friend pulled up to a traffic light and shots rang out, grazing the car and shattering a window. It was at that moment that Bennie knew he was getting in way too deep, and he quickly decided to reorient his life.

Unfortunately, by then, he had already had his first black tar heroin hit courtesy of one of the MVKs' weekend parties. Not long afterward, he started craving the sensation he felt—the warmth, euphoria, and freedom, however transient, from all bodily

6   www.johntedesco.net/blog/2012/04/19/how-mexican-cartels-launder-drug-money-in-san-antonio-hint-check-the-north-side;   http://www.mysanantonio.com/news/lol_news/article/S-A-ties-to-drug-cash-detailed-3483020.php.

7   http://www.ksat.com/news/texas-mexican-mafia-has-deep-roots-planted-in-san-antonio.

discomfort. Although he dropped out of the MVKs, he still went to some of his friends' MVK parties, mainly for the free heroin they were offering. He realized he needed money to support his new drug habit, and he started working at a fast-food restaurant near his high school. He struggled to eventually finish high school, but afterward, he faced the depressing realization that his life had started to revolve around a costly cycle of hits, withdrawals, and cravings, with the withdrawals becoming steadily more painful and the cravings stronger. He enrolled in a local community college for a couple of courses just to keep his parents off his back, but he was working forty—sometimes even more—hours a week just to pay for his hits. And he started to wear longer shirts to disguise the increasing number of injections he was making in his arms.

Then Bennie heard from a friend about some hiring going on in the oil fields south of San Antonio. The Eagle Ford shale was a large oil play made possible through the combination of hydraulic fracturing (a decades-old technique) and horizontal drilling (a more recent phenomenon). The tight oil in the horizontal shale seams could be unlocked by blowing the seams apart with the horizontal fracking, and beginning around 2009, a new oil boom was taking place in South Texas. [8] A classic Texas oil boom is always characterized by three stages: jobs at first for almost anyone who can move his or her arms and legs and doesn't have a serious criminal background, a belief the boom will never end, and the inevitable bust that follows. In the end, little is left of the boom except a lot of used Mercedes driving on potholed roads past boarded-up businesses and cars with bumper stickers that read "Please, God, give us another boom . . . We promise we won't screw it up next time." Bennie got hired, with minimal training, as a flowback operator recording initial well flows, making eighteen bucks an hour, 24/7. Not only could he afford regular heroin binges, but he bought a brand-new off-road pickup as well. Of course, there was always the problem of a failed drug test, but the nice thing about heroin was that it cleared within a few days,

---

8   https://en.wikipedia.org/wiki/Eagle_Ford_Group.

and he had a week off every other week so he could binge. While he was working, he was careful and would try to make do with some prescription painkillers, but he would feel lousy even a few days into his shift. Bennie knew he had to eventually get off the dope, but like all young addicts, he didn't really think beyond the immediate horizon, with each paycheck coming and going and his tiny savings never seeming to grow.

It turned out that Bennie didn't make it to the end of the boom. It wasn't even him that the undercover sting operation was after, but he got swept up by the random drug test he wasn't expecting, and his days in the oil patch were over. That didn't mean he was unemployable, but there was no way he was ever going to be able to earn anywhere near that kind of money legally again without a college degree. So he went back to live with his parents and tried to make do with low-pay temporary jobs such as warehousing, driving cars at auctions, and day-labor construction jobs. He started distributing meth, cocaine, and heroin for a friend who would then pay off the Mexican Mafia to operate as an independent dealer. But it wasn't long before his friend was arrested for dealing. When the police found that Bennie was a cell phone contact, had access to his friend's apartment, and had needles in his possession, he was slapped with a one-year charge for constructive possession. Bennie quickly pleaded *nolo contendere*, but because it was his first criminal arrest, he was placed on probation and sent to drug treatment, managing to remain clean for the remainder of his sentence.

One month into his probation, Bennie landed a construction job with the help of a friend. He earned only a few dollars above the minimum wage, but he was able to save enough of the pittance to pay off his lawyers. After leaving the halfway house, he took out a loan to resume his studies while living at home, a situation his father reluctantly acceded to. He managed to get through an additional year of college, riding the bus to classes now that his fancy pickup had been repossessed. He even developed a steady relationship with Mercedes Garcia, a former classmate from Balcones Heights who was in her last year of nursing school. He seemed determined to remain clean, the horrible memory of his last detox seared in his mind.

But like so many other heroin addicts, Bennie found it easier to dream about the future than escape the past. He was back working construction in the summer break between classes when, after stopping for a couple of beers at a nearby bar one Saturday night, he ran into one of his old friends from the MVKs. After a few reminiscences, they went back to his friend's apartment, and Bennie stared in disbelief when his friend pulled out some white powder and offered it to him. What for a normal person should have been an easy call turned into a fateful, eventually fatal mistake on Bennie's part. Someone who isn't an addict doesn't realize how easy it is to condition the opiate craving to all sorts of things, whether it be the image of the powder or tar, the image of a friend's face, almost anything. Nor can they appreciate how powerful that craving can be, even after years of staying clean.

Bennie took in the dope that night, and the next morning he woke up and finally realized that he wasn't just clever—he was self-destructively clever. In an instant, he had thrown away nearly two years of recovery, two years of a heartfelt attempt to build a normal, clean future. He now despaired that he couldn't hold back his cravings any longer. Within weeks, he was regularly smoking heroin, looking for his next hit, working any jobs—even illicit ones—to feed his addiction. He started moving down on the hierarchy of needs pyramid, his self-esteem and desire for human affiliation replaced by the daily grime of survival, anything to ward off the demons of withdrawal.[9] He sensed that this time there would be no second chances, that he was going to hit rock bottom and perhaps never get up again. Still, he couldn't manage to slay the cravings inside.

---

9   The "hierarchy of needs" is a psychological concept put forth by Abraham Maslow, which starts with physiological/survival needs and steadily works up through different stages to the final stage of self-actualization: http://www.simplypsychology.org/maslow.html.

Then on his final night on Earth, he injected this incredibly potent white powder with a "friend" who was working with a Nigerian courier and had invited him over for the first time. Bennie had no idea that its potency would be augmented because the familiar environmental cues that conditioned his tolerance and reduced his neural firing when the heroin started invading his endorphin synapses were all absent that night. Without telling his parents or girlfriend or brothers or anyone else who cared about him, Bennie Ybarra slipped off into the most amazing sensation he had ever had in his life—a warm, floating sensation that has been described at its best as a "hug from God." He never felt his heart stop and died with a peaceful smile on his face, the same one everyone likes to talk about at funerals when a loved one has "moved on."

Except no one talks about dying peacefully in one's sleep at the funeral of a heroin addict.

CHAPTER 2

Despite his status as a deceased heroin addict, Bennie Ybarra attracted a large gathering at his funeral. As was customary with large Mexican-American families, he had, in addition to his immediate family, two living *abuelas*, over a dozen *tias* and *tios*, and an even larger contingent of cousins. He also had a few friends from work and college as well as a few leftover ones from his MVK days and, of course, Mercedes, who had just found out she was two-months pregnant. Bennie's death came as a shock to all and a surprise to some. George Ybarra was not one of the latter, as he had unconsciously written Bennie off years earlier, notwithstanding the latter's efforts to stay clean in recent years. By contrast, Bennie's mother was almost hysterical when she viewed the body of her *mijo*, in whom she always had such great faith, even when he was disappointing her. His two older brothers' feelings lay somewhat in between those of their parents. Enrique, who left home when Bennie was about to start the third grade, had only heard bits and pieces about Bennie's drug habit and arrest, but he was too involved with his own family in recent years to give a lot of thought to his youngest brother. Carlos, who was living in Austin after graduating from the University of Texas at Austin, was much more aware of Bennie's addiction and was mostly nonjudgmental when Bennie would confide in him. He did everything he could to turn Bennie's life around, and he played a major role in getting some treatment for Bennie and helping his parents understand the nature of their youngest son's psychological malady. He was proud that Bennie had decided to return to college, but he felt a stab of betrayal when he learned of Bennie's overdose. *Dammit, Bennie! You were so smart. You could make people laugh all the time. Why couldn't you make yourself laugh in the end?*

****

After the service and burial and reception at the family home, George Ybarra grew quiet and spent the rest of the afternoon trying to comfort Maria, who held up well in front of the gathering but became distraught afterward. Enrique's wife, Monica, even though she knew that she wouldn't see much of her husband in the next several years as he was about to begin his fourth—and longest—overseas tour, decided to take the girls out to a movie, knowing that Enrique needed a long talk with his brother.

Monica Ybarra. née Cantu. still had feelings for her husband of seventeen years, but the long separations from his overseas service had strained their relationship. They had been friends at Balcones Heights High School even though they hadn't started dating until their freshman year in college. She fondly remembered Enrique as a broad-shouldered all-district linebacker and regional-class wrestler and president of the student council who, like her, took mostly advanced placement classes, especially in math and science. Enrique always struck her as more of a straight arrow than a lot of her friends. Unlike in the mostly Anglo schools in the northern suburbs, few of the students at Balcones recited the pledge of allegiance each morning; in the regular classes, some didn't even stand for it at all. But Enrique always stood straight with his hand over his heart, even muttering the pledge under his breath. He would take a mildly conservative, pro-military opinion in history and government classes, again in contrast to most of the other kids at the school. She remembered how one time, when a bunch of left-wing students tried to take down the American flag in front of the school in a political protest, Enrique led a group of football players to hoist it up again.

What Monica liked most about Enrique, though, was not just his athletic prowess or academic success: he also had a great sense of humor and an ability to make everyone feel at ease, from gangbangers to nerds. She would have dated him in high school except that her best friend was his steady, and she refused to break up that relationship, which ended in any case when Enrique went off to Texas A&M in College Station. She knew that he was going to be a leader somewhere—he had too much confidence and was too good with people not to be.

She wasn't too surprised that Enrique went to A&M because it was the most conservative public university in the state, although it had a reputation for being one of the "whitest" in the South as well, where relatively few Hispanics at that time went. She herself went to Southwest Texas State, a predominantly women's university up the road in San Marcos. When she heard about Enrique's breakup with her best friend, she made a point of contacting him that first Christmas holiday, and they started dating almost immediately thereafter. They tried to make the two-hour trip between San Marcos and College Station every other weekend, taking alternative turns on the drives. In addition to majoring in mechanical engineering, Enrique was in the A&M Corps of Cadets, the elite cadre of students at the heart of the A&M traditions, which required a considerable amount of time outside the classroom. His special unit was the Parsons Mounted Cavalry, where he learned to ride a horse with skill and fire off a cannon periodically, although his extra duties placed even further demands on his time.

Texas A&M was one of the most unique public universities in the country, once requiring military training of students but later restricting its official military regimen to only a portion of those in the Corps. Not having come from a military family, Monica wasn't really into all of the Corps traditions, but she enjoyed the occasional formal socials, and her heart always fluttered a bit when she would see Enrique in his military dress. Like a lot of the students at Southwest Texas, a former teacher's college that was partly known for being the alma mater of a young teacher who later went on the become the thirty-sixth president of the

United States,[10] Monica was studying to be an elementary school teacher. She figured she herself would never become a great leader or move about the country and the world on her own, so Enrique's military officer ambitions seemed exciting to her back then. She felt his strength when they embraced, but he never pushed her more than she wanted at the moment. He was always honest with her, and more than anyone else she had dated, he seemed genuinely interested in her own experiences and desires. She felt closest to him when they were alone together and he let his guard down. He seemed a bit rigid when he was at A&M, but when he would visit her at Southwest Texas he loosened up, and it was only natural that it would be there that they embarked on their first lovemaking.

They were married right after his graduation, but their honeymoon was brief, a few days at the Texas coast. By early June, Enrique was sent off to Fort Benning, Georgia, for the first of two basic Cavalry Officer Training courses—the second one offering specialized training in the Bradley Fighting Vehicle. Monica didn't mind her time in Georgia, where she made friends with some other young officers' wives, but it quickly became apparent that her life as a military spouse would always be on the go. In the first ten years of his army career, Enrique ended up at Fort Benning (twice), Fort Hood (twice), Fort Leavenworth, and the Pentagon, in addition to spending two tours in Iraq and one in Afghanistan. After his first Fort Benning stint, Enrique was assigned to Fort Hood as an officer in the Third Army Cavalry Regiment. It was in nearby Killeen that Monica applied and received her first teaching appointment, and it was Killen that she would ever after call "home" even though she didn't have all that much fondness for it and was frequently glad to leave it to accompany Enrique on his various stateside tours.

Monica would later marvel at Enrique's rapid progression through the ranks, with two straight below-the-zone promotions,

---

10 Lyndon Johnson was the only teacher since the 1800s to become a U.S. president, and he counted educational reforms among his signature accomplishments: http://www.ontheissues.org/Celeb/Lyndon_Johnson_Education.htm.

due to his exemplary leadership skills and valor in Iraq. She admired and respected him but worried incessantly about his safety during his overseas tours. He would tell her little about what was happening to him and his fellow soldiers, knowing she was anxious enough. But that also served as a barrier to their deeper communication and intimacy, underscoring how there would always be a large part of his life that was opaque to her. Nevertheless, two publicized episodes in which Enrique showed extraordinary leadership and bravery gave her a glimpse of the danger and chaos he regularly faced overseas.

The first of these was during his first tour, when, as a first lieutenant, his platoon was assigned to reinforce another tank unit that came under fire west of Abu Ghraib, in the heart of the Sunni tribal insurgency. Enrique led two Abrams tanks and three Bradley fighting vehicles as they left the town along the divided highway known as Route Huskies. As they made their way out of the town, fewer and fewer people were seen near the highway, and the ones who were stared silently at the platoon as it moved slowly through the outskirts of the town. Eventually, the traffic thinned, and what remained began to pull over. Enrique peered ominously outside the window of the tank, as it became so quiet outside that only the hum of the Bradley against the pavement could be heard. It was the silence before the impending attack that he and his platoons dreaded most. Once the fighting started, all the months of training and adrenaline kicked in.

Suddenly, almost out of nowhere, the platoon started taking fire from several directions. It took precious seconds to determine where the fire was coming from and several more moments for the two Abrams to set their sights on pockets of enemy soldiers in the fields. The main guns of the Abrams were deliberate but deadly, and over a period of several minutes, the fire from the fields and farmhouses began to diminish, but not before one of the Bradleys took a serious hit from a rocket-propelled grenade and caught fire. Quickly, Enrique rushed through the searing heat and rescued another first lieutenant, a sergeant, a corporal, and two privates from the damaged Bradley. They pried the rear door open and dragged out the mostly unconscious men, some laden with burns. With the medevac transport held up because of the withering ground fire, Enrique had to figure out how to transport the injured men back to the field hospital at Abu Ghraib. Quickly, he decided to remove enough armaments from one of the two intact Bradleys to accommodate the extra men. He and two enlisted men carried the five wounded men in one Bradley while two other soldiers switched to the remaining vehicle. He then commanded his Bradley back to Abu Ghraib, while the two Abrams and the other Bradley continued on. In the end, two men from the stricken Bradley later died, but one of the three who lived—First Lieutenant Travis Rackley, a good friend and fellow A&M Corps member— would forever remain indebted to his Aggie buddy as they both moved up through the ranks.

Monica was in attendance when they pinned the first Silver Star on Enrique just as she was present when they pinned his second one four years later. The latter was for an incident that had occurred during his second tour in Iraq, in Nineveh Province. Enrique, by that time, had been promoted to captain and was in charge of a company of the Third Cavalry Regiment. It had been positioned at a forward operating base near Tal Afar, where the insurgency was particularly violent and resupply convoys from Turkey were constantly being attacked. Four tankers had been struck by rocket-propelled grenades about eight kilometers northeast of the town, just after the junction with Route 1 going to Mosul. One of the Bradley escorts had also been damaged by an improvised explosive device hidden near the road. After a radio call, Enrique led two Abrams and an undermanned Bradley to the rescue, taking heavy flak as they approached the scene. As with the other firefight, the Abrams guns quickly took charge of the situation, but there was still incoming fire when Enrique left his vehicle to tend to the wounded. Two of the contractor drivers were already burned to death, but two others had managed to escape and somehow survive the assault by hiding in a nearby drainage ditch. All the damaged Bradley occupants were still alive, but some had sustained head injuries, and one was even unconscious for several minutes. Enrique later learned that the unconscious soldier was a fellow captain Terence Jackson "TJ" Matthews, the son of Army Major General Loren Matthews, who had once led the First Cavalry Division. Enrique called for a Huey and his men were all successfully evacuated, but not before Enrique himself was hit in the right shoulder by sniper fire. Once the evacuation was complete and the enemy fire had died down, Enrique's small contingent made it safely back to base. Enrique's shoulder took months to heal, and it never again would be completely free of pain.

Enrique's heroism and leadership were impressive even amid the multitude of similar exploits of junior officers throughout Iraq during the American occupation. His valor was duly noted by senior officers who rewarded Enrique with the second of his below-the-zone promotions, this time to major. Monica was truly glad for Enrique, whom she knew was a good man, but she chastised herself for not being more of a "military wife". She had come to hate war, and she hated even more the long separations that were putting a strain on their marriage. She had her own problems—corralling and instructing increasingly impulsive students every day and playing single-parent to their two daughters, who were conceived just before each of Enrique's two Iraq tours, which prevented him from being at either of their births. It was after the birth of Sydney, their second, that she developed a postpartum depression that lingered, leading her to struggle with her moods for much of the next two decades. When Enrique arrived back from his second tour, she realized he too had changed. He no longer smiled or laughed as much, and he was even uncharacteristically curt with her at times. There were even times when, late at night, he would awaken moaning and in cold sweats. Although he wouldn't divulge what his nightmare was about, it was clear that part of his unconscious was still back in the treacherous sands of Western Iraq.

Enrique was assigned to the Army Acquisition Command at the Pentagon for the next two and a half years, working mainly on the upgrade program for the Bradley, which was suffering large losses in Iraq due to the improvised explosive devices lying about everywhere. He made several well-received suggestions pertaining to the strength and materials for the armor, location of escape hatches, and other strategies to improve survivability of the crew. He also participated in initial evaluation of the MRAP armored troop carrier,[11] designed to supplement the Bradley in high-risk areas laden with explosive devices. Although some of his suggestions were not taken up—to later regret by the manufacturers—he continued to pile up decorations for his contributions to the development teams. Although he felt more bureaucratically constrained in the Pentagon than in the combat arena, his bold suggestions and overall critical thinking abilities stood out in the staid Pentagon bureaucracy and were noted by his superiors just as his field leadership had been in Iraq.

Monica had quit her job in the Killeen Independent School District, accompanying him to Northern Virginia, where they rented a house across the Potomac in Alexandria. Things were still not the same for her and Enrique, with him working long hours at the Pentagon, but she did enjoy living in the Washington metro area, where there was so much to do and history was everywhere. She helped out at the girls' preschool and did various other volunteering. When, however, Enrique was selected for army's General Staff College at Fort Leavenworth, Kansas, where he would gain his first master's degree, she decided against going with him. She did permit the girls to stay with him over the autumn months as Enrique's mother had agreed to take her place in the household, taking care of the girls.

She was fortunate to get the teaching position at her old school back, although she was transferred to the fifth grade, where the kids were more rambunctious. She was hoping that Enrique would return to her at Fort Hood, but instead he moved on to Afghanistan, where he was assigned to the headquarters staff of the International Assistance Force in Kabul. She knew his overseas

---

11 The Mine-Resistant Ambush Protected (MRAP) carrier was fielded in Iraq and Afghanistan from 2007 to 2012: https://en.wikipedia.org/wiki/MRAP.

tour would place further strain on their marriage, and she went into another mild tailspin, which she tried to hide from him.

She was relieved initially when she thought he would be mostly spending time in Kabul, and his regular Skyping to her and the girls helped. But when she found out that he was spending the majority of his time at forward operating bases in the area, which were constantly under shelling and suicide attacks, her anxiety level increased. To avoid discussing his experiences and her fears, she and Enrique engaged in mostly small talk and businesslike communication—what to do with the house, when and where to take the car in for a maintenance check, where to send the girls for after-school care, etc.

His ensuing stint in Afghanistan showed him to be in the mold of the "soldier's general"—General Omar Bradley—for whom his fighting vehicle was named.[12] In addition to helping with the training of Afghan officers and working with the First Cavalry's Fourth Combat Brigade Team (the Long Knives) at Mihtarlam and other forward operating bases to improve logistics, tactics, and leadership, he supported the general staff by consulting with junior officers in nearby provinces. On his trips to the forward bases and command posts, he would listen and take notes as the soldiers would describe what progress had been gained and, more typically, what further assistance was needed to perform their task. Field officers were pleasantly surprised at how many of their basic requests were met within a short time after his visits. He genuinely felt the pain of every injured soldier, and he vowed that good lives wouldn't be wasted for some politically relevant but militarily insignificant objective. He was blunt and tenacious, although not always politically correct, in his dismal assessment of the Afghan army's prospects and the need to change tactics on the American side.[13] One of the aims he fought for early on was to bring the

---

12   http://www.history.army.mil/brochures/bradley/bradley.htm.

13   Enrique's fictional assessment of the capabilities of the Afghan army seems to be confirmed by actual analysis: https://sputniknews.com/military/201606111041166692-afghanistan-army-us.

infantrymen into more defensible positions—too many were being lost in remote outposts that were designed to bolster the American government's facade that every inch of Afghan territory was under the control of the government. Some outposts had already been abandoned,[14] but as Enrique's more extensive recommendations were adopted and large sections of the eastern provinces were either ceded to the Taliban or transferred to the Afghan army, American deaths started to decline. For his service in Afghanistan, the higher-ups gave Enrique another award—the Meritorious Service Medal—that led to yet another below-the-zone promotion to lieutenant colonel after only twelve years of service, which was extraordinary in an era where some of the best junior officers continued to languish without support from their commanders. Few among the junior officers and enlisted soldiers he dealt with objected to his meteoric rise, as his growing legend far transcended any medals or promotions. Everyone knew it wouldn't be Enrique's last promotion, that he was headed for far bigger commands in the United States Army someday.

When Enrique returned to Fort Hood, Monica had even more trouble than before connecting with him, and she surprised him by requesting that they attend marital counseling. By the end of the year, though, she was once again at his side during his promotion ceremony, performing dutifully as the supportive wife receiving her bouquet of roses. During his eighteen months at Fort Hood, Monica and Enrique worked hard through counseling and other means to regain some of the intimacy that had been lost during his long overseas career, and a sense of normalcy returned to their lives. By the end of the middle of the next summer, Enrique was selected to attend the Army War College in Carlisle, Pennsylvania, and Monica and the girls once again picked up their roots. Being selected for the school basically meant that it wouldn't be long before he was selected for colonel, which she desperately hoped would mark the pinnacle of his army career and, within a few short

---

14   http://www.nytimes.com/2010/04/15/world/asia/15outpost.html?_r=0.

years, be followed by retirement. Then perhaps she could finally relax and enjoy the stable family life she longed for.

Carlisle was a historic town, scenically nestled at the foothills of the Appalachians, a half hour west of Harrisburg. It hosted Dickinson College, one of the oldest colleges in the United States, and the Army War College, located on the grounds of the old Carlisle Indian College, an abandoned experiment in the assimilation of Native Americans that did, however, produce one famous legacy—the world's greatest athlete, Jim Thorpe.[15] While Enrique studied for his second master's degree in strategic studies, Monica enjoyed playing stay-at-home mom again and helping out at the girls' schools, with Sofia having entered her second year of middle school and Sydney still in elementary school. Enrique had majored in engineering at A&M but now reconnected with some of his previous interest in history, commensurate with the realization of how important a knowledge of geopolitical affairs was as he rose to a senior officer rank. One thing they managed to do as a family was horseback riding, which Enrique hadn't done since his A&M Corps days, and even Monica rode for the first time in her life at a nearby farm situated at the base of the Tuscarora National Forest. She even managed a little wobbly skiing at a couple of resorts in the Allegheny mountains during the long winter, but although Enrique and the girls seemed to take to it, she found the downhill slopes a little too hairy for her tastes.

When the news came for Enrique's next assignment, Monica's mood turned dark once more, this time requiring a prescription for antidepressants that she hid from Enrique. He would spend eight months at NATO headquarters in the Hague, serving as a NATO attaché, and receive his expected promotion to full colonel—that she could handle. But it was understood that his promotion and involvement with the international organization were merely preludes to his next assignment after that—commanding the largest American army base between Italy and the Persian Gulf, Camp Bondsteel in Kosovo, for a minimum of two years. Monica

---

15   https://en.wikipedia.org/wiki/Carlisle_Indian_Industrial_School.

and the girls would spend the summer in the Netherlands, traveling partly on their own as far south as Paris and as far north as Amsterdam, but then they returned to the States for the beginning of Sofia's eighth-grade year. While her mother could help take care of the girls, Monica didn't know if their marriage could take yet another long forced separation after that, since families were not allowed at Bondsteel. Though she could return to their old house in Killeen, even her old job with the Killeen Independent District was in jeopardy, as she was informed just before returning from the Netherlands that there were no immediate openings at her old school and that she would have to apply to other schools in the district without a guarantee of a position.

Then to make matters worse, right before they were to move from Carlisle to Holland, sudden word of the death of Enrique's brother arrived, which stunned both of them.

CHAPTER 3

Carlos and Enrique sat a table near the bar of a pub off Interstate 10, a few miles north of the church they had attended every Sunday with their parents and Bennie and where they had grown up playing Catholic youth sports year-round. They hadn't seen each other in almost a year since Enrique left for the Army War College. Enrique bought the first round and quickly started draining his Coors Light.

"Man, it's great to see you again, Carlos," he said as he bumped his fist to his brother's.

"The same, bro!"

"Seems like you're doing well in Austin. I read your stuff now and then on the Internet—you're really a great writer, Flaco. I wish I had your talent in that area. I was always good at math, but I never felt that strong at writing. Fortunately, Monica was able to help me with some of my grad papers."

"Yeah, how is it—or was it—up there? Monica and the girls liking it?"

"It's been pretty good. All of them have been having a good time—they really dug seeing the snow, and we've even gone skiing a few times. Of course, there're only a couple of places nearby that serve even halfway-decent enchiladas."

"I'm sure you've been to places with worse ones."

Enrique smiled and then turned to Carlos. "Yeah, and I may be going to another one . . . for a long while. You know about Kosovo?"

"Of course, all that shit Clinton and his gang pulled back in the '90s to break up Serbia and get rid of Milosevic? I bet Monica isn't thrilled about heading there."

"She's even less thrilled because she *can't* go there—no wives allowed at Camp Bondsteel, the base I'll be commanding there."

"So you'll be apart for up to three years?"

"Hopefully, not any more than that." Enrique glanced about at the bar television that showed some hockey action on ESPN, and then he quickly changed the subject. "So how about you . . . You ready to settle down?"

"Not quite. You know Austin's a singles town. Everyone's having too much fun hangin' out together. Why spoil it with marriage and kids, huh, Enrique?"

Carlos's good-natured gloat wasn't lost on Enrique, who showed his irritation before again abruptly changing the subject. "So what the hell do you think happened to Bennie? You've always been closer to him. I know he had way too much *chulo* in him, but I thought he was starting to get his act together."

"So did I. He seemed to be going straight . . . Mercedes seemed to have been a good influence on him. I don't believe in that shit about 'once an addict, always an addict'—it wasn't so much the drug addiction he couldn't escape as his friends who got him started in the first place. But it might have happened again later on. Bennie always thought he could beat the odds, but in the end, it was all a bunch of *chorrada*."

"I just can't believe it. I know we're different, but we both succeeded in our different ways. Bennie had a lot going for him, but it doesn't seem like he saw us as role models at all."

"We were too separated in age. His role models were his peers, and that was his biggest problem."

"And what about his kid? I don't know even if it's gonna be a boy or girl. Did he even let anyone know Mercedes was pregnant?"

"Not me. Maybe he didn't even know himself."

"Shit, I never thought I'd be an uncle for the first time to someone I might never know. Do you think Mercedes will ever let us see the kid?"

"I don't know. She's probably feeling pretty upset right now. I understand your situation, what with your own family and you moving all over the place. But I'm just up the road and hope to stay a part of the kid's life . . . if she'll let me."

"So how do you figure Mom and Pops are taking it?"

"I don't know about Pops so much since he always considered Bennie a pain in the ass, but I think Mom's really feeling a lot of hurt inside."

"Yeah, for sure. Mom always had a soft spot for Bennie, her *mijo*, despite his shit."

Enrique quickly ordered another round, and Carlos stepped into pay even though he hadn't finished his own beer.

Changing the subject, Carlos asked, "I hope you don't mind me asking, Kiki, but I've always wondered how you could stay in the military so long. I personally would never make it as a soldier, always questioning authority. Don't you have any regrets over what happened in Iraq and Afghanistan, all the misery not just to our own soldiers but also to the people over there?"

Enrique paused before replying, "Flaco, you have no concept of what it means to be a soldier, at least in overseas combat. It's not because of your leftist ideas or because you're not brave enough. I've known guys even more way out than you and who aren't as tough. The problem is you don't understand the concept of duty. In combat, you do what your commanders tell you to do, and you do everything you can to protect your team. They're everything to you in those situations. Outside of me, who could you really count on to risk their own life to save yours? I personally know lots of guys who'd do it over there."

"The ol' band of brothers."

"Yeah, but I don't like to use that term because it's being overused these days."

"Okay, but weren't there ever times over there when you felt uncomfortable with what you were doing under orders? I mean, surely it must have dawned on you that people weren't dancing in the streets when you first arrived there. Did it ever occur to you that, in their minds, they were just average people defending their towns and families against a foreign army? Did you ever think of them as anything but 'evildoers' when you were firing at them?"

Enrique smiled faintly and shook his head. "Again, you don't think of those things when you're over there. Now I do sometimes but not then. You're doing a job, and if you don't do it the way you were trained, you end killing one of your buddies—or yourself."

"So you never thought of countermanding an order?"

"I can't say that I did. Look, when it comes to a one-on-one interaction with the population, yes, you ask, 'Are these people really the bad guys?' If you take a prisoner, of course, you're supposed to treat them according to the Geneva Convention. What went on at Abu Ghraib and elsewhere shouldn't have happened.[16] I certainly wouldn't have given the orders to do all that shit, but I'm not going to lie to you, it's hard as a first lieutenant to step up and complain, and as for the political stuff, it's up to guys like you if you want to change that. It's not our job in the military to go against the president if he decides to send us in."

"You know I admire you, Kiki, despite our different views on things. You were always a great older brother, although I hated how you'd always beat the crap out of me when we'd get into fights when we were little. I have my doubts about our military, but not about you. The military *needs* guys like you. If there ever comes a time when the military really has to step up and protect all of us in the States or even around the world against some bastard of a president, I know we can depend on you, Kiki."

Enrique nodded and then changed the conversation.

"So how about you? What're your plans . . . to move up gradually through the ranks at the *Statesman*? Or do you plan to make a break for it and go to one of those big-time papers up North?"

"Oh, I don't know. Every now and then, I get to do something interesting, whether it involves Texas politics or fracking or some legal issue, like voting rights or immigration or abortion. But

---

16 https://en.wikipedia.org/wiki/Abu_Ghraib_torture_and_prisoner_abuse.

now I'm thinking of digging into the drug cartels in South Texas, maybe publishing a big exposé. I want to find out where that heroin that killed Bennie came from, who was pushing it up from Mexico or wherever, who was *letting* it be pushed up. I feel as though I owe it to Bennie, maybe even more to his kid—to show Bennie wasn't the bad guy in all this."

"Do what you want, Carlos, but even though I know he was my brother, I can't let Bennie off the hook . . . especially if he knew his kid was on the way. In the end, we all have to take responsibility for our actions."

Carlos nodded as if to signal at least partial agreement.

Then Enrique turned to Carlos with a serious face. "And that includes you, Flaco. You'd better realize that the cartel dudes you're planning to take on don't like to see their names in papers."

"Hey, you risked your life over there. Now it's time for me to risk my life over here for something. But—and I don't want you to take this the wrong way, Kiki—maybe if you guys were risking your lives on the border and not all over the Middle East, I wouldn't feel compelled to risk my life . . . and maybe Bennie wouldn't have lost his."

Enrique gulped down the rest of his beer and nodded but said nothing.

CHAPTER 4

After taking a week off after the funeral, Carlos returned to Austin in a conflicted mood. On the one hand, he felt despondent, even guilty, over Bennie's death. Bennie was his little brother, and despite all the kidding and grief older brothers may give their younger siblings, there is a protective bond that is felt. *Why didn't I do more to get him out of that environment, maybe even get him to live with me in Austin for a while?* Yet Carlos also felt a new determination to use his journalistic tools to track down Bennie's killers—all those who were promoting and profiting from the drug trade from its source to Bennie's doorstep.

As he vowed to press on with his research and eventual story, Carlos started reminiscing about his entrance into the journalism field. He had always been an excellent student like his older brother, but even from early on he had been much more interested in writing and literature, reading all sorts of adventure and science fiction novels and, most of all, books about history and those who made it. His feverish mind was both a secondary teacher's dream and nightmare, as he constantly challenged this or that statement and proffered strong opinions on a wide range of esoteric issues ranging from Tesla's grand free energy schemes to transhumanist neural technologies to the chemical poisons that were getting into Americans' bodies and, most of all, to the corruption of the American political system. Above all, he could write, showing a mature style by middle school that most college students couldn't match. He was fortunate in that Balcones Heights was not only his local high school but also one with an array of magnet schools and programs, from the science and technology one in which Enrique was enrolled to ones in international affairs and the creative arts. After submitting a few samples of his writing, Carlos was easily accepted into the writing program at Balcones, where he studied both creative and nonfiction writing throughout his four years. He managed to churn out a variety of literary output, from essays on various political topics to short stories and a few works of poetry. He even managed an op-ed on the *Huffington Post*, discussing how local police could gain better trust among young Mexican-Americans, especially males. With his impressive scholastic literary corpus, plus his near-perfect score on the reading and writing portions of the college entrance exams, Carlos was a shoo-in for a spot at one of the top private universities in the nation, but he decided to stay close to home and attend the University of Texas at Austin's Plan II Honors Program with a full scholarship in hand. There he earned magna cum laude honors and worked his way up to becoming editor in his senior year of the campus literary magazine, *Analecta*.

Carlos's facility at writing could be attributed mainly to his belief that all writing, whether fiction or nonfiction or poetry, should be anchored solidly in its rhythms and timing. He believed that every sentence should have a complex of frequencies, the lowest being the general rise and fall of the sentence and the highest harmonic being the onset and offsets of the words themselves, and he could actually feel the cadences as he was creating a passage. In his view, sentences should build up and deliver, much as a comedian sets up to a punchline. But occasionally, sentences should exhibit a type of syncopation, with the outcome of a situation (for example, "So-and-so died . . .") preceding an exposition of the events leading up to it: this reverse chronology, applied to sentences and even paragraphs, was designed to pique the reader's interest. The half-cycle rise and fall of each sentence also ideally repeated itself in the buildup and denouement of each paragraph and chapter and even the entire work. He appreciated the role of metaphors, especially in poetry, but long-drawn-out ones struck him as pretentious. Simplicity is what he strove for—parcels of wisdom presented in brief but firm verbal handshakes with the reader. It didn't matter to him if the novel was long or short— Clavell, Hemingway, and Tolstoy were all favorites—as long its prose was clear and contained an engaging narrative that smacked of authenticity and left the reader wiser about the human condition than before.

As he progressed through college, his interest in literature waned as he grew more enamored with politics. His politics were mostly left of center, as he chafed at everything from the military-industrial complex and income inequality to religious intolerance and the stereotyping of minorities. Never, though, did he go so far as to disrespect the American military, given the military service of his father and brother. His politics eventually turned to protest, and he was even arrested once at a pro-immigration gathering. By the beginning of his senior year, though, a switch had flipped in him that led to a rapid transformation of his political *weltanschauung*. A friend had introduced him to some conspiracy websites and invited Carlos to a meeting of the Austin chapter of We Are Change, a motley group of conspiracy theorists, libertarians, and New Age proponents.[17] He devoured the 9/11 "Truther" literature, from David Ray Griffin to Daniel Estulin,[18] and he became very agitated and even horrified as he reached the conclusion that September 11 was a classic false flag massacre[19] carried out by United States

---

17   http://wearechange.org.

18   David Ray Griffin is the author of many exposés about September 11, 2001, including *9/11 Ten Years Later: When State Crimes against Democracy Succeed* (Olive Branch Press, 2011); Daniel Estulin is the author of the most definitive work about the shadowy but powerful Bilderberger organization, entitled *The True Story of the Bilderberg Group* (Trine Day, 2009).

19   The term "false flag" is a widely used term in conspiracy circles that describes covert governmental operations that are designed to appear as though they are being carried out by entities, groups, or nations other than those who actually planned and executed them. It is derived from naval warfare, when ships would fly a different flag as a ruse before a sea battle: https://en.wikipedia.org/wiki/False_flag.

government and that politicians of both parties and journalists and law enforcement agents and even judges and scientists were all part of the cover-up. It is less traumatic for a conservative or libertarian to accept that the American government—not just a particular political party or administration—could have been behind such a diabolical event as September 11 because they have less faith in government to begin with. But when a leftist who believes in the promise of big government to humanize society comes to the conclusion for the first time that the government is itself owned by ostensibly liberal people who usurp the courts, media, intelligence agencies, political elites, and financial system all for their own grandiose self-aggrandizement, then disillusionment sets in. At a breakneck pace, Carlos began to shed most of his previous leanings, forsaking his prior infatuation with income equality, gay rights, climate change, and other elements of the leftist agenda as he now railed against amorphous elites trying to take away the liberties of the American people. He started contributing to several conspiracy blogs and even started a few of his own, in the meantime participating in a libertarian political campaign and even attending a national Truther convention. This went on for over a year after graduation until he realized that he couldn't earn enough to pay his bills and that he had to make a hard decision—whether to borrow to pay for graduate school, or find a job with his writing and political skills.

He knew the Austin *American-Statesman* had postgraduate internships available, and since he had already spent time there on a summer internship, he decided to apply. He was initially hired by the paper on a part-time basis, but the salary was minimal, and he continued to do some outside politicking and blogging. When the newspaper offered him a full-time position doing local and state reporting, though, he decided to give it a go. The one request was that all his outside political activities had to cease to maintain the guise of "objectivity." He mostly agreed to do so, although he did continue to contribute to various political websites and even some conspiracy sites under a pseudonym, and he also began writing his first work of conspiracy fiction on the side. His reporting was mostly boring, local stuff, like school-district matters and crime and transportation issues, but he did get into some state politics when the Texas legislature was in session, every other year for a few months. On occasion, he would be given a more extended assignment, such as investigating immigration reform or voting-rights or the impact of the fracking oil boom (and later bust) on South Texas communities. For these and other stories, he would win several Texas Associated Press print and online journalism awards, but the more valuable national awards eluded him. He had itched to do a story on some Truther movements and their doubts about the official American government theory of September 11, given that Austin was the home of one of the Internet's leading alternative news site, *Infowars,* but he was always turned down. As his boss, a crusty middle-aged Texan named Travis James "Jimbo" Burnett once noted, there were three things no one was allowed to advocate in the *Statesman*—"more gun control, less football, and any insinuation that September 11 might have been an inside job."[20]

Carlos vowed that he wouldn't let anyone deter him this time from embarking on his drug trade expose. He was determined to find out who killed his brother—the players involved, the protections they received, the route of the heroin, and so on. He was doing it to defend his brother, to expose the corruption of authorities, to protect others like Bennie in the future, and maybe finally to get some national recognition. When he proposed the story to Burnett later that year and added that he would need extended time to investigate it along with some extra travel funds, the latter demurred, saying that he needed to think about it a little more, given that it was an election year and there was more than enough work for *Statesman* reporters to cover. He suggested Carlos do some serious background research before delving into anything

---

20 It has been frustrating to the Truther movement that virtually the entire the mainstream media—sometimes explicitly—has refused to research or even discuss any account of September 11 other than the official government conspiracy version (see David Ray Griffin, 2011, op. cit., p. 53).

too quickly, and he further advised him to keep his personal loss at a journalistic distance. So Carlos waited patiently throughout the fall, but shortly after the New Year began he confronted Burnett again.

"Jimbo, you remember that drug story I talked to you about last spring, right?"

"Yeah, I do. Did you do a little research the way I asked?"

"Some." After listing the names of the some of the books he had read concerning the international drug trade, he pressed his case. "You promised me you'd let me go ahead with it once the election stuff was out of the way. You going to honor your word?"

Jimbo sighed. "Yeah, I am. But give me a little time to make your case to the brass—they need to know from the beginning what you're up to, especially if they're footing the bill. I have to make it clear that it's not some personal vendetta you're after."

Carlos was angry. "Personal vendetta my ass!" he exclaimed. "Bennie was one of almost fifty thousand overdose deaths that year . . . almost twenty thousand cocaine and black tar heroin deaths alone pushed by the cartels, and it keeps getting worse every year!"[21]

When Burnett didn't reply, Carlos continued in a steely voice, "Look, Jimbo, if some other country dropped a whole bunch of nerve-gas on us and killed twenty thousand Americans, we'd send half our military over there to practically nuke 'em. But nobody gives a political shit about twenty thousand deaths due to poisons coming across the southern border and through our ports. Bennie was a son, a brother, a father even, just like everyone else killed— you're talking about *real people*, Jimbo!"

Burnett finally acquiesced. "Okay, Carlos, I get it. Go ahead with it . . . I'll handle the big boys here. You're damn right, it's an important story for the *Statesman* to cover. It'll leave a powerful impact on a lot of our readers, but if your little exposé turns out anything like I think it will, it's gonna make an even bigger

---

21   For 2014 data, see https://www.drugabuse.gov/related-topics/trends-statistics/overdose-death-rates.

impression on the high and mighty in this country who are gonna give us hell for it. So just be ready to take the flak, pardner."

****

In the ensuing six months, Carlos began to do serious background research on the drug problem in America, including its sources, extent, and most of all, why drugs were still flowing mostly unmolested across the borders despite the nearly fifty-year-old war on drugs. He didn't know where it would all lead as he charged ahead, which was fortunate from a journalistic standpoint. Had he known the result, he probably wouldn't have begun the story at all.

The first thing Carlos did was to look at the basic statistics, starting with President Nixon's War on Drugs in 1973. Although the drug addiction rate remained fairly constant throughout the next four decades or so, the number of addicts increased by 50 percent, and the drug arrest rate increased by over 400 percent.[22] That failure wouldn't have been so glaring, except that over one and a half trillion dollars had been spent fighting the war on drugs, including prison costs.[23] The costs of fighting drugs kept soaring, from less than one hundred million dollars in 1973 to over twenty-five *billion* dollars in 2015,[24] even as the wholesale price of cocaine and heroin per gram dropped almost 90 percent from 1980 to 2001 alone.[25]

The continuous increase in drug use for over four decades, despite the United States government's huge expenditures to eradicate it, clearly meant that powerful forces were continuing to promote and protect the drug trade. It didn't take long for

---

22 https://www.nap.edu/read/18613/chapter/4#45.

23 http://www.thewire.com/national/2012/10/chart-says-war-drugs-isnt-working/57913.

24 DPA_Fact_sheet_Drug_War_Budget_Feb2015.pdf).

25 Office of National Drug Control Policy (October 2001). *The Price of Illicit Drugs: 1981 Through the Second Quarter of 2000* (http://www.abtassociates.com/reports/price_illicit.pdf).

Carlos to figure out that one of those forces was the American government itself and its shadowy intelligence circles, spearheaded by the Central Intelligence Agency. It seemed that wherever the United States had a dog in a fight—whether it be in Southeast Asia fighting communist China during the Cold War and then later on in Vietnam or in Central America battling leftist rebels or in Afghanistan overthrowing the Taliban—drug trafficking was sure to follow.[26] There were those who argued the United States was the biggest drug dealer on the planet, or at least the primary manager of the global drug trade, but Carlos quickly realized that those claims were too simplistic. As his research progressed, he concluded that the United States wasn't a large global drug player so much by intent as by expediency. Whenever covert support was needed for groups the American people and its Congress were unlikely to fund directly, intelligence agencies such as the CIA could always count on the drug trade to provide the desired funds clandestinely to its allies. In many cases, the intelligence agencies would override honest drug-enforcement agents committed to their work, and in rarer cases there were allegations that intelligence operatives actually put drug enforcement agents in danger.[27] It was obvious that the twin goals of prohibition and protection were irreconcilable, and it was also clear which goal was winning out.

The American government's philosophy of "expediency first" started in World War, when mafia capo Charles "Lucky" Luciano was freed from jail in exchange for Cosa Nostra assistance to the

---

26 There are many excellent accounts of the U.S. government's role in the drug trade, but the most authoritative is generally considered to be Alfred W. McCoy's *The Politics of Heroin: CIA Complicity in the Global Drug Trade* Second Edition (Lawrence Hill Books, 2003).
See also http://www.salon.com/2014/03/08/35_countries_the_u_s_has_backed_international_crime_partner.

27 There have been many allegations of these betrayals, but the most infamous one involved Drug Enforcement Administration officer Enrique Camarena: http://www.laweekly.com/news/how-a-dogged-la-dea-agent-unraveled-the-cias-alleged-role-in-the-murder-of-kiki-camarena-5750278.

allies in the invasion of Sicily in 1943 and afterward during the Italian campaign of 1944.[28] It continued on into the late 1940s and early 1950s with American support of the Corsican gangs involved in drug trafficking, which were used to beat back communist-led unions in the port of Marseilles.[29] It was in Southeast Asia, though, that major American involvement in the drug trade began, initially with the United States support of Nationalist Chinese factions fighting the communist Chinese along the Chinese-Burma border in the aftermath of World War II. The Nationalist force at one time numbered over twenty thousand soldiers, exerting control over a large swath of Northeastern Burma. The Nationalists greatly increased poppy production and then traded the opium for munitions and other supplies in Thailand. Thailand itself began to increase opium production, and the Golden Triangle comprising the regions of Northeastern Burma, Northern Thailand, and Northwestern Laos emerged as the leading opium producing region in the world. Planes from Air America, owned by the CIA, began to transport not only supplies in but also opium out of the region to processing labs in Hong Kong primarily.[30] Once the Chinese Nationalist Army remnants were effectively disbanded, the CIA continued to support anti-communist activity in Laos during the Vietnam era, mainly by purchasing large amounts of opium from Hmong tribesmen, who turned their agricultural plots into poppy fields before eventually being forced out of Laos altogether after the Pathet Lao victory in 1975.[31]

One of the ironic twists in the CIA's opium business was that some of the opium that was carried on Air America planes from the Golden Triangle to the processing labs in Hong Kong was later sold to American soldiers in Vietnam, which led to a phenomenal increase in heroin consumption there, with estimate of

---

28   See McCoy (2003), op. cit., chapter 1.

29   See McCoy (2003), op. cit., chapter 2.

30   See McCoy (2003), op. cit., chapter 4.

31   See McCoy (2003), op. cit., chapter 5.

up to 40 percent of all soldiers becoming addicted to heroin.[32] Drug smuggling to the United States from Southeast Asia even took place within the military system, mainly in postal and other shipments, but there were more lurid allegations of drugs being smuggled in the coffins and corpses of dead soldiers.[33]

The United States was by no means the first or only Western nation expediently involved in the drug trade in Asia. The British started opium trading in 1773 because the trade between India and China—controlled by the British East India company—was so lopsided that something from India needed to be exported to China in return for all the tea and spices exiting the Middle Kingdom. That something turned out to be opium. Although the Chinese resisted the scourge of opium and tried on multiple occasions to resist its importation, British gunships—later backed by French and American and other Western forces—eventually prevailed militarily.[34] The British weren't the only ones involved in the forced drug trade, as American clippers competed directly with them for the opium trade to China. The Dutch, meanwhile, exported opium from India to their colonies in Indonesia, while French cartels got involved in the opium trade in their Indochina colonies. Ironically, some of the same French drug connections assisting the French government against the Vietnamese communists during the Indochina War of the early 1950s were used by the Americans a decade later during the Vietnam War.[35]

Within a decade of the American exit from Vietnam, the American government was again providing support for the drug trade, but this time it was a new drug (cocaine) and a new venue

---

32 Stanton, M. D. "Drugs, Vietnam, and the Vietnam Veteran: An Overview." *American Journal of Drug and Alcohol Abuse* (1976), *3(4)*: pp. 557–570.

33 See McCoy (2003), op. cit., chapter 2.

34 https://en.wikipedia.org/wiki/Opium_Wars.

35 See McCoy (2003), op. cit., chapter 3.

(Latin America).[36] In the face of opposition from the United States Congress, operatives within the Reagan administration decided, after the Sandinista overthrow of the Somoza dictatorship in 1978, to support the anti-communist Nicaraguan rebels known as the Contras by engaging in a wide array of illicit fund-raising activities, from selling advanced missiles and other armaments to Iran to protecting what became the first lucrative drug trade from Latin America to the United States. The Contras served as middlemen for the Colombian cartels, which produced the cocaine that was then transported to the United States by Contra leaders such as Danilo Blanton. The base cocaine was then converted into crack cocaine, which first became widely available in Los Angeles and spurred a multibillion dollar industry involving nefarious gangs such as the Crips and Bloods and dealers such as "Freeway" Rick Ross. [37] Cocaine went to *el norte* in massive quantities, to places such as Mena, Arkansas,[38] while guns and ammunition went south. For much of the 1980s, attempts to apprehend and prosecute the major players in the Contra-cocaine network always seemed to be sabotaged by higher-ups, as were media and congressional exposés.

---

36 Again, there are many in-depth accounts of the involvement of the United States in using drugs to support intelligence operations in Latin and South America, but the most widely acclaimed is Gary Webb's *Dark Alliance: The CIA, the Contras, and the Crack Cocaine Explosion* (Seven Stories Press, 1999).

37 Webb, 1999, op. cit., chapter 7.

38 For an exposé concerning the role of Mena in the CIA-sponsored cocaine smuggling of the 1980s, see http://www.serendipity.li/cia/c_o_mena.html. It was the downing of a plane originally based out of Mena's airport piloted by Eugene Hasenfus that led to the exposé of the Iran-Contra covert funding operation: http://www.ticotimes.net/2014/10/06/the-exposure-of-eugene-hasenfus.

In the process, the CIA was ridiculed with the nickname "cocaine importing agency."[39]

The defeat of the Contras in the early 1990s didn't end the cocaine-importing business. Instead of Nicaraguans and Hondurans and Costa Ricans arranging the shipments, the new kingpins were the Mexican cartels. Cocaine and black tar heroin ended up being transported up the west coast of Mexico primarily by the Sinaloa and Tijuana cartels and through the eastern provinces by the Gulf cartel and, later on, Los Zetas. The implementation of the North American Free Trade Zone further expanded the traffic across the Mexican-American border and played into the hands of the cartels, which suddenly had access to a large arsenal of trucks and cars and bridges for transporting their drugs to the heartland of North America.[40]

In carrying out his research, one trend stood out at Carlos like a deer in headlights. It seemed the drug trade was first and foremost a product of capitalism and free markets. Communist countries were very hostile to drug cartels, as evidenced by the dramatic reductions in drug production and addiction when the communists or socialists took over in once heavily drug-infested nations such as China, Vietnam, Cuba, Bolivia, and Nicaragua.[41] By contrast, the breakup of communist or quasi-communist states such as the Soviet Union and Yugoslavia led to an explosion of the drug trade in the newly created nations. Carlos recognized that communist antipathy toward the drug cartels wasn't necessarily out of altruism for the people but rather because drug cartels with their paramilitary forces posed a threat to the dominance of the state. The same held true for theocracies such as Afghanistan and Iran, which also had a serious drug culture that was vigorously

39   https://en.wikipedia.org/wiki/North_American_Free_Trade_Agreement.

40   http://www.democraticunderground.com/discuss/duboard.php?az=view_all&address=104x4061234.

41   For a discussion of China's efforts against drug addiction, see http://www.cnn.com/WORLD/9705/27/china.drugs.

attacked after the Iranian Revolution of 1978.[42] By contrast, the Western nations themselves might try to restrict their own drug production with varying degrees of success, but they wouldn't hesitate to turn to the overseas cartels when they wanted to topple existing governments, whether popular or not. Nor did they have any aversion to propping up entire narco-states if they agreed to play ball with the West.[43]

Carlos was somewhat fascinated as he researched the details of the CIA involvements in the Southeast Asian and Latin American drug trades, but he knew that wasn't where the heroin that killed his brother came from. Bennie had injected the white powder paste, which the Mexican cartels traditionally didn't ship, and the white powder probably didn't come from East Asia since that production had been severely curtailed after the mid-1990s and currently supplied only a small portion of the North American market. Instead, the most likely source was Afghanistan, which now produced over eight thousand tons of raw opium, by far the most of any nation on Earth. The Taliban, with their harsh rule, had nearly eradicated opium production in 2001; but when the United States bombed them out of power in "Operation Enduring Freedom," the red opium poppies quickly began to re-carpet the many valleys

---

42 See http://iranian.com/Opinion/2007/February/Opium110/index.html. Interestingly, the most hostile nations in the world for trafficking drugs are predominantly ones with theocratic governments: http://www.thegooddrugs guide.com/blog/0801/7-countries-you-dont-want-to-get-caught-with-drugs-in.

43 Narco-states are those in which government officials, to varying degrees, permit the drug trade to flourish. One of the first to be designated as such was Colombia, while current ones include Afghanistan, Guinea-Bissau, Guatemala, and Mexico (see Haupt, D. A. 2009). *Narco-Terrorism: An Increasing Threat to US National Security*. Norfolk VA: Joint Forces Staff College (JFSC 25789).

tucked beneath the mountains of the Southern Afghan provinces of Helmand and Kandahar.[44]

What Carlos couldn't figure out completely was where the opiates that ultimately killed Bennie went after they left Afghanistan and ultimately arrived in San Antonio. There were several routes available, a circuitous one through the Central Asian republics, another involving a sea route from Pakistan across the Arabian and Red seas into the Mediterranean, and a more direct route across Iran to Turkey. Carlos surmised that the Iran-Turkey route was the most likely one, given that Iran and Turkey seized more heroin than any other nations in the world. Once leaving Turkey, the heroin could flow from the Bosphorus Strait to the Adriatic Sea with impunity, given the low interdiction rate among the Balkan nations. Carlos's research pointed to the major role of the Albanian mafia in the Balkans, a mafia that had been set loose by the political disintegration of the former Yugoslavia in the 1990s.

Once Albania, the most tightly controlled of the communist states, underwent a democratic transformation in the late 1980s, the Albanian mafia sprang to life, and its fortunes were given a large boost by the rise of the Kosovo Liberation Army (KLA) in the adjacent Serbian province of Kosovo, where ethnic Albanians were a majority. The KLA, once deemed a terrorist group by the United States, was a shadowy mob that began to draw Western support in the run-up to the Kosovo conflict of 1999.[45] Even before Serbia vacated the rebellious province after heavy bombardment by NATO air forces, the KLA was heavy into the drug business, selling heroin in exchange for arms. There were lots of theories as to why NATO had such an interest in Kosovo. Ostensibly, it was to protect the Kosovars from the Serbs, who were alleged to have engaged in a bunch of massacres against them while denying them their previous autonomy, but most if not all the "civilians" killed

---

44 http://www.breitbart.com/national-security/2016/09/11/post-911-afghanistan-opium-cultivation-production-increases-nearly-20-fold.

45 http://www.iacenter.org/warcrime/2_kla.htm.

in the so-called massacres later turned out to be KLA soldiers.[46] So counterviews held that Western financial interests wanted to wrest control of Kosovo's significant mineral wealth or that Kosovo was merely a means of toppling the Serbian government and gaining control of the Balkans for strategic purposes, such as the control of oil pipelines from the former republics of Central Asia.[47]

Why the West flip-flopped to support the KLA over more peaceful mainstream Kosovar parties was also the subject of speculation, but it was clear that the KLA was willing to do the bidding for Western financial interests in exchange for political domination of the province and unfettered control of sex and drug and even organ trafficking.[48] The choice of the KLA was typical of the CIA and other Western intelligence agencies, which often sought out the most violent and fanatical rightwing or religious paramilitaries to do their dirty work—whether it be the various death squads in Central America, the ultranationalists in the

---

46   NATO's allegations of a massacre of Kosovar civilians by Serbian police at Račak and other places was used as a pretext for invading Serbia in 1999, but evidence for the alleged massacre has been widely disputed: http://www. mediamonitors.net/gowans1.html. In fact, the original forensic report of Finnish pathologists was altered to support the allegation: http://www.b92.net/eng/news/crimes.php?yyyy=2008&mm= 10&dd=23&nav_id=54430.

47   https://hendersonlefthook.wordpress.com/2014/12/01/the-kosovoalbania -golden-triangle.

48   https://en.wikipedia.org/wiki/Human_trafficking_in_Kosovo; http:// www.motherjones.com/politics/2000/01/heroin-heroes; http://global-politics. eu/2017/01/26/kosovo-europes-mafia-state-hub-eu-nato-drug-trail/.

Ukraine, Al Qaeda in the Middle East, the French cartels in Vietnam, or the mafia in Italy during Operation Gladio.[49]

Before the KLA could gain control of Kosovo, NATO would engage in the most devastating aerial campaign in Europe since World War II. A total of thirty-eight thousand combat missions in less than three months destroyed bridges, power plants, factories, broadcast stations—even the Chinese embassy.[50] The immediate result was an elevation of a small NATO-backed paramilitary with limited popular support—the KLA—to the status of the main Kosovar political party during the war's aftermath and its leader, Hashim Thaci, becoming prime minister. The charismatic Thaci was a graduate dropout who once flirted with Marxist-Leninism but soon became a key figure in the gun-running and heroin dealings that provided the major funding for the KLA.[51] The longer-term result was the transformation of Kosovo into a narco-state under the control of the KLA—renamed the Democratic Party of Kosovo—and its descent into one of, if not the poorest, regions of Europe.[52] The KLA would, in the process, become a major player in the transport of Afghan heroin to Europe, especially after NATO's overthrow of the Taliban and the subsequent massive increase in opium production there. In the center of it all, seemingly protecting the Kosovars from everyone

---

49   Operation Gladio was one of many "stay-behind" covert operations to thwart communist influence in Europe after World War II: https://en.wikipedia.org/wiki/Operation_Gladio. For a detailed discussion of the role of drug trafficking in Operation Gladio, see Paul Williams. *Operation Gladio: The Unholy Alliance between the Vatican, the CIA, and the Mafia* (Prometheus, 2015), chapters 2 and 3.

50   https://www.rt.com/news/243545-nato-serbia-bombing-yugoslavia.

51   For a brief synopsis of Thaci's transformation from underworld to political kingpin, see http://axisoflogic.com/artman/publish/Article_57430.shtml and https://www.theguardian.com/world/2010/dec/14/kosovo-prime-minister-llike-mafia-boss.

52   http://sputniknews.com/europe/20150217/1018391877.html.

except the cartels running the country, was NATO's Kosovo Force, known as KFOR, with its largest contingent based at Camp Bondsteel.[53]

****

Carlos's investigation revealed that the KLA and other Albanian cartels, the Camilla being the largest, were crucial intermediaries in the international heroin trade, transporting anywhere from 40 to 70 percent of the Afghan heroin. [54] They had enough muscle to handle the heroin as it passed through Iran and especially Turkey, but they needed help to get it to points beyond. Their biggest ally was the largest narcotics trafficker in all of Europe—the 'Ndrangheta, based in the southern Italian province of Calabria. The 'Ndrangheta were like big brothers to the Camilla, making sure they were taken care of as the Calabrian cartel distributed the heroin all over the world, from Amsterdam and London to Nigeria and even Central America.[55] Carlos quickly recognized that a major key to unlocking the secrets of the international heroin trade—and the path taken by the heroin that caused Bennie's death—was to zero in on the Albanian-Calabrian connection.

An Italian journalist who had collaborated with the *Statesman* on a story about the fracking boom a few years earlier had fortuitously offered help when Carlos first mentioned he wanted to do a story on the trade in white powder heroin. He had a contact within the Italian State Polizia's Anti-Mafia Division—a Commissario Ranieri—who could give him lots of information

53 See https://en.wikipedia.org/wiki/Camp Bondsteel for a brief description of the base; for the KFOR's alleged role at Camp Bondsteel and elsewhere in Kosovo in protecting the drug cartels, see http:// thoughtcrimeradio.net/2012/04/kosovos-mafia-state-and-camp-bondsteel-towards-a-permanent-us-military-presence-in-southeast-europe.

54 https://search.wikileaks.org/gifiles/emailid/2652224.

55 http://countervortex.org/node/1768.

and leads on the 'Ndrangheta's heroin smuggling operations. When Carlos called Captain Ranieri in early September, the latter seemed very excited that the American press might finally be willing to delve into the international heroin trade, which he considered a great scourge that was destroying millions of lives not only in Italy but around the world. He even provided Carlos with the contact info for a Serbian official involved in narcotics interdiction, who could help him if he ever visited the Balkans.

Fortunately, Carlos had a means not only of getting to the Balkans but of getting right to the heart of the Balkan drug trafficking—Kosovo itself. Not only Kosovo, but the large American/NATO army base supporting the KFOR effort there— the very Camp Bondsteel commanded by his older brother, Col. Enrique Ybarra.

CHAPTER 5

As the Turkish airliner dropped its landing gear on final approach, Carlos peered down through the late-morning gray November sky at the rooftops of Pristina, the capital of Kosovo. The concrete apartment block buildings had some lingering patches of snow on them, which broke up the city's dark-monochrome facade. He had been told that Pristina itself had very little charm, although the surrounding countryside was scenic, especially when it turned green in the spring. Aside from a few visits to Mexico, this was Carlos's first trip outside of the United States since his foreign study in Barcelona during his junior year at UT-Austin. While Burnett had gotten him permission to do the story, the *American-Statesman* refused to cover the international trip, although they did give him the time off. He felt bad that he had and would continue to lie to his older brother about the purpose of his visit to Kosovo. It wasn't the friendly visit he had let on to Enrique when the latter returned home on leave the previous summer but a pretext for a series of clandestine meetings with his Serbian narcotic agent and the latter's informants, who could tell him firsthand what was going on with the drug trade in the newly formed nation.

When he got off the plane, Carlos was feeling hungry and decided to pick up a sandwich at the airport. He then went outside to the curb, where he saw the white KFOR jeep that Enrique had arranged to pick him up. It would take him through the drab streets of Pristina and its outskirts before heading south on the E65 (Adriatic highway) to the town of Ferizaj, home to Camp Bondsteel. As he passed the brown countryside, Carlos peered out the window. *I've never lied like this to Enrique before. Someday soon, I'd better apologize—before he finds out.*

****

The young lieutenant rang Enrique in his office. "Sir, your brother has arrived. Should I send him in?"

"By all means, Lieutenant. Thanks."

Less than thirty seconds later, Carlos appeared in the doorway of the small office, smiling at his brother. "*Que onda vato?*"

Enrique got up and hugged his brother and offered him a seat. "I'm doing great, bro!" he replied, smiling.

"So I take it you had a good trip? I see you've gained a little weight, Flaco . . . or should I call you 'Gordo' now?"

"Look who's talking. You'd better be nice, Kiki. Just because you're some fancy commander now doesn't mean I won't lay you on your ass!"

"Right . . . when I'm an old man, Flaco. Just remember, I'm still your big brother!"

"Yeah, so what are we going to do for fun in this shithole?"

"I expected you to tell me. You're playing the tourist, right?"

Carlos looked directly at his brother and smiled wryly. "Who says?"

Enrique looked directly back at his brother, not hinting at any concerns, and ignored the question. He then replied, "I think we'll do some skiing tomorrow afternoon. There's a resort at Brezovicki near the Macedonian line, with some good snow right now. You've skied, haven't you?"

"Hell no, but do you forget all the rail stuff I could do with my skateboard when I was younger? I'm still doing a little wakeboarding now and then in San Marcos, so I should be a cinch on the snowboard."

"Good then. It'll take a little over an hour to reach. You know, Kosovo isn't a big place—less than three times the area of Bexar County back home. We can leave around noon and eat on the way.

You'll like the skiing, and the local town, Pritzen, is pretty nice and has some good little restaurants."

"With enchiladas, right?"

Enrique deadpanned, "Not quite. You have to go to Pristina to get some so-so Mexican food, but you might at least be able to order a good lamb and goat-cheese fajita—if you brought along your own tortilla."

Both laughed, and then Enrique continued on, "Skiing is about the only outside thing you can do around here in the winter. You'll be impressed when you see your older brother cruising past you down the slopes. Course I'd already tried it out when I was on my two tours up north. But can you believe I still haven't dented a knee yet?"

"Yeah, right, but isn't it dangerous cruisin' around here? I mean, I assume this base is here because there's trouble all around."

Enrique smiled. "No, bro—there's *no* trouble around here *because* the base is here. Don't worry, you'll see lots of traffic, including tourists and UN vehicles on the road. There'll be no problems on our way there."

Flaco grew quiet. *There's no trouble now . . . but what about after I start poking around?*

Enrique continued, "So you're going to spend some time in Rome after here?"

"Yeah, I'm going to spend some time in Italy touring around. I have a couple of weeks, maybe longer if I can dig up a story."

"'Bout what?"

"Oh, maybe about the immigration mess in Italy and Southern Europe," he lied. "I'm thinking of doing some in-depth analysis and perhaps even make some comparisons to the border immigration crisis back home."

"And the *Statesman*'s paying for all this?"

"Maybe. They're hoping that if it's good enough, it might be picked up by a few other national papers and create a little good national publicity for the paper."

"Must be nice."

Carlos didn't want any more questions about his trip, so he changed topics. "So do you get out of this shithole very often?"

"Stop calling it a shithole. Compared to some of the other places I've been stationed, Kosovo is halfway to heaven. But I do travel to Washington and sometimes in Europe, mainly for meetings. It's hard to get away as the commander of a large base."

"And Monica and the girls?"

Enrique looked away briefly. "Because of the time difference, I rarely get to speak with them directly except on weekends, usually by Skype. As you know, no dependents are allowed here."

Carlos didn't reply for a few seconds. He knew that one of the great regrets of his brother's military life was not being around his family more. He also knew that Enrique's marriage was suffering since when he would visit Killeen, Monica would sometimes confide in him about her depression over the long separation.

Enrique asked about their parents.

"Pop's doing okay," Carlos replied, "but Mom's getting so *loca* these days. She's constantly praying and claims to see Bennie everywhere. I told Pops to get her on some meds, but he's refused thus far. Now even he thinks it's starting to get creepy."

Enrique stared at the window, deep in thought . . . and sadness. Moments later, the young lieutenant at the desk stopped by and told Enrique that a visitor was waiting for him.

Enrique turned to Carlos and stood up. "Why don't you get a little rest now? I'll get someone to drive you over to the visiting quarters. I'll pick you up for drinks around five thirty . . . then we'll have dinner at the Officer's Club."

"Sounds good, bro." Carlos gave his brother a high clasp and a quick hug before retreating from the office. *Yes, we're going to enjoy a good dinner tonight, but the real work starts afterward.*

****

The dinner was a foursome, with two of Enrique's junior officers joining them. Most of the conversation was small talk about the local scenery, especially the young Albanian women and the local brews and brandies. Carlos sensed that most of them felt indifferent about their assignment. On the one hand, they were in Europe—more or less—and had a lot of greenery and mountains about them, but they didn't really understand what their purpose in Kosovo was, and their duties followed mostly the same dull routine every day. Bondsteel, built in 1999 by American contractors, was once home to seven thousand personnel and had a large detention facility; but there were now less than fifteen hundred soldiers and civilians, as violence between Serbs and Kosovars had long since quieted down. Despite its amenities—it still had a small hospital, a few fast-food restaurants, a building for college classes, a large gym, and even a movie theater—soldiers were mostly confined to base and eventually grew bored living there. This was less true for Enrique, who, as base commander, had to deal with all sorts of maintenance and personnel issues and had more extensive interactions with other officers in the multinational KFOR group. He noted how his year at the Army War College and his courses European military history there had prepared him well for his mission, as had his stint at NATO headquarters. As they drove back to quarters, though, Enrique let on to Carlos how much he missed being with his family, especially now that Sofia was about to enter high school, and Sydney wasn't far behind. He still had another year and a half left in his tour, so in characteristic fashion, he added he would just have to "suck it up."

When he returned to his room, Carlos sat down on the bed but didn't rest. He took out his Android and quickly typed an encrypted message to his Serbian contact, Zoran. "When & where 2 meet?"

The reply came back swiftly. "2200 . . . the Apache. Enter club, have drink, and then leave. Don't get noticed."

Carlos checked at the front desk to arrange and see if there were any cabs that could take him into town. While American troops at Bondsteel were generally forbidden to go off-base except while on duty—creating an almost-prisonlike atmosphere within the camp—civilians were under no such restrictions. Just before nine in the evening, a white Volvo taxi arrived outside the main gate that took Carlos along the R122 into the potholed older part of town, where the Apache was located.

Carlos entered the smoky bar area, which faced the stage where a couple of partially nude women were dancing provocatively. Carlos ordered a vodka and lime and rapidly scanned the room. He tried to imagine what Zoran might look like in the unlikely event he was in the room. In his previous conversations with him, Zoran had conveyed, in a low-tenor voice, a tough and pragmatic persona as well as faintly idealistic bent, as he described the opiate scourge that was afflicting not just the Balkans but all of Europe. Carlos tried to imagine how a man who was involved in undercover work would look. Most likely, he had a moderate build and slight facial hair and wore nice clothes, perhaps a silk shirt or even blazer. Carlos then glanced at the dancers, who seemed to be going through the motions, undoubtedly with ample drugs in their systems. He thought about where the girls came from, which could be anywhere west of the Urals and north of the Sahara but most likely from some poor Balkan country dominated by organized crime syndicates. He knew from his research that, as Kosovo declined, more and more of the girls were of Albanian ancestry, usually in their late teens, intent on leaving the countryside. Just before ten, Carlo downed his second vodka drink and wandered out of the club.

The crowd milling about had grown in size, containing a sizeable number of Westerners seeking entrance, and he tried to mix inconspicuously with it. As he neared the curb, he received a text to get into a black Mercedes cab sitting to the right of the entrance on the street. Zoran's dark-haired, bespectacled face was much as he had imagined it, but the Serbian didn't bother with any small talk as he said, in flawless but accented English, "Check to see if anyone is following us. At 2215, I'm going to swing by the Coco club and pick up our contacts. In the meantime, we're going to drive around a bit and even stop to get some petrol and a takeout."

"So do you think they suspect anything at this point?"

"The cartel watches everything here. The last thing they want are outsiders nosing around. As with all underworld operations, you're dealing with some very ruthless men."

Carlos remained silent while taking in Ferizaj's downtown. There were a few modern buildings, and the gas station looked like the typical self-serve ones with food marts in the United States. Although there were no McDonald's in the town itself, there was a quasi-fast-food burger place nearby that Zoran stopped at before getting gas. The whole time Zoran was relaying in rapid-fire fashion the history of the drug cartels and assorted other criminal activities in modern Kosovo.

They drove further south on Besem Rexhepi Road before slowing down just past the Coco Club. Zoran drove into the parking lot and signaled to a young man and woman who were waiting outside. Carlos didn't know who the couple was, but Zoran had promised they would provide him some with good information. The couple quickly got in the car, and Zoran made a quick turnaround onto the Rexhebi motorway and then onto the R122 before speeding off to Camp Bondsteel.

Just before they arrived at the entrance to Bondsteel, Zoran ordered the man and the woman to exit the car and move to the trunk while he brought out a vodka bottle for Carlos. "Hold this and act drunk and make sure the guard knows you're Colonel Ybarra's brother. Ordinarily, taxis aren't allowed on base, but I'm sure he won't challenge you."

Sure enough, although they were briefly stopped at the gate, the guard was taken in by Carlos's act. Not wanting to create a scene and upset his commanding officer, he waived the taxi on through, albeit without the vodka bottle and with strict instructions for the cab to immediately exit after dropping Carlos off. After arriving at the officer's quarters, Zoran opened the trunk, and the young man and woman got out and quickly followed Carlos to his room. Inside, they all sat down, the two guests keeping their coats on. Carlos offered them a couple of miniature liquor bottles before he took out his laptop and flash drive. He then began recording while at the same time taking notes of their conversation as the night progressed.

****

The young woman, a red-haired beauty from a small rural town in Southern Moldova south of Chisinau, mostly looked down when she answered the questions. Natalya's English was broken, and she frequently switched to Albanian, which the man translated for Carlos.

Her basic tale confirmed what Carlos's previous research had shown—that there were thousands of young women from the Balkans and Eastern Europe who had been lured away by phony job prospects and then sold into the sex slave trade, dominated in the Balkans by the Kosovo drug cartels. She remembered little of her journey, except that she was supposedly hired for a maid position in Western Europe but then transferred to an underworld pimp in Romania. She was gang-raped on the way as a means of "breaking her" and fed her first heroin just before stripping nude at an auction, at which she was sold to a Macedonian who took her passport away and deposited her at a brothel in Skopje. After working for over a year and nearly paying off her "auction fee," she was transferred to various locations within Kosovo, where she continued to dance in strip clubs and sometimes service several men at night.

Then the man, who said his name was Zamir, interjected that he had joined the Kosovo Liberation Army as a teen and, after the Serbian withdrawal, had been moved up the ranks of one of its main spinoff cartels—the notorious and powerful Camilla. He began to regularly see Natalya as a client, but for some strange reason, he started to see beyond her tarnished exterior and began to want to know her "in her soul."

"Once I showed interest in Natalya as person, she begin to open up and trust me," Zamir said in thickly accented English, replete with rolled r's. "I don't know what happened to me—I had done lot of nasty things in life, never cared about anyone, even my former girlfriends. Now all I wanted to do was to be with Natalya, but cartel boss also wanted Natalya, and now there is friction. I knew I'm in trouble and have to decide quickly. I got Zoran's info from a Serbian narco-friend who tell me if I ever want to get out of the business to contact him . . . that he could help me if I give info."

"So what information can you give me?" Carlos asked. He felt somewhat guilty in that he knew he couldn't promise them any sort of safety without his brother intervening.

"I tell you anything you want to know about drug trade here. Perhaps you already know Kosovo and Albania are big to bring heroin from Asia to Western Europe—and America."

"Yes, I know the general picture . . . but not a lot of the details."

Zamir paused and then looked Carlos directly in the eye. "I am midlevel 'soldier,' so to speak, in Camilla, but because I'm fluent in Serbo-Croatian and know some English and even a little Turkish and Italian, I go outside Kosovo a lot, keeping watch over various Camilla routes. I watch heroin all the way from the East to when it leaves for Italy and Serbia and other places to go north. I count and weigh bags, sample dope, guard money, things like that. I'm not alone or even biggest person, but I do most of talking and sampling. Believe me, total heroin controlled by Camilla is huge—several tons a week![56] And that's not counting other Albanian gangs. I see it with my own eyes, hold it with my own hands, tasted it with my lips! We watch out when we are outside Kosovo. We know sometimes police tipped off and eager to do their jobs, maybe only to show people they do something about all the drugs everywhere, but here in Kosovo, we never worry, not even for a second! We control all policemen and officials here. All are in with us or too afraid and keep quiet. Even the Kosovo president himself used to be involved in these things—you know his Drenica Group back in the '90s?[57] And your KFOR troops—they don't care a bit! They just hang out at their base all day or drive right past our

---

56 Officially, only eighty-five tons of heroin cross the Balkans every year, representing 40 to 70 percent of all Afghan heroin that passes through the Balkans, primarily Kosovo (http://www.balkaninsight.com/en/article/balkans-remain-major-drug-transit-point-us-report-03-03-2016).

57 See footnote 47 and http://www.pri.org/stories/2011-03-27/kosovos-mafia-how-us-and-allies-ignore-allegations-organized-crime-highest-levels.

vehicles loaded with heroin.[58] And lots of them even try out our girls."[59]

Carlos asked, "So when you mean 'from the East' . . . do you mean Afghanistan?"

"Yes, there most of it comes . . . especially after 2002."

"When the United States overthrew the Taliban," Carlos interjected.[60] Then after a shrug from Zamir, he continued, "And where does most of it go?"

"The biggest stash goes through Albania. It has long and rough coastline that is hard to control. Most heroin then goes to Italy, some France, some through Balkans. Getting drugs through Montenegro and Serbia and Croatia is not too risky, but Slovenia and Hungary are tighter."

"Okay, thanks, but I know most of this. What I need is for you to state that you have personally transported drugs to this or that place."

"I already tell you. I once hold twenty kilos of heroin in my hands. Once I even take load of *two hundred kilos* across Macedonian border to Skopje, running right down the E5 from here. I can tell you where are all our labs, where refined white powder from East is stored." After Carlos handed him a piece of paper, Zamir quickly and studiously proceeded to draw out the locations of five laboratories, mostly in and around Pec in the western part of Kosovo.

"And can you tell me how much, if any, of the white heroin makes it to the United States . . . if you know?"

Zamir paused. "I don't know numbers. But I do know some does because boats that smuggle cocaine from Americas leave with white powder bags hidden inside. I see it myself."

Carlos turned toward Natalya. "And did the girls help transport any of the drugs for the Kosovo cartels?"

---

58 Despite various allegations (see footnote 53), direct evidence is lacking that KFOR has promoted or refused to interdict the heroin trade in Kosovo.

59 http://www.dw.com/en/german-soldiers-spurring-sex-trade/a-1365134.

60 See footnote 44.

After Zamir translated for her, Natalya shook her head and said in broken English, "No, Camilla do not trust us, but they give us any drugs *we* want, very cheap in Kosovo." She then imitated shooting up her vein, even showing some marks.

Zamir interjected, "Almost all girls at clubs are addicted."

Carlos nodded somberly. Then he turned to Natalya and Zamir and asked, "So where would you go if I tried to help you out of here?"

Natalya understood and quickly replied, "I want go back to Moldova . . . to get new passport. Then we can go someplace nice—maybe America?"

Carlos smiled uneasily when he heard that. "Of course, but you know life's not easy in America for young people without educations who have been in the drug and sex trade."

Zamir retorted angrily, "Not easy? How about here? Most young people don't have jobs, and ones that do—well, look at us. Life never easy here, but once Serbs left, all industry go too. Our land is good for growing, in beautiful, fertile valleys with mountains all around, but on the people side Kosovo, even Albania, is mostly wasteland. Most of good young people try to leave. You will help us leave?"

Carlos nodded. "I will try my best. First of all, I need to talk to my brother about getting you safely out of here. Don't worry about tonight. You two can have the bed to sleep on. I'll sleep on the floor. I'll get you some breakfast, and then I'm going out with my brother tomorrow. At this point, there is no reason to worry. No one knows you're here."

But upon entering his first stage of sleep, well past two in the morning, Carlos didn't realize that lots of people knew where Natalya and Zamir were hiding, and another would soon know—his brother Enrique.

****

The Camilla had been closely monitoring Zoran and everyone he was meeting. They didn't have to tail him because Ferizaj was a small town, and the Camilla had lots of informants and police officers under its command. Even though the Camilla stronghold was Metohija in Western Kosovo, in reality it had its tentacles everywhere in the state. When he heard the news about Zamir's meeting with Zoran and the American, Zamir's friend and boss, Pirro Gjoni, was more than unhappy—he was worried: Zamir knew too much. He had traveled too far and could name names and places better than anyone else could. *Zamir was a good soldier, until that damn whore came along.* Pirro knew that he had to tell his bosses even as he regretted that he probably wouldn't see his friend ever again.

When Enrique arrived at his office at seven o'clock, he saw his phone light flashing. After he started up his computer and started on his coffee, he checked the message. It was from the Ferizaj chief of police. "Colonel, we have a serious problem on our hands. Evidently, some drug cartel members were brought to your base last night. Please call as soon as possible."

Enrique was dismayed. This is all he needed, what with Carlos here and the two of them supposed to go skiing in the afternoon, one of his few breaks in the past month. When he returned the call, he was even more alarmed at the police chief's message.

"Colonel, thank you for returning my call. I am sorry about this problem, but what happened last night is very serious. The individuals that apparently entered the base are dangerous criminals. We ask your cooperation in being able to retrieve the drug suspects."

Enrique was skeptical. "How do you know this? No one has reported any breach here. KFOR is well protected."

"Well protected against hostile forces . . . but not against friendly ones."

"So you're saying that someone brought these suspects on base. I don't believe you."

"It's happened before, no?"

Enrique recoiled at the allusion to the previous incident. It had happened a year earlier, when a couple of frisky soldiers decided to sneak dancers from a local strip club on base. Evidently, the entire barracks had coughed up the money to pay for them for the night. But after the show, the three women, all from Romania, started crying and refused to leave, requesting asylum because their lives were "in danger." Enrique had to personally meet with the women and then quickly decide what to do. In the end, he had a United Nations vehicle under diplomatic cover transport them to the Romanian Consulate in Pristina, where they were eventually issued new passports and flown to Bucharest. The local cartel boss was very upset, not because he lost a very modest financial investment in the women, but because of the message it sent to the hundreds of other women enslaved in the Ferizaj area as well as those beyond. Enrique had avoided any lingering tensions by promising not to let that happen again and confining all his soldiers to base for the next sixty days, except on duty.

"Yes, but things changed after that," Enrique replied. "So where's your proof that it happened this time."

The police officer waited for a few seconds before replying carefully. "The proof, Colonel, is sitting in your brother's room at the officers' quarters."

****

Enrique was stunned. *Carlos couldn't have been involved in this, or was he?* If he was, it would be bad news for everyone involved . . . but especially for their relationship.

Enrique rang Carlos's room, with no answer, and then his cell phone.

Carlos answered, still half asleep. "Yeah, who's this?"

"It's Kiki. We need to talk, Carlos . . . *right now*!"

"Okay, okay. What do you need, bro?"

Enrique could barely conceal his concern. "I want to come over to your room. In fact, I'm on my way."

"Jesus! Why now, man? I'm half asleep and haven't even showered or dressed!"

"Doesn't matter," he said curtly. "I need to see you right away."

Carlos was worried. *Someone had squealed on them!* Was it Zoran, or was it someone else? He had a mind to call Zoran right away, but there wasn't time. He had to get Zamir and Natalya into the closet, hidden, and make sure everything was in order. He briefly thought about moving them outside under cover, but he realized that they'd be quickly spotted. Since Zamir and Natalya were already awakened by the phone calls and knew the situation, it didn't take long for them to hide.

When Enrique rang, Carlos was still feeling a bit groggy, but he immediately turned on the coffeemaker. When Enrique arrived, he immediately asked him if he wanted a cup of coffee.

"No time for that," Enrique said. "Mind if I take a look around."

"Suit yourself. After all, you own all this, right?"

Enrique ignored the jab and started looking in the bathroom, behind the shower stall, and then in the closet. At first, he didn't see anything, but then he heard a heavy breath from Natalya and pulled the clothes apart to expose her and Zamir. Then he turned back to Carlos.

"What's this all about?" he asked angrily. "Why'd the hell you bring them back to the base? Don't you know you've caused a big headache for me?"

"You mean your narco buddies in Ferizaj are all over your case?"

"What the fuck are you up to, Carlos? Why'd the hell did you come here? Obviously, it had nothing to do with seeing your brother—more like using me for your fucking story!"

"What the fuck are *you* up to, Kiki? Don't you know what you've got here—a fucking narco-state that transports most of the heroin in the world to Europe and beyond—including Texas, *where your brother Bennie once lived*? Not to mention all the trafficking in women and organs and everything else? What are you doing at this fancy base—protecting the Camilla? Or do you even know what the Camilla is? This is all *gacho*, Kiki!"

"Shut the fuck up, Flaco! You don't know what the hell you're talking about."

"Then maybe Zamir here can tell you. He was high up in the Camilla. He knows names, places, routes, everything! He could help you shut down these bastards!"

"That's not our mission, goddammit! Our mission is to protect these people from the Serbs, to make sure there's no more of the shit that happened in '99."

"Like what? All those fake massacres that NATO blamed on the Serbs? All the thousands supposedly killed by the Serbian police in Kosovo? There were less than two thousand killed *in the entire Kosovo War*—including KLA, Serb soldiers, all those Serbs killed by the KLA, and all the civilians killed when NATO bombed the auto factories, the power plants, the TV stations. *So where were the big Serb massacres of civilians, Kiki?*[61] It was all about us and NATO deciding it was time to steal part of Serbia so they could control some of the oil and gas to Europe. And to create a narco-state headed up by the big capo, Thaci."

"Carlos, you're all fucked in the head!" Enrique yelled. "I don't know where you get all your anti-American bullshit. Our mission here is to protect the people . . . you should see the smiles we get when we go into town and into the countryside. Once Serbia and Kosovo agree to territorial swaps and Serbia recognizes Kosovo and they both join the EU, we'll be gone. In fact, our mission is already winding down. Your stuff about protecting the so-called drug trade is total shit."

"Yeah, then how come wherever we stick our nose into other people's business, drugs just happen to start flowing? What about Vietnam? Hell, the CIA was flying out opium for our allies, which became the very heroin that was being pushed on your army buddies over there. In fact, some of the drugs ended up being carried in their dead bodies on their way home! And what about all the crack cocaine the CIA started moving from Central America to help the Contras, killing our cities in the process? And how about Afghanistan, where the opium crop had been burned away until we knocked the Taliban off and now it's producing over seven

---

61   See footnote 46.

thousand tons—more than the rest of the world combined! And do you know who's on the receiving end of all of it? Guys like Bennie—*your brother*!"

"Bennie did it to himself. He came from a good family . . . There was no reason for him to get involved in that gang stuff."

"You still don't get it, Kiki. You think wearing that uniform makes all the crap slide off you? Did you ever think about *who* you were blowing up in Iraq and Afghanistan or *why* they didn't want you in their country? Did you ever think of the hundreds of thousands dead in those little ventures over there and the millions of homeless orphans roaming around? The trouble with you, Kiki, is that you never once thought about what the hell you were going to do in the military. You liked pleasing Pops and looking impressive and getting all the accolades, but you never gave one thought to all the misery we were causing over there."

Enrique became enraged, his eyes bulging. "You don't know what the fuck you're talking about, so why don't you keep your mouth shut so I don't have to rip your goddamned tongue out!" Enrique jutted his fist in the direction of Carlos in a mock threat. "I'm sick of that left-wing bullshit you've been spouting all your fucking life." After an extended period of silence, Enrique looked at Carlos and then Natalya and Zamir. In a calmer voice, he said, "You're going to have to leave the base. I'll have our motor pool take you wherever you want to go, even to the border if needs be."

Natalya and Zamir looked down but didn't respond. After a brief silence, Carlos interceded.

"Look, Kiki, I'm sorry for what I said. I was out of line, okay? But what you don't understand is that Natalya, from Moldova, doesn't have a passport. They took that a long time ago from her. And Zamir and she have no chance staying around here. They'll be dead before the next sunrise if they don't check out of Kosovo. Look, there must be some other way to get them out of here."

Enrique thought about his options. *Carlos is right, dammit . . . I can't let them out on the street.* He knew there was no Moldovan embassy in Kosovo. Moldova was still among the almost half of the world that didn't recognize Kosovo,[62] and he didn't trust the American Embassy in Pristina because he suspected it would be in bed with the Kosovars and wouldn't hesitate to release the man, who evidently had lots of damaging information. He quickly decided he would circumvent NATO protocol and make an unauthorized flight into Macedonia—regardless of the consequences for his career. There he would wash his hands of Natalya and Zamir and, of course, Carlos, and then he'd be done with the whole mess.

Enrique turned to Natalya and Zamir. "Don't leave this room under any circumstances." Then to Carlos, he said, "I'll be back in less than an hour. You'll get your answer then."

---

62 Currently, only 109 of 193 members of the United Nations recognize Kosovo as a sovereign state.

CHAPTER 6

After returning to his office, Enrique quickly searched through his computer to find the phone number of the American Embassy in Skopje, the capital of Macedonia. He had met the ambassador once at a KFOR function, and he remembered him as very knowledgeable and professional.

He explained the situation to the ambassador, and the latter agreed to provide refuge to Zamir and Natalya and to get Natalya a new passport to replace the one stolen from her. He also indicated that Zamir's information could be valuable to not only the Drug Enforcement Administration, which had agents in the embassy, but also the State Department in general. The ambassador didn't elaborate, but Enrique knew what he was implying. The United States was allied with both Macedonia and Kosovo, but Macedonia had a large Albanian minority population and was fearful of the Kosovar Albanians, whose National Liberation Army forces would periodically stir up unrest in the republic. While none of these actions had, in recent years, amounted to much, Macedonia was perpetually concerned about calls for a Greater Albania that had the potential to redraw the map of the Balkans.[63] Anything that would put the Kosovars on the defensive—such as the potentially explosive testimony of Zamir—could increase the Macedonian's trust in the United States.

---

63 http://republic-macedonia.latestnews365.com/newsfile/the-destabilization-of-macedonia-greater-albania-and-the-process-of-ldquokosovizationrdquo---center-for-research-on-globalization.html.

Before returning to Carlos's room, Enrique swung by the helipad and asked that a UH-60 Blackhawk helicopter be made available immediately and that clearance into Skopje be requested. Although cross-border flights were not routine, they did occur periodically, and clearance was usually obtained quickly. In the meantime, Enrique went back to Carlos's room and told Carlos to arrange his checkout and to make sure he and his friends brought all legal documents with them. Fortunately for Zamir, Zoran had already instructed him to have his passport and plenty of cash on him. After returning to the room, Carlos sat Zamir down again and began to enter an enormous amount of information from Zamir quickly into his computer. Clearance finally arrived about three hours later, and shortly thereafter Enrique drove up to the room and whisked them all off to the helipad. Enrique offered Zamir and Natalya some fast food he had obtained on his way to the quarters, but pointedly, he had brought nothing for his brother.

The army captain flying the Blackhawk was somewhat surprised to see Carlos and Zamir and Natalya accompany the colonel, but it wasn't his place to ask questions. After all, NATO personnel were always taking flights here and there when visiting Bondsteel. Enrique asked the captain briefly about the flight path, which usually tracked the E-5 to Skopje. It was a very short flight— only about forty-five kilometers in the air, less than fifteen minutes for the Blackhawk—but instead of landing at the NATO base in Skopje, Enrique instructed the helicopter to land directly on the premises of the American Embassy.

As they crossed the border from Kosovo into Macedonia, Enrique pointed out Mount Ljuboten to the right of the aircraft. "If you open your eyes wide, you might even see the ski resort beyond . . . which we were supposed to go to this afternoon, *if you recall*." Carlos remained silent. He knew he had said enough in the morning.

Landing at the embassy was no problem. The building and its grounds were surprisingly huge—one of the largest American embassies in the world. It looked less like an embassy than a large office or even military complex, situated on a bluff overlooking the city. It was long rumored to contain a skyscraper underground and serve as the hub for a huge military and civilian intelligence network for the Balkans.[64] When the Blackhawk landed, the deputy chief of mission came out to greet Enrique and the others and escort them into the compound.

The four met with the deputy in his office. He explained to Natalya and Zamir that they could stay there for a few days, maybe more, as the guests of the ambassador while things got "sorted out." Based on other cases, it would probably take a week or two to get a new passport, if she indeed had a valid one previously issued. In the meantime, there were people in the embassy who would like to talk to Zamir, whose info could be very helpful on a number of fronts. They would be allowed to return to their countries, or in Zamir's case, an extended-stay visa to Moldova or elsewhere could be arranged if he already had a valid passport. He then asked Zamir if he had enough money for flights since any ground transportation could be risky. Zamir indicated that he did, without telling the deputy of mission that he also had a couple of kilos of heroin stashed on him and Natalya that they were going to unload at the Skopje Airport to a friend for over fifteen hundred Euros.

The deputy's eyes bore down on Zamir and then Natalya. He then warned them about their plight. "I wouldn't linger too long in Moldova or anywhere else between here and there. I hope you know they're not going to forget about you. Their power comes from fear, and letting you off the hook would lessen the fear among the others. If I were you, I would scrape enough money to buy a ticket to the Americas or even Australia. Stay there a year or more, and you'll probably be okay."

Zamir translated for Natalya and then nodded for both of them. "Okay, we understand situation." He paused and then added, "How much it cost from here to Australia?"

"Your best bet would be leaving from Athens. Last-minute flights from there are under one thousand euros per person, one

---

64   http://www.abovetopsecret.com/forum/thread424954/pg1.

way. Of course, you would need an electronic visa. It's generally no problem . . . under ordinary circumstances."

Zamir nodded again. "It's okay for us. All we need is Natalya's passport."

The deputy then turned to Carlos and asked what he needed. After Carlos hesitated, Enrique chimed in.

"He's good. He's planning to go to Italy on the next flight out, right, Carlos?"

"Yeah. Hopefully, I can get on a late-afternoon or early evening flight."

"That shouldn't be a problem . . . There are several airlines that head out around that time. I prefer the Alitalia flight, which leaves around five. I'll have my secretary check on flights to Rome." Then after a pause, he added, "I assume you'll be needing a ride to the airport."

Carlos was about to decline the offer, but then he hesitated. *Why should I assume I'm safe even here in Macedonia?*

The deputy read his concern. "Look, I'm going to strongly recommend that you let us take you to the airport." When Carlos nodded his assent, the deputy then sat back in his chair and opened up about the situation in the Balkans. "You know, the people of the Balkans used to be the friendliest people on Earth—to outsiders. To each other, they couldn't shed their ethnic and religious histories and prejudices despite fifty years of socialism and the strong rule of Tito and extensive intermarriage in the urban areas.[65] While many observers were surprised Yugoslavia lasted as long as it did, when it crumbled, there were incredible centrifugal forces unleashed in the various ethnic wars of the 1990s.[66] As the governments and even

---

65 Josip Broz, more widely known by his assumed name, Tito, was prime minister and/or titular president of the former Yugoslavia from 1944 until his death in 1980. He kept the Slavic states together in the Yugoslav Federation through personal popularity, diplomacy, and mild authoritarianism. See https://en.wikipedia.org/wiki/Josip_Broz_Tito.

66 For a summary of the various ethnic conflicts that tore the old Yugoslavia apart, see https://en.wikipedia.org/wiki/Yugoslav_Wars.

nongovernmental social institutions weakened after the civil war, criminal syndicates started to take over like a cancer. It's true that the worst ones are out of Albania and Kosovo . . . I'm not going to tell you anything you don't already know, but there are dangerous ones all over—here, Serbia, Bosnia, Croatia, even Montenegro. Their tentacles reach into Southeastern Europe as well—Romania, Moldova, you name it. Danger is everywhere now once you tick off the wrong person." He paused before continuing, "Maybe I shouldn't be so frank, but personally, I've come to realize how it's best not to mess with nation-states. The breakup of Yugoslavia was probably inevitable, but most of the ones we've gotten involved with were not. And I can't see how the average person has benefited from all the disintegrations." The deputy paused again. "I'm sorry, Colonel, I know it's not the party line, but that's the way I've come to feel."

"You don't have to apologize, sir," Enrique said. "And I appreciate your going to bat for these individuals." Turning to his brother, he added, "They would have been in serious trouble otherwise."

"That's what we're here for, Colonel." Then glancing at Enrique's military jacket, he added, "It's the least we could do for a soldier who earned two Silver Stars."

Enrique nodded to the ambassador and then turned and said goodbye to Zamir and Natalya and left the room. Carlos followed after him. After they had both left the office, Carlos thanked his brother and added, "I know you're pissed off at me, Kiki, and I don't blame you. I'm sorry, if it still means anything, but I want you to know I did it for Bennie. I want something to happen to the bastards who gave him—and millions like him—that ugly shit."

Enrique stared at Carlos for a few seconds, still miffed. "Take care of yourself, Flaco. You're still in a lot of trouble—even in Italy. I hope the next time we meet isn't at *your* funeral." Then he turned around and left for the waiting Blackhawk nearby.

****

Carlos checked with the secretary and managed to get booked on the late-afternoon flight to Rome. He still had about two hours before leaving for the flight, but he didn't want to linger too long at the terminal. So he decided to text Zoran. Zoran immediately texted back, thanking Carlos for ensuring the safety of Natalya and Zamir. *I wonder how he knew I was able to get them to safety. Is everyone watching everyone else here?*

Carlos later found out that Zoran Josipovic, as a member of Serbia's Security Information Agency posing as an anti-narcotics agent, had been tasked with exposing the corruption and criminality in the leadership of Kosovo in an attempt to delegitimize its international status and ultimately block Kosovo's bid to join the European Union. As a Serbian patriot, Zoran mistakenly thought safety was bestowed upon him upon crossing the border into his homeland, but it wasn't long afterward that he fell victim to a fellow Serb working for the Zemun clan. Evidently, the Zemuns, despite having ratted on Albanians during the Kosovo conflict, were now working with the Camilla to move heroin into Eastern Europe through Serbia. As a favor to their Kosovo partners, as well as themselves, they made sure Zoran Josipovic met not a hero's welcome but an ugly death. Such was the twenty-first century, where drug lords and syndicates were rapidly replacing nation-states as the dominant force of modern societies.

****

On the return flight to Bondsteel, Enrique gazed out the front window of the Blackhawk, a window he had peered through a countless number of other times in his army career. This time, though, felt different—the view was tinged by a veiling glare of anger and sadness and disillusionment. He was angry because he had been played and compromised by his brother, and he was sad because he felt more alone than ever before. Carlos and he were close when they were young, and despite their differences, they had remained close over the years in a strange way that only brothers could fathom. *But now?* After all the tours, he barely knew his daughters, and his marriage to Monica had suffered to the point that he didn't know if it could even be resuscitated. While he kept in touch with many of his platoon buddies and some of his fellow cadets from A&M, as base commander he no longer felt the camaraderie he once shared because everyone was now in his chain of command and he couldn't let his guard down. So with his parents rapidly aging and growing sick with diabetes and who knows what else, Carlos was the only one left who was a constant in his life. He hadn't had the same relationship with Bennie, who was so much younger than him, but he understood that Carlos had one with Bennie more like his was with Carlos. This, no doubt, was why Carlos was plunging along in his crusade, trying to protect his younger brother, even in death. *Maybe that's what I need to do— forget all his bullshit and protect Carlos against not just others but also himself.*

Beyond the anger and sadness and loneliness, Enrique was disturbed by Carlos's rant about Kosovo, which was echoed to some extent by the deputy chief at the embassy. When he joined the army as a first lieutenant, he never thought about what he was going to do in it, who he was going to fight, and why. He helped topple Saddam Hussein in Iraq, helped stave off the resurgent Taliban in Afghanistan, and he was now in Kosovo protecting against—*what?* The American incursion into Iraq proved to be a disaster, the American incursion into Afghanistan was worse, the NATO bombing of Libya was an even greater catastrophe, and even the bombing of Kosovo—*what had it accomplished?* Where drugs and criminal activities were once mostly contained in the Balkans, now they resonated everywhere in the open . . . like that Ferizaj police chief prick who was snooping around *his* base, working for the Camilla or some other narco clan. *He and his buddies are the goddamned assholes we're protecting!*

Enrique still clearly loved the military and its camaraderie and teamwork and discipline, but in the end those were only collateral benefits, ones that depended ultimately on whether the missions were morally justified. For the longest time, he had had no doubts that they were, but after all his Southwest Asia tours and now this, he started to think about something he had never really put his mind around before. *Maybe it's time to think about getting out, to move onto something else in life.*

The Blackhawk pilot sensed Enrique's inner turmoil as he approached the KFOR base. "It's not always easy being a commander, is it, Colonel?"

"No, it's not, Captain."

****

When Enrique got back to his room, he checked to see if Carlos's flight arrived safely in Rome. It had, and there had been no incidents at Skopje International Airport. Enrique was relieved that his brother had made it out okay, even though he knew he was still surrounded by danger. *Godspeed, Flaco.*

CHAPTER 7

Shortly after landing at Fiumicino Airport, Carlos texted Franco Ranieri, a commisario in the Italian State Polizia's Anti-Mafia Division, who had been referred to him by his Italian journalist friend and who, in turn, had led him to Zoran. Ranieri had let on that he had recently brought a Calabrian into the witness protection program who could be helpful to Carlos. Danio Chiapetto was a young but relatively well-connected member of the 'Ndrangheta mafia[67] operating out of Catanzaro who was facing over twenty years in prison after being charged with several counts of extortion and bribery and drug trafficking. Having been orphaned at an early age and taken in by a sympathetic local boss, Danio rose very quickly in the local ranks of the Calabrian cartel, but his lack of familial affiliation turned out to be his ticket to the state's witness protection program. Unmarried and without any close relatives, he had no one to jeopardize except himself, and he could avoid that by moving to safety by ratting out his former cartel members.

After a fitful night of sleep in a cheap hotel near the airport, Carlos hailed a cab to the modern office building on the Via Tuscolana housing the National Police headquarters. He was greeted by Captain Ranieri, an outgoing but imposing man who briefed him in fluent but Neapolitan-accented English. "Signore

---

67 The 'Ndrangheta is the most powerful of Italy's crime syndicates, operating out of the southern region of Calabria: https://en.wikipedia.org/wiki/%27Ndrangheta.

Ybarra, welcome to Rome. I understand your stay is short, which is a pity because there is so much to see and do here, but I understand your circumstances. So I gather you would like some information from us to help you in an article for your newspaper. Was Zoran helpful to you?"

"Very. Almost too helpful though. His informants and I are lucky to have gotten out alive, but things should be okay now."

"Good," Ranieri replied.

Carlos gazed at the police chief and then said, "Yes, I'm hoping you might provide me greater insights and information than I've already gathered for my story. I appreciate your meeting with me on short notice."

"I see. But why is it that you are interested in the drug trade over here? Your cocaine and most of your heroin come from Mexico and South America."

"Yeah, but I have a personal reason." Carlos paused to take a deep breath. "You see, my younger brother was an addict and not long ago overdosed on heroin—not the black tar from Mexico but the white powder. I'm trying to trace how it made its way here and, more generally, why drug smuggling continues to grow in the modern era. Drugs like opium have been around for centuries, but international drug cartels are a much more recent phenomenon."

Ranieri looked sympathetically at Carlos. "I am very sorry about your brother. Drugs have killed many friends of mine in different ways. Sometimes people in high places forget about such things." After a slight pause, he continued, "And unfortunately you are right about the general situation about drug trafficking. The cartels were the first beneficiaries of 'globalization,' it seems, dating back to the British, who moved drugs from India and Burma to China in the 1800s. Now the increasingly porous borders, expanded international air and shipping, and weaker governments all play into their hands. And our nations seem to be somewhat 'schizoide,' if I may use that term, about these matters. For instance, Italy has suffered as much as any country in fighting this scourge. Our police, public officials, journalists, and even judges— many of whom I personally worked with in my career—have been targeted and killed by the mafia. Yet our governments still participate in the very 'actions' that lead to the creation of narco-states—as in Afghanistan."

"Yeah, especially in the case of my own government," Carlos retorted. "Our national 'war on drugs' has been a failure mainly because we've been using drugs to fight wars."

"I agree, and unfortunately, even when we try, we don't always follow through with our own efforts. It's like we chop down part of the toxic forest every now and then but let other sections remain standing. In time, the forest grows back even bigger than before, and its unwanted foliage begins to spread into once-healthy areas. For example, the various Italian mafias are not just in the south anymore. Even Lombardy, the richest province in Italy and the center of our industrial and commercial activity, now has mafiosi running all over it."[68]

"I understand that the mafia controls about 3 percent of Italy's economy now. Is that true?"

"Probably a lot more. By some estimates, the take from narcotics alone is around sixty billion euros—about 4 percent of the national output.[69] It is larger than all but a few corporations in the world. Very sad, isn't it?"

"I read where the 'Ndrangheta really came to the fore when the West started supporting the Kosovo Liberation Army. Do you agree?"

"Yes and no. There is no question that the 'Ndrangheta are the major distributors of the Afghan heroin transported by the Albanians, and the KLA funded itself to some extent out of drug proceeds, even before they took over in 1999. But our tough actions against the Sicilian Mafia in the 1980s were probably even more

---

68 Lombardy contains Milan, the commercial hub of Italy. For a brief introduction to the extensive spread of the various mafias beyond their traditional homelands, see http://www.metropolitiques.eu/Northern-Mafias-the-territorial.html.

69 http://gangstersinc.ning.com/profiles/blogs/crime-does-pay-how-italian.

instrumental in allowing the 'Ndrangheta to take over some of the traditional markets."

Ranieri's demeanor then turned businesslike as he stared directly at Carlos. "I can help you with general things, but you understand I cannot give you information on specific operations." He paused, glancing at the door. "Danio, over there, he can tell you more . . . but he needs something from you."

"Like what?"

"He wants to go to America—your Texas. Danio has helped us out quite a bit, but he's made it clear he doesn't want to spend his whole life in our custody. We can help him financially, but he needs a sponsor before we can let him leave. If you agree, he will talk."

"What do I have to do as a sponsor?"

"You must put him up for a period . . . a few weeks, maybe months perhaps. You must find him housing and transportation and help him with employment, which shouldn't be too hard since he knows English, and his new papers will all be in order. Danio said he wants to work out in the country somewhere." After sensing Carlos's hesitation, Ranieri added, "Don't worry, it's not a lifetime commitment, and Danio's not a bad man—although he's done some bad things."

Carlos remained wary, but he didn't see a showstopper in the whole scheme. After all, he wasn't married. He didn't even have a steady girlfriend at the moment, so a few weeks or even months at his place shouldn't be a problem. Since Danio would still technically be in Italian Police custody, it was highly unlikely he would try anything stupid.

After a few seconds, Carlos replied, "Okay, tell him I'll help get him started in the United States. Can I talk to him now?"

Ranieri left the room and returned with a slightly built man who looked in his late twenties or early thirties. He introduced Danio, who spoke semi-proficient English requiring only occasional translation. Danio began by elaborating on the same thread that Ranieri had hinted at, how he was orphaned as a little boy and hung around some of the young gangsters in Catanzaro growing up. He was smitten with their lifestyle, with its adventure and danger and swagger and, above all, power. Before he even entered middle school, he was running errands for his *'ndrina*—the local chapter—learning to handle knives and other such things. By sixteen, he had dropped out of school and was already involved in drug trafficking, although he had yet to hold a gun. Danio described his blood oath at nineteen, in which he swore eternal allegiance to the 'Ndrangheta, to "respect the rules of the clan," and to "disown his father, mother, brother, and sister."[70] He acknowledged how easy the latter was for him because his parents were dead, and he barely knew his two sisters.

While most of his activities dealt with the drug trade, he also got involved in extortion and loan-sharking, mostly enforcement. At first, he felt important, being part of a "family" that he never had before, marveling at how much respect men twice his age who were not in the mafia would show him. He learned the arts of arson, explosives, and kidnapping, and he even spent time in prison, returning home with even more prestige because he maintained the *omerta*—the code of silence. Eventually, he moved up higher in the drug trafficking network, which was the source of most of the revenue for his clan. Although his English was spotty, he would nevertheless travel abroad, from the Balkans to Amsterdam and, even on occasion, to New York and Colombia, in the latter case to hook up with the Cali cartel.

In time, though, he began to see through all the pseudo-romantic trappings of the 'Ndrangheta and see his partners for what they were—cold-blooded businessmen and assassins, who only observed the "code" as a matter of convenience. He witnessed what to him were senseless vendettas spawned by petty egos, and he was always looking over his shoulders not at his enemies but at his *camorristas*. He saw the ill treatment of most of the women from the *'ndrina* families, and he was glad to remain single, not being pressured into marrying because he was not one of the blood

---

70 http://www.dailymail.co.uk/news/article-2537140/Police-crack-coded-mafia-initiation-message-reveals-members-drink-blood-swear-eternal-allegiance.html.

families that needed the intermarriages to keep the peace. In time, he did increasingly gruesome acts, including two murders. One involved a drug dealer who cheated Chiapetto's boss out of the equivalent of over one hundred kilos of heroin; that one didn't affect him so much because the dealer was "scum" and the hit was quick. The second one was on a local businessman who was over his head in debt to the *'ndrina*, though no fault of his own. He pleaded for his life, but Danio shot him all the same in front of his young children. That one affected him in a big way, for in the weeks and months afterward, he would see the man's face every night in his dreams and wake up in terror. Even now, years later, he continued to experience flashbacks. It was when he was asked to carry out a political killing on a Catanzaro politician demanding action against the 'Ndrangheta that he finally balked and decided it was time to leave the only family he had ever known. He contacted a local prosecutor who he knew could be trusted and turned state's evidence. In the end, his testimony put eight men, including the *'ndrina* capo, in jail for a total of over one hundred years, although the case was still on appeal.

After hearing his brief story, Carlos started on a train of specific questions, to which Chiapetto quickly replied.

Did Danio ever transport heroin from Kosovo? Yes, many times.

How did he usually bring it? Overland to the Albanian coast, usually near Viore, and then across the Tyrrhenian Sea in fishing boats.

Where would it end up? In his case, usually Catanzaro, but depending on conditions, anywhere along the Southern Calabrian coast.

Did they ever get interdicted? Never by the Albanians, sometimes by the Italian navy; for that reason, the Puglia coast north of Lecce was often used since it was very close to Viore, although it meant paying off the Apulian gangs and using the backroads to Calabria.

Was there ever trouble with the Apulian mafia—the Sacra Corona? Generally not since they depended on our large network in Europe to move the drugs.

How about with the Albanians? Sometimes, but we had ways to "make life difficult" for them. (Ranieri interjected that the Calabrians would snitch on the Albanians when they threatened to move more of their drugs through the Balkans.)

And how did the heroin eventually make it the Northern European cities? Predominantly by boat, on trawlers, freighters out of Gioia Tauro, even on cruise ships like the *Costa Concordia*, one time even using a submarine.[71]

And the heroin to the Americas? Mainly through the New York mafia clans, some through Nigeria, but also some through Honduras, although the Latin and South American connection was mainly used to import cocaine to Gioia Tauro and then onto the rest of Europe.[72]

The entire interview lasted a little over one hour. At the end, Carlos thanked Danio for providing such important details for his story. Then he looked at him and said, "I understand you want to come to America."

"Yes, I want to live in Texas." For the first time, Danio showed a glimpse of a smile.

"Why Texas?"

Danio switched to Italian, with Ranieri translating. "When I was little, I always dreamed of being a cowboy. Most of my friends liked the action movies dubbed from America, but I preferred the westerns, and I dreamed of the wide-open spaces, the ability to be free. You might think because I was an orphan all I want to do is be around people, but it is the opposite—I don't have a lot of

---

71 http://listverse.com/2015/11/15/10-chilling-facts-about-the-secretive-ndrangheta-mafia.

72 For an account of the relationship between the 'Ndrangheta and Los Zetas and other Mexican cartels, see http://www.coha.org/the-relationship-between-the-italian-mafia-and-the-mexican-drug-cartels-part-2-the-business-relationship.

close attachments. I imagine myself sitting out in the high desert watching the raptors and the sunsets. And at night, I want to look up at a clear sky and see *la via lattea*."

Carlos kidded him. "But you know cowboys have to ride horses. Can you ride one?"

Danio seemed perplexed and then Carlos let him in on the joke. "Actually, folks on the ranch use pickups now, but really, if you want to live in the country, it might be easier for you to start out working the oil fields. With the price of oil going up, companies are starting to hire again, for all sorts of positions. It's tough work, but if you end up somewhere like West Texas, in the Permian Basin, you'll experience all those things you've imagined, and nobody will bother you out there."

As Danio nodded, Carlos thought about what kind of life he must have had, what could happen to your mind if you killed someone. He thought about his brother: he must have killed people in Iraq and Afghanistan . . . How could *he* live with it?

Carlos turned serious. "Danio, I don't know if the captain told you, but I'm doing this story because my brother died of an overdose—on white powder heroin, perhaps handled through your people. Whether you realize it or not, you committed a lot more than two murders—your victims were men, women, kids all across the globe." He paused to gauge Danio's reaction, but the latter's face revealed little. "But because you turned, you may well have saved a lot more people than you killed, so that's why I'm going to help you start anew in America."

Danio looked at the captain and then turned to Carlos. "You are very kind, signore. I promise that I will not be problem to you."

They shook hands, and then Danio left the room. Afterward, Ranieri went into a few more details on what was going to be required of Carlos. In the end, he assuaged most of the latter's worries.

"It will be okay, my friend. Only you and I and Danio know where he'll be staying. He'll get a check sent to a post office box every month, and you will report back here on his status, using encrypted e-mails, of course. If he disappears someday, the checks will stop, and he will be on his own. It's his choice. As far as we're concerned, he owes us nothing more."

Carlos started to ponder everything he had learned about the heroin trade, its complexities, intrigue, and sheer enormity of it. It supported whole nation-states from Afghanistan to Kosovo to Albania, and its economic muscle was felt even in a modern industrialized country such as Italy. *How can any of us really make a dent in it when our own governments are facilitating or at least tolerating it?*

His next question surprised the captain. "So why do you keep at it?"

Ranieri smiled and looked up for a moment and then grew somber again. "I am a protector, by nature. Everyone drugged or murdered by the mafia was someone's brother, sister, son, daughter, mother, father . . . but they were also mine. I am proud to protect the living—that's my code. The 'Ndrangheta talk about a code of valor, but they have no code—only fear!"

Carlos stared for a moment at Ranieri. "I wish I could claim your same admirable convictions, Captain," he said. "Yes, as a journalist, I'm supposed to lay out the truth for people. In this case, though, I am more interested in vengeance."

CHAPTER 8

When he arrived back in Austin, Carlos began writing his series; but shortly after the holidays, his workload increased, and he had to turn his attention to other assignments. In addition to the regular parade of murders and trials, flaps over growth and zoning, and other more mundane issues, there was a lot more state business now that the Texas legislature was again in session and stirring up its usual controversy. He also had to prepare for Danio's visit, rearranging the second bedroom and reaching out to some contacts in the oil business to see if Danio could get started sooner rather than later in his new life. He figured Danio would be inside most of the day, so he bought some Rosetta Stone programs for teaching English and Italian. As for the newspaper article on the drug trade, that would have to take a back seat temporarily.

He planned his article as a five-part series—about three-thousand words per piece. The first, already mostly complete, would describe in general terms the failed War on Drugs, the heroin epidemic raging across the country, and what was behind it. It would entice the reader to enter the rest of the series by offering glimpses of the topics to be covered. The second part would be entitled "A Brother's Tale," describing how such a smart and impish little kid such as Bennie could fall into the clutches of heroin addiction. This piece would describe the drug culture of San Antonio, the teen gangs, and the cheap heroin and other drugs coming from Mexico. The third part would trace the heroin that killed Bennie from its source in Afghanistan through the Balkans and onto Calabria before making its way to Nigeria and westward across the Atlantic. It would describe the various mafia organizations, using Zamir, Natalya, Danio, and others to bring the story to life. It would stress that a veritable Pandora's narco box had been opened, that there were now too many addicts, mafia cartels, narco-states, "legitimate" businesses, and even world powers involved to be able to corral easily the illicit flows. The reference to "world powers" would presage the fourth part of the series, the most controversial one, in which he would discuss how the great Western powers—primarily England, France, and the United States—from the 1800s on used the drug trade to support and topple governments all around the world, in the process creating narco-states. He would illustrate his point by describing how the heroin that killed Bennie was grown in a narco-state (Afghanistan) rebuilt by the United States and transported through a narco-state (Kosovo) created and protected by the United States and onto mafiosi in Europe, who were in cahoots with cartels operating out of Latin American narco-states that emerged during the CIA wars of the 1980s. The series would conclude with a final chapter on how many more young men like Bennie would end up dying before the country took notice. He would argue that it was hopeless to try to stop demand in a stressed-out society already using a variety of dangerous prescription drugs, especially when so many of its young people found their lives with heroin and cocaine much more rewarding, at least initially, than the dysfunctional and impoverished lives they were currently leading. He would argue it was senseless trying to stop young men, and now even women, from transporting and protecting the drug trade when the immediate gratification in terms of money and power and privilege was so much greater than the career prospects they would ordinarily entertain.

No, he would argue in the final piece the solution to the drug scourge was to create a worldwide commitment to strong borders and strong nation-states. It had been shown time and again in history—whether it be the communist takeover of China in the 1940s, Cuba after its revolution in the 1960s, the victory of the Vietnamese communists in the 1970s, Singapore after the imposition of the death penalty for trafficking, or the rise of theocracies such as the Taliban in Afghanistan—that strong-armed governments could, with enough will, snuff out most of the drug trade under their purview.[73] It was easy to understand why. Shadowy cartels with paramilitary capabilities were not just a threat to the citizens of a nation, but they were also a threat to the state itself. Conversely, weak but ostensibly emerging democratic states—South Vietnam in the 1950s and 1960s and Afghanistan and Kosovo and Mexico currently—were actually havens for the drug trade, in which the cartels acted as money banks and enforcers for candidates and political parties. The United States, in its efforts to fight communism and terrorism and tinhorn dictators around the world had, either intentionally or unintentionally, done more than any other country on Earth to spawn the failed states that lubricated the global drug engine.[74]

The complete series would be long by newspaper standards, but it could be spread over several days or even weeks, if it only ran in the Sunday edition. If it attracted a lot of interest, Carlos felt he had enough additional material to easily extend it into a full-length nonfiction bestseller, which he could write in his spare time after the initial series was published. He looked forward to turning the bulk of his attention to it once the Texas Legislative session finished up in May, but in mid-March Carlos received a lengthy encrypted e-mail from Captain Ranieri. Danio would arrive in Dallas from Rome in late May and would need to be picked up and transported to Austin, where a post office box would have to be set up for him. The captain emphasized that all this had to be done clandestinely, using aliases and encryption, because Danio's life would be in danger for the near term. Carlos agreed to everything and mentioned he had already developed some strong leads for oil field rig work, so Danio's stay in Austin could be fairly brief.

The ensuing encrypted text message was simple: *"Molto bene."*

****

---

73   See footnotes 41 and 42.

74   http://www.voltairenet.org/article175898.html.

As planned, Danio's arrival at Dallas-Fort Worth International Airport on a hot Texas Memorial Day weekend was brief and discreet. Danio rarely spoke during the three-and-a-half-hour trip down to Austin, gazing intently out the window of the car. He revealed little but did seem to relish the burger and fries they picked up on the way. *I wonder what he's thinking. Is he wary of his new life or hopeful, or does he even care?* Carlos tried to forget about Danio's murders, but that thought kept swirling in his mind. He argued to himself that he could have done the same had he been born under different circumstances. After all, hadn't even Bennie, born into a solid family, succumbed to the gang life for a while?

When they got back to the apartment, in one of the nondescript modern complexes that were springing up all over the major cities of Texas faster than the oil coming out of the ground, Carlos explained to Danio what their relationship was going to be like during his stay. Basically, Danio had to hang out the entire day either in the apartment or on the apartment grounds, perhaps the pool, unless he was granted permission. There was a grocery store within walking distance and various other shops, which Danio probably wouldn't need to frequent on his own. The most important thing for Danio was to improve his English, and secondarily, he needed to review postings on Internet job sites. With a one-year work visa and a false resume embellished by the Italian State Police, Danio could quickly manage to get some unskilled position, but the goal was to get a more permanent job within a few months. Carlos tried to explain to Danio that America offered lots of opportunities but that he had to learn a completely new way of interacting with people—a normal way that didn't involve threats and vengeance.

Carlos initially didn't know how Danio would take to his new life, but he was surprised at the resilience and entrepreneurism that Danio quickly demonstrated. The latter took his online English courses seriously, and his English began to improve rapidly. Carlos would even hear Danio practicing when he was cooking at dinner, which he ended up doing most of the time since he had more time than Carlos to prepare, and his dishes ended up being a lot more savory. Danio quickly became friends with the apartment maintenance man, with whom he began to hang out. The apartment manager, in turn, knew other individuals who were looking for temporary laborers. Before long, Danio was making lots of money off the books, which didn't diminish his witness protection funding. Carlos mused that Danio was still engaged in scamming of sorts, but this was the garden variety and harmless, unlike the former career of his that ruined lives. With his new income and the Italian government's checks and Carlos's hospitality, Danio ended up with enough money to buy a used off-road pickup by the end of July. Carlos figured Danio would have to work another month or two before he rounded up the cash for protective clothing, monitors, specialized tools, and commercial auto and worker's liability insurance that were all needed to start as an oil worker on contract. Eventually, Carlos was able to get Danio in contact with a company that hired workers doing rig completion in the Permian Basin, and it agreed to hire him beginning in mid-October.

As the summer wore on, Danio became more comfortable with his life in Texas, filled with his day labors and tinkering with his truck. Being handsome and exotic with his Italian accent, Danio also started to hook up with some of the young women in the complex, even bringing back a couple to his room on occasion. As his English improved, he started opening up even more to Carlos about his previous life and the criminal world of the Southern Italian mafia clans, all of which Carlos wrote about in his journal. In return, Danio was intrigued by the larger story being told by Carlos and would pore over some of the drafts on Carlos's computer, with his Italian-English translations in hand.

One night in mid-August, Danio asked Carlos to tell him about his brother. Initially offended by the question, he understood this was part of Danio's rehabilitation process, to personalize his victims, even if Bennie was a remote one.

"Bennie was very smart . . . too smart for his own good maybe. Unlike my brother Enrique, who followed in my father's footsteps and became an army officer, and me, who rebelled politically but was just as driven as Enrique to succeed, Bennie didn't get enough discipline when he needed it. At first, he would do things that would bother my parents, but he could always make us laugh afterward. After I went off to college, though, Bennie really changed because there was no one else to keep him in line. My dad was in his late forties, but his health was already starting to deteriorate, and his tough parenting style, which worked for Enrique and sort of for me, was completely ineffective for Bennie. He started hanging out with his friends at all hours, even staying with them overnight, when Pops started getting on him too much. My mom, on the other hand, babied him so he would often go around Pops to get what he wanted. Mind you, he wasn't an orphan like you, but he started drifting away from the family."

"And so did he join in—what you call it?—a 'gang,' like me?"

"Yes and no. His gangs were kids of his own age or a little older—creating a little mischief here and there but nothing like the 'Ndrangheta. Don't get me wrong. We have gangs just as violent as yours in my hometown, but Bennie was smart enough to learn early on to keep away from them. What he wasn't smart enough to do was avoid heroin. Initially, he thought it was something like weed—marijuana—but he got too heavy into it before he realized what it was doing to him. You've tried heroin, right?"

"Actually, I have not. We may have earned big money with it, but we were forbidden to mess with it ourselves. I would use cocaine now and then, but never heroin."

Carlos turned away from Danio. *Fuck the 'Ndrangheta, fuck all those bastards with their fucking double standards! They'd at least have some honor if they injected their own shit instead of feeding it to kids like Bennie!*

"I know what you are thinking, *dottore*. I don't blame you to hate me even though I provide you and the *polizia* with lots of information. I am truly sorry about your brother Bennie—he was very smart and fun and good boy, but once he got hooked on dope, his life was mostly full of pain. He would have deep down envied death all the time. Now he doesn't have to suffer."

Carlos looked Danio in the eye. "You're right, Danio, he's not suffering anymore . . . but the rest of us are."

****

On Labor Day weekend, Carlos held a little barbecue for Danio and some of his newfound friends. The maintenance man and his wife came, along with a couple of Danio's day-labor coworkers and their girlfriends and a pair of young women that Carlos had seen hanging around the pool with Danio. Carlos mused at how unpretentious and carefree all of them seemed to be, enjoying life in the moment, in contrast to the upper-middle-class wannabe strivers he so often encountered at UT-Austin. Carlos was impressed, even mystified, by the transformation in Danio. In contrast to his initial wariness and seeming introversion, Danio was irrepressible among his newfound clan. *He's made more friends around this complex in a couple of months than I have in almost two years.* In a way, it made sense—Danio wouldn't have grown up with a lot of structure or religious teachings or lofty moral ideas, so he had to survive through his childhood and young adulthood by being good at reading people. But his newfound zestfulness? *It's probably because daily life, despite its vagaries, seems to him like heaven after his escape from the hell of the 'Ndrangheta.*

A few weeks later, just before he was about to leave for West Texas, Danio surprised Carlos by bringing home a puppy—a presumed mixture of lab and pointer—from the local pound. "Don't you worry, Carlos"—he smiled—"I'll make sure that Capitano here doesn't destroy your place. In any case, I won't be here for much longer, so enjoy him while you can!"

Carlos said in a serious tone, "As they say, Danio, they tend to be our best friends—as long as they aren't trained to sniff out drugs and explosives."

Danio was perplexed, but then he realized the joke when Carlos started laughing and playing with Capitano.

"Ah, signore, tu es molto cattivo!"

Carlos sensed the meaning of the latter word and merely winked.

CHAPTER 9

Danio's departure in October coincided with the completion of Carlos's lengthy series on the drug trade. A few days after handing it in, Jimbo Burnett called Carlos into his office.

As Carlos was about to seat himself, Jimbo beamed and shook his hand vigorously. "Carlos, this is terrific work! We always knew you had the talent, but it's finally come all together in this baby. Congratulations, man!"

Carlos was a little taken aback. "You mean you're planning to publish it . . . as is?"

"I wouldn't go quite that far, pardner, but we're going to leave most of it in place. What I'd like to you do to do is cut it down to four parts, and we'll run it Thursday through Sunday. I'd cut out the first part about the history of the global drug trade and throw it into what would have been the fifth part. Let's start with your brother's overdose. I know it sounds bad, but that'll hook the reader into the larger picture. The total word count will drop to around ten thousand, part of which will come from reducing the background material and part from me helping you tighten it up here and there."

Carlos thought about what Burnett was saying and agreed it made sense. Burnett, beneath his paunchy midsection and good ol' boy demeanor and Texas twang, was a damn good reporter and an even better editor who combined a down-home populism with a knack for understanding his readership. He had once won a Pulitzer for an expose on the safety problems at the proposed nuclear waste dumps in West Texas and Southeastern New Mexico, and he had turned down several offers at the *New York Times* and *Washington Post* because, in his words, he considered those papers "about as honest as a nun working night shifts at a whorehouse."

"Okay, I'll rework it to four parts and start reducing the word count. If you go easy on me for the next couple of weeks, I think I can get you something by mid-November. I appreciate you're not scrapping it altogether though. After all, I'm sure you've thought about how it maybe could get the *Statesman* in trouble."

"*Maybe* get us into trouble? Hell, the shit's going to be flying at us from all directions faster than greased lightning, starting with the *Times* and *Post*, just like they did with Webb's expose in the '90s.[75] But an article like this can also raise the stature of the *Statesman*—if we live to enjoy it." Burnett winked but then paused to let that thought sink in with Carlos. "Carlos, I'm not going to lie to you, there are a lot of people who'll want your scalp after this appears—maybe even your brother. Didn't you tell me once he's the head of that Camp Bondsteel over there you write about? How is this going to affect your relationship with him?"

"I honestly don't know, but Bennie was *his* brother too . . . and if he doesn't care enough about him to take his blinders off and see how our goddamned government conspired with all those assholes over there who ended up killing him with their dope, then I don't give a flying fuck what he thinks."

Burnett stared at Carlos but didn't say a word.

****

The first part of the series appeared the Thursday after Thanksgiving, and the next day, Carlos's voice and e-mail were swamped. Most of the comments were positive, but Carlos knew that the third installment—the one that would run that Saturday—would be the most controversial. There were several

---

75 See Webb, 1999, op. cit., chapter 27; see also Alexander Cockburn and Jeffrey St. Clair's *Whiteout: The CIA, Drugs, and the Press* (Verso, 1999) chapter 2.

requests to be interviewed and a few to reprint the entire series, mostly by Midwest and West Coast dailies. For the first time in his life, Carlos got a glimpse of what journalistic fame was all about— both the good and the ugly. He received lots of congratulatory texts from friends and a *bellissimo* from Captain Ranieri, but it wasn't long before the blowback began.

The first piece was by a *Washington Post* columnist who claimed the articles relied too much on recycled accusations, anonymous sources, and a biased view of the efforts of the United States government to tackle the drug problem. A *Los Angeles Times* writer echoed those criticisms and implied that Carlos was assigning blame to everyone but the one to whom it really belonged—his own brother. Finally, the *New York Times* offered a scathing frontal attack on the motives of Carlos and the *American-Statesman*, claiming that shoddy journalism bent on sensationalism shouldn't be allowed to impugn the efforts of so many dedicated law enforcement agents and other personnel of the United States government.

But the most chilling reception to the article came from a completely unexpected place. Less than two weeks after the publication of the series, a letter arrived with an Australian postmark. When Carlos opened it, he was horrified see a postcard with the bloodied faces of Zamir and Natalya at the bottom of a grave pit. The caption on the card read "Greetings from down under." When Carlos saw the photo, he immediately began to puke.

The next day, Carlos knocked on Burnett's door. The garrulous editor greeted him a jovial, "Well, if it isn't the big dog popping in to brag about the Pulitzer he's about to win."

"I wish. Jimbo, you've got to stop plugging the story from here on out . . . quickly!"

"Now hold on for a second, what do you mean 'stop plugging' it? It's already out there, hombre, and I'm getting requests from all over the country and even outside the States to reprint it. This story is putting us on the big map once and for all. No way I'm going to back us out."

"But you saw the *Times* and *Post* articles. Do you really want to take them on?"

"I don't give a rattlesnake's ass about them. Everybody knows they're just shills for the Deep State these days. Hell, criticism from them feels almost as good as the top prize itself!"

Carlos slumped in the chair opposite and looked down without replying.

"Okay," Burnett said, "there's obviously something else bothering you. What is it—the fact that you brought the Camp Bondsteel stuff into the mix, knowing it would embarrass your brother and possibly damage his career?"

Carlos didn't look up but shook his head in disagreement. He handed Burnett the photo of Natalya and Zamir. Burnett looked it over, and then his expression changed.

Carlos exclaimed, "Three informants dead already! And who's next . . . my Calabrian, maybe even me?"

Burnett looked out the window and then leaned back in his chair and sighed. In a somber voice, he looked directly at Carlos and opened up about a similar predicament he once faced. "You probably never heard about it, Carlos, but early on, in between a couple of brief stints with the *Express-News* down in San Antone, I spent a year in the Valley with the *Monitor*. I stood out like a sore thumb down there with my paleface and freckles, but I spoke good Spanish and I was pretty headstrong, so I didn't shy away from anything from the start. Well, it's not hard to find corruption along the border . . . the *mordida's* everywhere. I was cocky enough to think I could get away with publishing something about the local sheriff bein' in cahoots with the bail bondsmen. Well, the next thing I knew, I was at lunch one day, and a shot came right through the café, plugging my arm." Burnett lifted the half sleeve to reveal a still-prominent scar at the top of his right bicep. "I'm not going to lie to you, I wanted to get out of town faster than a hog at a barbeque, but then my editor got hold of me and said, 'Where the hell do you think you're goin', son?' He sat me down and reminded me, just as I'm going to remind you, that journalism at its best isn't all about the glory. It's about standing up for the truth and staring down the evildoers."

Carlos continued to look down, seemingly nonplussed.

Burnett glowered at Carlos and asked, "So aren't you gonna ask me what I did next?"

"Well, I assume you lived," Carlos replied sarcastically.

"You're dammed straight I lived . . . In fact, I did a lot more than that. I got myself a Smith and Wesson and a flak vest and started swaggering all over the town, showing the sheriff I wasn't going to back down. It was all pretty damn stupid in a way, but lo and behold, two weeks later, the federal prosecutor out of McAllen arrests him and a bunch of his posse and my stock shot higher than a gusher."

Carlos still didn't look up, but Burnett knew he had his attention. "Dagummit, Carlos, our field is polluted these days with shills, liars, whores, and cowards . . . It's enough to make a buzzard gag! Even here at the *Statesmen*, there are things we're never going to touch either, like all that 9/11 crap. But every now and then, we show a little balls and let the public know what's really going on in the world." Burnett then looked Carlos in the eye. "Tell me, are you going to let your brother be the only one in your family putting his life on the line for something?"

Finally, Carlos looked up and stared impassively at Burnett and said curtly, "No."

Burnett then asked, "So are you going to let us sell the story?"

As he got up to leave Burnett's office, Carlos smiled wryly. "Yeah . . . but only after I buy my Smith and Wesson and flak vest first."

****

Carlos remained uneasy in the days that followed, concentrating on two major tasks at hand. First, he had to contact Danio via Captain Ranieri to let him know the danger he might now be in. Second, he sent off an alert to his brother about the series that had just come out and apologized for his earlier deception and for possibly damaging his career due to the Bondsteel links.

The first reply was from his brother. Enrique's e-mail was surprisingly gracious, congratulating him on one "helluva exposé." Carlos was more than surprised at Enrique's reaction and e-mailed back to wonder why Enrique wasn't madder at him. Enrique replied that, despite a few minor quibbles he had, it was clear that "you had your facts straight." He also wrote that he admired that "you did it partly for Bennie, to show that he was a victim as much as a self-victim." As for his career, Enrique said, "No worries—FIGMO. Returning soon to the States . . . for good!" Carlos knew what FIGMO meant—"finally got my orders" in military parlance— which explained the strange way military officers seemed to care a whole lot less about their jobs when they knew they were about to leave a post.

The second reply came about a week later. The e-mail from Danio read, "Congratulations on your article, *dottore*. It is the work of a true *erudito*. Don't worry about me . . . No one even knows who I am out here except Capitano. Attached was a picture of Danio in his cowboy hat, kneeling next to Capitano with an oil rig and beautiful sunset in the background. The e-mail closed with a cryptic inscription that read, "*La vita è sublime quando non si teme la morte.*"

CHAPTER 10

As the months dragged on after the publication of his drug trade series, Carlos's unease continued to grow, not only for himself but for Danio. He was glad to receive one correspondence from Danio in early February from Carlsbad, New Mexico. The letter contained a photo of Danio with a young Hispanic-looking woman, with the inscription on back that read, "Sabrina, the girl of my dreams! *Non e bella la vita?*" Carlos smiled. *Yes, life is beautiful now for you, Danio, but . . .*

Then Carlos thought about his own life. True, he had had a good career as a journalist, and his story on the drug trade had propelled him into the national spotlight, although it was unlikely he would ever win a top national journalist prize, given how critical much of the article was of the American government. Yet he never found relationships as easy to muster as most of his friends, or even Danio, seemed to. He'd had a couple of on-off relationships in college, but nothing like his brother's, which quickly led to marriage and a family. His first infatuation was with Maricela, a beautiful transfer student from Mexico City whom he had met at the literary magazine and continued to date after graduation, but she ended up going back home after college to be with her family. He had a few brief flings while starting out at the *American-Statesman* before eventually entering into his longest and most serious relationship—with Catherine Czesek, a fellow journalist at the newspaper. She was a tall blonde of Polish descent from a suburb of Chicago who had come to UT-Austin for college and had done the same internship with the *American-Statesman* only a year later. She mostly covered the social scene, including events, trends, and music. Catherine was the only woman ever in his life for whom Carlos could honestly say he could ditch work in a heartbeat any hour of the day. He and Catherine saw each other almost daily at work and then spent much of their free time outdoors, bicycling together around Lady Bird Lake, camping in nearby state parks, or sometimes on long weekends heading out to Big Bend National Park in West Texas. He would accompany her to restaurants, concerts, plays, and various social events she was covering, often standing around while she would interview people. After she had finished her business, they would frequent one or more of the Sixth Street bars, where they occasionally had friends playing in house bands. After a few tequila shots, Catherine was known to dance a bit provocatively, which both chagrinned and titillated Carlos as he watched.

Carlos admired Catherine for her vivacity and zest for people, but he didn't really think of her as the kind of "serious" reporter he was becoming. Every now and then, she would write a decent story with social significance and commentary, but he never realized how ambitious she was underneath it all until the day she informed him she had been offered a job by the *Chicago Tribune*, doing pretty much the same things she did in Austin but for a much larger audience and salary. He stared at her in disbelief as she told him she was going to accept the offer and, by the way, would he like to join her in Chicago? He was devastated initially but then began to ponder whether he could really leave Austin for a place where it regularly got below-zero in the winter and he would be a long way away from his family and didn't have even the inkling of a job. *I don't blame her for wanting to go back to her roots and, in the process, get a big promotion; but why does she have to ruin our good life down here?*

He did some half-hearted searching for journalistic opportunities in the Chicago metro area for a while, and he visited her monthly for the next six months, but it became evident during that time that their relationship was doomed. As much as he tried to rationalize why he couldn't join her in Chicago, he finally had to admit the truth: Catherine, with her strong personality and accomplishments, was his equal in Austin despite the fact that

Austin was *his* territory and his career was going well there; but in Chicago, it would be far different. Without a decent career position, he would be in Catherine's shadow, and he feared growing alienated without any close family members there. *Maybe I could handle her being the leading breadwinner, but could she?* He felt she would inevitably lose interest in him, so he would end up far worse off than if he stayed in Austin.

The problem was that he never again could find anyone who could match up to Catherine, someone with whom he could establish the same intimacy. He eventually started dating again, but in his longing for Catherine the younger ones seemed too immature and most of the older ones struck him as to ready to settle down and have kids. As the years passed, he got more set in his ways and started closing off his emotional side and becoming more resigned to living life without a close partner. He didn't think too much about having kids, although he enjoyed visiting his two nieces in Killeen on a frequent basis. Austin being what it was, he still had a lot of single friends to hang out with if he needed to, so he didn't experience the loneliness that he might have felt in other cities full of older, married couples.

Despite the uneventful months since the deaths of Zamir and Natalya, Carlos couldn't quite shake the premonitions that he was a marked man. *If they get to me, maybe it's better if I don't have a spouse or significant other to burden emotionally.* True, his mom—already reeling from the loss of her youngest son—would be devastated, possibly preventing her from ever again leading a normal life, but Pops was different. Although he always credited Carlos for his academic accomplishments—unlike Bennie, whom he considered pretty much of a disgrace—he mostly treated Carlos's liberal views as an irritant. Pops believed in discipline, individual responsibility, and respect for America and her military. He either dismissed or became angered at Carlos's antiwar and bleeding-heart sentiments. He couldn't deny Carlos's arguments that, until recent decades, Mexican-Americans suffered from discrimination in South Texas and elsewhere or that predominantly Hispanic San Antonio urban schools were not at par with the predominantly

Anglo ones on the Northside. Pops's retort, though, was that even in the old days, if a person worked hard, he could succeed and that it was the kids themselves nowadays and all the broken families and lack of discipline that turned the inner-city schools so bad. Pops would really get ticked when Carlos would spout off about the American military being everywhere overseas and all the trouble it was causing and how the populaces in the occupied countries were turning against us. Pops would rail at how Carlos was disrespectful of the family's traditions and especially of his older brother, who was putting his life on the line for what he believed in. *I doubt that he ever thought I was putting my life on the line writing this drug series, especially since he never commented about it. No, as long as Kiki, his favorite, is still alive and doing well, Pop's worldview isn't about to be shaken by anything that happens to me.*

He knew Enrique would take it harder. Despite their differences, they were still close as brothers, and Carlos knew he owed him for the mess he had created in Ferizaj. Kiki was a proud soldier, but he wasn't dogmatic like Pops, and he could bypass any superficial differences in his relationships. Kiki had his family, frayed as it was, and he had his "band of brothers," which, in the end, really wasn't the same as an actual brother because an actual brother was there when you were growing up, when you were undergoing the metamorphosis from a boy to a man, and, in most cases, when you needed support later in life. He vowed that, even if it was the last thing he did, he'd make amends with his brother as soon as Enrique returned to the States.

****

In the end, Carlos didn't get the chance to make his amends with Enrique, or for that matter, anyone else. Less than six months after his series first appeared in the *American-Statesman*, less than a year and a half after his fateful trip to Kosovo and nearly three years after Bennie's death, Carlos turned on the ignition switch going to work on a warm mid-March morning when a huge explosion blew out from under the hood, sending car and body parts flying everywhere. Although the murder was never solved, rumors quickly spread how the 'Ndrangheta, irate at the detailed analysis Carlos published of its worldwide operations, called in a big request of its partner in the cocaine trade, and Los Zetas performed the favor. It wasn't the typical Zeta killing, but it sent the same message: *Don't mess with our business.* In the end, the flak vest and gun, which Carlos had agreed to buy but never did, wouldn't have made much of a difference.

Enrique, already short in his tour, hurriedly packed his household and personal items and sent them off to storage in advance of his new assignment at the Pentagon beginning later that month. He stopped off only briefly in Killeen before heading off the next day with Monica and the girls to San Antonio to be with his parents. His mother was too distraught to arrange anything, but Enrique convinced his father that the main funeral service should be in Austin, where Carlos had spent all his adult life, while a smaller religious ceremony could be held in San Antonio the next day at the local parish.

Carlos's memorial service, in contrast to his brother's, was well attended by friends and journalistic colleagues. Many family members also made the trip to Austin, although some decided to attend only the San Antonio service, like Bennie's ex and Carlos's niece Jasmine, now a toddler. There were several national journalistic figures in attendance since it was so rare that an American journalist would be killed on American soil, and even his old girlfriend Catherine flew in from Chicago to pay her respects. One prominent journalist spoke briefly and stated that Carlos's sacrifice would be honored with a new annual prize in his name that would be bestowed by the National Press Club to the journalist who showed "exemplary courage in uncovering the truth." Several people got up to talk personally about the man they knew, starting off with Enrique's oldest daughter, Sofia, who told of how generous and fun her uncle was with her and her sister, trying to fill in while her dad was overseas serving his country, as when he suffered through a Dad-Brownie campout when she was a little scout. A few speakers later, Enrique got up and told of Carlos's life while growing up, their hanging out together in the neighborhood, the love they had between them, and Carlos's amazing writing talent, which led him to his prestigious position with the *American-Statesman*. He concluded by admonishing everyone not only to honor those in uniform but also all those who, every day of their life, were sacrificing to make this country a better place. "My brother may never have worn the uniform," he said as he started choking up, "but he was as fine and brave a soldier as there ever was." His display of emotion was infectious, as most of those in attendance started to cry or well up as well. Then the main eulogy was delivered by Jimbo Burnett, who told of Carlos's stellar career with the *American-Statesman* and how he had set such high standards for himself and others to follow. He then started talking about the events that led to Carlos's writing the story about the drug trade, and he talked about Carlos's reluctance to further propagate the story nationally and internationally after the deaths of three of his informants and how he talked Carlos out of it. Repeating the words he told Carlos almost verbatim, Burnett recalled how he looked Carlos in the eye and admonished him, "Are you going to let your brother be the only one in your family putting his life on the line for something?" Then Burnett started to lose his composure and had to be helped off the lectern. No one had ever seen Jimbo Burnett even cry a tear before, let alone crumple in a heap of emotions.

Carlos would have been surprised at two things that day. First, contrary to his predictions, Pops welled up along with everyone else in the church that day. Mixed with sorrow was a self-admonishment that he had all too often favored his older son while now belatedly realizing that Carlos was every bit as patriotic and brave as Enrique. Secondly, Carlos would have been surprised that a visibly distraught dark-haired thirtyish-something man wearing jeans and a cowboy hat with a young pregnant woman at his side slipped in almost unnoticed in the back of the church, shortly after the celebration of Carlos's life was under way. No one in the audience knew that it was Danio Chiapetta, who was still alive because of an assumed name and identity that only Captain

Ranieri now knew. Nor did anyone at the mass know that it was his detailed account of the 'Ndrangheta's role in the global drug trade that helped bring Carlos's story to life . . . but Carlos himself to his untimely death.

****

On the way back to Killeen after the memorial services, Enrique was mostly silent. His two brothers' deaths had shaken him, and even more it had shaken his faith in the government he was defending. He didn't blame himself for Carlos's death. His brother had his act together and knew the risks he was taking. *But Bennie—what if the heroin that killed guys like him really did pass right under our nose at Bondsteel?*

He had rented a townhome in Alexandria, about fifteen minutes from the Pentagon, and he planned to start work there soon without returning to Bondsteel. He didn't want to leave his family again, even for just a few months, and he sure as hell didn't want to go overseas again, at least for an entire tour. He also started to think about his life beyond the military. He'd have his twenty in a little more than two years and could retire with full benefits, but it was unclear what he would do afterward. If he and Monica stayed in the area, his options would be limited—Killeen had a lot of retired colonels and was too dependent on Fort Hood to support a diversified, high-tech economy. Perhaps he could work in Austin, which had a lot of small high-tech companies that could use his executive skills, or even Round Rock to the north, which he noticed was expanding rapidly as he passed it on the way. Either way, he was looking at a long commute.

Later that night, he asked Monica about what she was going to do about the house and her job. Somewhat to his surprise, she told him that she wasn't going to do anything with either.

"I'm sorry, Kiki, I'm not planning to join you in Washington. I've been torn between going and not going, but I've decided that I'm tired of moving. I figure now that you're a colonel, you can

101

retire on a good salary in a couple of years and come back to Texas if you want."

Enrique was at a loss for words. *Yes, I can retire as a colonel*—"*if I want*"—*but you're forcing the decision on me. There's no way I'm going to make it to general without a wife at my side.* Enrique was upset, but he was relieved that at least Monica hadn't intimated that she was seeing someone else—yet.

After an awkward pause, Enrique asked, "Well, are you at least planning to come up with the girls this summer?"

"Of course . . . but I'll have to leave by the first weekend in August to prepare for next year. The girls could stay a little longer."

"And what if the girls wanted to stay with me next year?"

"Well, Sofia is old enough to make her own decisions, and Sydney will probably want to go where Sofia goes. I want to caution you, though—Sofia's starting her junior year at Killeen High and is involved in a lot of activities. She may not to want to go."

Enrique pondered her words. *So is our marriage effectively over? I can't blame her for refusing to be uprooted again, along with the girls, and for not wanting to start over in her job again. But is there something more she's not telling me?*

"I understand. Then let's play it by ear. I'll respect her choice." He paused before he broached the question that had been worrying him. "Tell me honestly, though, does this mean you want to stay in the marriage . . . or not?"

Monica hesitated and then said, "Yes, I want to stay in the marriage . . . for now. I know that's pretty wishy-washy, Kiki, but it's not that part of me doesn't love and respect you still. Things have changed, though, especially since you took that Bondsteel assignment, and I don't feel the same way about things as in the early days of our marriage. It's probably not you who's changed the most but me. The sad thing is you haven't been around to see me—or the girls—change."

He stared at her. She was still attractive, although she had put on some weight over the years and was starting to show some wrinkles. It wasn't her physical appearance that had been altered so much as the psyche that projected through it, revealing a sterner and, in some ways, sadder countenance than she had once had, products of loneliness, regret, and even resentment. *This isn't the time to probe her . . . Better to push it aside and end my stay here on a positive note.*

Then he smiled at her. "You know, hon, I'm really looking forward to June. We're going to have a great time this summer. Tonight, I want to take you and the girls out for a really nice dinner. We all need a little to cheer us up."

"Sure, that would be nice." Then she gave him a brief kiss on the cheek.

PART II

CHAPTER 11

Enrique stared at the line of cars that snaked along the George Washington Parkway against the backdrop of the dreary late-March sky. It was his first commute since his arrival back in the States, and he was not used to traffic snarls after spending years outside a major urban center. Most of the trees were still denuded of their leaves, but he knew from his previous stint in Washington that spring was just around the corner, with the splendor of the Cherry Blossom Festival rapidly approaching.

Ahead of him, still out of sight, was the behemoth known as the Pentagon, the nerve center of American military power. Over twenty-five thousand military and civilian personnel toiled away inside its immense halls, performing operational and strategic planning, intelligence analysis, program management and acquisition, accounting and budgeting, and a host of support services. The Pentagon was renowned for its mass (over six hundred thousand square meters of floor space), its prodigious budget (officially less than six hundred billion dollars but, by some estimates, closer to one trillion dollars, with overseas operations and "special" military-related expenses figured in), and the incredible speed at which it was engineered and constructed (sixteen months during World War II). There were various theories as to its peculiar shape, ranging from its association with the Masonic pentagram (since so many other symbols and layouts in the nation's capital had symbolic significance) to an offshoot of an older building plan, designed to fit an irregular shape of land. Regardless of its origins, the pentagonal design was surprisingly efficient, for despite the nearly thirty kilometers of highways in its corridors one could walk from any location to another in it in less than ten minutes.[76]

As a senior officer, Enrique was assigned to the Army Chief of Staff, General George Johnson, primarily as a liaison to the various operational commands. Given his two previous overseas theaters, he focused mostly on EUCOM (in charge of European operations) and CENTCOM (in charge of Middle Eastern operations). In his positions, Enrique was privy to a unique vantage point, available only to a small percentage of the top officers and civilians of the United States military. Although he would sit in on briefings by others before the Joint Chiefs of Staff, he never actually provided any himself; instead, he would help develop presentations for others to give and ensure their content and presentations were flawless. A good bit of the background material he handled was classified "top secret," since it constituted the military's most closely held operational scenarios and plans.

Enrique's review of CENTCOM's plans and analyses for the Middle East gave him special insight into a dramatically shifting Middle East. It turned out that, contrary to what the American public was led to believe, the United States never really had any serious plans to attack Iran. There were some in high circles who still relished the thought, but such an operation was now considered militarily infeasible. After years of sanctions, Iran had become more self-reliant in advanced technologies and was no longer some third-world power. Most importantly, it had a credible air defense system—relying mostly on the S300 PMU-1 and its domestically produced version[77]—that was highly mobile and resistant to computer and cruise-missile attacks and would result in massive attacking-aircraft attrition. Iran also had the means of disrupting the oil flow through the Strait of Hormuz through a combination of supersonic antiship missiles, mine-rocket

---

76   https://en.wikipedia.org/wiki/The_Pentagon.

77   https://www.rt.com/news/332807-s300-defense-system-iran; see http://www.thedailybeast.com/articles/2015/04/13/putin-s-missile-could-make-u-s-attacks-on-iran-nearly-impossible.html for military implications.

assemblages, and swarms of small explosive-laded surface vessels. Enrique now understood why the Iranian nuclear deal agreed to in 2015 seemed so lopsided in favor of Iran.[78] The economic sanctions against Iran were extremely leaky, and everyone (including Iran) knew that the American threat of a military strike and occupation was no longer credible.[79]

Enrique was also surprised at the dire situation CENTCOM was portraying for Saudi Arabia. Once relatively stable, Saudi Arabia had become the most repressive of all nations in recent decades and faced mounting pressure from its increasingly educated but largely unemployed youth and its restive Shia populations in the east and south. The war with Yemen had proven to be a disaster, and the creaking monarchy was itself becoming increasingly divided.[80] CENTCOM was worried that an implosion in the kingdom could threaten its presence in the entire Middle East, and it had plans to use whatever means to help its favored Saudi royals fend off any uprisings. This would include naval aircraft from the Fifth Fleet, bombers from the 379th Air Expeditionary Wing based in Qatar, and special ops units sent in to hold strategic infrastructure. Until the Yemeni war, these were thought by CENTCOM to be enough, but the terrible performance of Saudi troops along the border with Yemen—in which many Saudi troops fled, leaving their weapons behind[81]—greatly alarmed American

---

78   See https://en.wikipedia.org/wiki/Joint_Comprehensive_Plan_of_Action. Expert opinion continues to be divided over the "Iran deal," which enabled Iran to remove all sanctions against it in exchange for a delay in its enrichment of nuclear fuel. One thing is certain: the deal was far more popular in Iran (many polls showed over 80 percent approval) than in the United States (no poll showed more than 60 percent approval).

79   http://www.nytimes.com/2009/10/05/world/middleeast/05sanctions.html?_r=0.

80   http://www.strategic-culture.org/news/2016/04/14/the-implosion-of-the-house-of-saud.html.

81   https://syrianfreepress.wordpress.com/2015/04/26/cem-45188.

planners. Enrique quickly realized that there would have to be at least one combined cavalry-infantry battalion available for immediate deployment in Qatar to help quell any unrest the Saudis couldn't cope with.

The other major strategic planning he was involved with was in Eastern Europe, where the United States had, for several years, been prepositioning heavy weapons, including Abrams tanks and newer Bradley fighting vehicles, in nations bordering Russia.[82] The crisis in Ukraine had clearly caught the United States off guard, with its political posturing getting ahead of its military capabilities. After the overthrow of the elected Ukrainian government by the American-sponsored coup in February of 2014,[83] Russian president Vladimir Putin shocked the West by quickly annexing Crimea without firing a shot and then covertly backing Donetsk separatists in their standoff against the Ukrainian government.[84] In the blink of eye, the two most valuable areas of Ukraine were gone before the United States military could even react.

Enrique was especially alarmed to read the intelligence emanating from Ukraine front regarding Russian capabilities. The Russians were obviously helping the Donetsk rebels, but even so, the latter's effectiveness surprised, even shocked, the Ukrainian army and its American backers. The separatists' success partly rested on the electronic superiority of the Russian arsenal, whose jamming capabilities proved far superior to what had been believed

---

82 http://www.stripes.com/news/europe/carter-us-to-position-armor-in-baltics-poland-southern-europe-1.354008.

83 https://www.rt.com/op-edge/228379-obama-power-transition-ukraine.

84 For a view of the conflict in the Eastern Ukraine, see https://en.wikipedia.org/wiki/War_in_Donbass; for an alternative view, see https://piazzadcara.wordpress.com/2014/05/18/the-popular-uprising-in-east-ukraine-rebellion-against-the-first-neo-fascist-regime-in-post-war-europe-by-lionel-reynolds.

previously.[85] The United States military and its NATO allies had moved a lot of firepower in Europe to the Russian border,[86] but they had become reliant on satellites and networking for much of their technological advantage. Any inability to secure those communications could be a very ominous development, rendering all that prepositioning of armor much less effective.

During his first few months on the staff, Enrique carried away several general impressions. The first was that, despite the political bluster, the American military was not seriously planning for any large ground-based conflicts anymore. The size of the army was shrinking, and agile military components such as special operations were being increasingly relied on and incorporated into operational planning.[87] It was also clear the United States was planning to rely on proxies for most of its engagements in the future, which were more about upending hostile regimes than taking back large swaths of territory from highly mechanized adversaries. Part of the reason was that the American people had lost their taste for direct American involvements overseas after the failures in Iraq and Afghanistan,[88] but Enrique still had trouble fathoming the implications of it all. Did this mean that the great armored divisions that had dominated every conflict, from the Civil War to Operation Iraqi Freedom—the divisions that he himself had been a part of—were now mostly a relic of the past?

Enrique's second major impression was that nations such as Russia and China were leapfrogging their military technologies on budgets that were but a fraction of that of the United States. Defensive systems, such as the S400 missile system Russia was now

---

85　http://www.defensenews.com/story/defense/policy-budget/warfare/2015/08/02/us-army-ukraine-russia-electronic-warfare/30913397.

86　http://www.nationalsecurity.news/2016-04-01-u-s-troops-armor-moving-to-natos-eastern-front-full-time-as-deterrent-to-russia.html.

87　https://www.democraticunderground.com/10024297587.

88　http://politicalticker.blogs.cnn.com/2013/09/09/cnn-poll-are-you-war-weary.

fielding, or the super-cavitating torpedoes China was building, or all the jamming and cyberwarfare technologies being perfected, were substantially cheaper than the expensive aircraft and fleets and satellite communications they were designed to take out.[89] He sensed a certain inertia, even staleness, about his own military's thinking, and congressmen who were more interested in defending jobs in their home districts than challenging the military establishment were no antidote to the bloated defense budgets. *It's been so long since we ever faced a foe with advanced defensive capabilities . . . Can we even be confident anymore in our technological advantage?*

Enrique's final impression was related to the other two. It seemed as though the foreign policy posture of the United States was unrealistically bellicose in an age when the American military was stretched so thin. With troops based in over 150 countries,[90] it was easy for policymakers to delude themselves into thinking that they could control everything anywhere in the world, often on the cheap. Special ops and proxies only went so far, though, given that they were unable to hold ground and, in the latter case, of questionable reliability. *Who, behind the scenes, is pushing us into all these engagements that our military seems hard-pressed to handle? And where is the pushback from our highest military leaders?*

In addition to his work for the army brass and his liaisons with the commands, Enrique was also assigned to some "purple suit"—i.e., army, navy, air force, and marine—advisory exercises. These tiger team reviews were designed to be probing and open-ended, with his teams typically posing as adversaries (red teams) whose mission was to poke holes in the planning scenarios. Enrique found these to be challenging but also extremely stimulating, allowing him to use critical thinking skills that had largely gone dormant while he was in the Balkans. As a colonel, he was usually the highest-ranking officer on these teams, and he was selected to lead the very first one in which he participated. Enrique's red

89 http://www.economist.com/blogs/economist-explains/2015/06/economist-explains-9.

90 https://en.wikipedia.org/wiki/United_States_military_deployments.

panel was charged with thwarting an operation near the Horn of Africa, where American troops, along with some friendly Arab ones, were involved in securing some inland military bases. In the scenario, a couple of armored battalions with infantry support quickly overtook the main port and moved to the interior of the country. All seemed to be going well for the blue team coalition until Enrique's red team, representing the local regime, destroyed the ports and key airfields by means of an extensive network of prewired explosives, effectively trapping the coalition armored division in the interior without resupply capability. The specter of a regime setting up an ambush by destroying its own key infrastructure and then launching a guerrilla campaign was unforeseen, as was its devastating effect on the coalition's campaign. The startling results of the exercise quickly made its way upstream, and shortly thereafter, Enrique's entire team received a commendation from General Johnson.

While the team may have caught the eye of the top brass, one particular individual caught the eye of Enrique—a striking young lieutenant commander who had played a major role in devising the team's strategy. Jessica Beasley, a Naval Academy graduate and naval intelligence officer, was Enrique's first direct experience with the new breed of young female commissioned officers who were now graduating in large numbers from the academies. He was so impressed and fascinated by her that, at the end of the exercise, he couldn't fathom the thought of her disappearing into the bowels of the Pentagon without him gleaning more about her and her background.

After the team's last briefing, Enrique stopped Beasley in the halls. "I want to personally thank you, Commander, for your decisive role in the exercise. You really showed a lot of intellectual boldness and leadership. I could see the way the others started to respond to your ideas."

Beasley smiled. "Well, yes, sir, every now and then we sailors come up with a good idea."

Enrique smiled back. "Well, I hope you didn't find working under an army officer too stifling. We tend to be a little more cautious, you know."

"On the contrary, I wish I could work with someone like you for the rest of my career. You're good at critical thinking, but more importantly, you're a fantastic leader. You listened and brought out the best in us even though you could have easily pulled rank, especially with your credentials."

Enrique smiled again. "What would you know about my credentials, Commander? You haven't been spying on me, have you?"

Beasley's eyes gleamed. "Of course, sir, that's what intelligence officers are paid to do."

Then Enrique broached what could have been a sensitive subject. "I hope this isn't the end of our association, Commander. I would like to think my knowledge of the navy could stand a lot more improvement."

"Of course, sir. You know where to reach me."

****

Enrique held off calling Beasley for over a week. Monica and the girls had just arrived, and he was busy settling them in. He arranged for a few high-school summer camps for Sofia and Sydney, and he rented a cabin the third week in July in one of the West Virginia mountain resorts, where they could go rafting and horseback riding. With their activities and all the other attractions in the Washington metro area, Enrique figured the girls wouldn't get totally bored. At the very least, he could hopefully wean them a little bit from their smart phones, in which they always seemed to have their noses buried.

Monica was polite but distant when she arrived. She clearly had misgivings about being with him, but she put on a good face. Enrique vowed he would make her feel loved again, and that part of her she claimed still loved him would reciprocate. Enrique took her out for a swank dinner for their seventeenth wedding anniversary at the Fiola Mari in Georgetown, and the entire family went on a dinner cruise the next weekend along the Potomac. Monica seemed nonchalant in bed, however, almost going through the motions. *There has to be another man she's interested in . . . Her heart's definitely not in it anymore.*

By the end of the month, Enrique's fingers could no longer resist dialing Beasley's number. He initially thought about asking her to one of the nicer restaurants in Pentagon City, but he ruled it out because it might give the wrong impression. Instead, he invited her to a delicatessen in the Pentagon itself, where it would appear more businesslike, which he convinced himself it was in any case.

After they sat down and ordered, he asked her to tell him five things about the navy he should know but probably didn't. "The navy's addicted to tradition," she said as she proceeded to tell him about the bell, which still rings on naval vessels every half hour to mark the passage of a watch, and a few other ones such as the cannon salute. Then she jokingly relayed the long-standing tradition that women were not allowed on board naval vessels because they were considered bad luck, inviting disastrous storms to wreck the ship. [91] Ironically, she added, "Ships were usually referred to in the feminine and had female mastheads, supposedly because Prince Henry the Navigator back in the 1400s said that ships were like women because they had to be 'powdered and painted to look good.'"[92] Enrique laughed and had to reciprocate with a few tidbits and traditions about the army, including how uniform colors were based on the whim of George Washington. Then he started asking more seriously about her involvement with the navy. She relayed that her father had been in the navy, that she had never considered any other service academy, and that she prided herself on her academics—first in her class at Annapolis, majoring in political science with a minor in computer science. She had already been on three tours with the fleet, twice in destroyers and once as chief

---

91   https://en.wikipedia.org/wiki/Naval_tradition.

92   http://chicagotonight.wttw.com/2013/11/12/ship-shape.

naval intelligence officer with the USS *Tripoli*, the second of the *America*-class amphibious assault ships.

Enrique asked her how she managed with all the marines on board the *Tripoli*, which totaled over fifteen hundred from the expeditionary and aviation units.

"The jarheads never bothered me as long as they stayed in their part of the ship cleaning their rifles. Just kidding, of course. It was the sailors I had some problems with now and then, mostly just keeping them on track. Intelligence gathering, as you know, can be pretty tedious."

"Did you ever have problems with your subordinates?"

"Not very many . . . Intel analysts aren't, by and large, high-maintenance. Of course, I was well trained at the academy in leadership."

"How so?"

She paused and smiled. "My senior year, I was selected commander of the Drum and Bugle Corps. It was actually a pretty big responsibility for a midshipman, and it gave me a lot of confidence in my leadership. I've never since doubted my ability to be an effective commander."

"Well, it seems like with your credentials, you'll have a clear path to admiral someday . . . if you want it."

She didn't take the bait but instead surprised Enrique with an invitation. "Sir, if you want to know a lot more about the navy, let me see if I can swing an invite to a party over the Fourth of July weekend hosted by Admiral Dennison. He works for the chief of naval operations. He's a good friend of the family's and has always been a bit of a mentor to me, even nominating me for the academy. There'll be a lot of naval officers there with their families, but there'll be some others as well. I'm sure he'll want you to bring your whole family along."

"That sounds great, Commander . . . as long as they don't bring up the umpteen straight years of Navy victories over Army. Of course, I'm an Aggie, not a West Pointer."

Beasley laughed. "Don't worry, Colonel, at the party, we'll all be on the same team."

CHAPTER 12

The next Monday, Enrique received a call from Vice Adm. John Dennison. He personally invited Enrique and his family to his gathering and apologized for such short notice. "You know, you must have really impressed Jessica Beasley because she rarely suggests that I meet someone outside the fleet. Don't worry, though, everything's going to be informal and, for the party at least, no rank privileges."

Even though he figured he probably wouldn't know anyone at the party, Enrique nevertheless was pleased at the invite. He had bought tickets for the July Fourth National Mall celebration the next night, but he hadn't made any plans for the Saturday before. When he told Monica and the girls, they seemed less enthused. In fact, the girls started pouting that they didn't want to go to a party for the "geriatric crowd."

The admiral's address was in Maclean, a few miles west on the George Washington Parkway. When they arrived, Enrique was surprised at the opulence of the two-story Georgian mansion as well as the large estate's view of the Potomac below. Monica and the girls warily got out of the car and ventured up to the house, with Enrique reminding Sofia and Sydney to be on their best behavior. Admiral Dennison, followed quickly by his wife, came to meet them at the door and welcome them to the party, where fifty or so guests dressed casually were already assembled. Dennison epitomized the stereotype of an admiral, trim for his age and tanned, with slightly graying hair, but he was a little shorter than Enrique thought he would be. His gracious manner couldn't disguise an assuredness, even steeliness, that Enrique picked up on immediately. Dennison showed Enrique and Monica around the living area and introduced them to another couple their age, a marine colonel also stationed at the Pentagon. He told Sofia and Sydney that there was a pool and badminton court out back along with "a bunch of young men eager to meet some pretty young ladies from Texas." The girls' dispositions changed immediately, and it wasn't long afterward they made a beeline to the backyard.

The marine officer—John Hernandez—was also of Mexican-American ancestry, but from California. Like Monica, his wife Kayla had just joined him, and they were residing in Washington for his second Pentagon tour, although he had spent additional time at Quantico. It turned out that Hernandez's tour in Iraq overlapped Enrique's, but though they shared many similar experiences, neither wanted to talk about them at the party. Monica and Kayla hit it off well, which pleased Enrique. *Maybe a good military wife-to-wife friendship can really lift Monica's spirits.*

After about a half hour, Beasley arrived at the party. Enrique was very surprised to see her in a tight blouse and shorts, which revealed her lithe figure, and with her hair in a ponytail rather than her usual bun. He was also surprised to see a good-looking tall young man at her side. Beasley and her friend made their way to where Hernandez and Kayla were talking with Enrique and Monica, and she quickly introduced herself.

"Hi, I'm Jessica Beasley, and this is my friend, Jerry Lear." After all the handshakes were extended, Beasley said, "I hope you ladies don't mind, but I've had the pleasure of working with both your husbands on some tri-service operational planning teams." Monica and Kayla both glanced at their husbands somewhat suspiciously before Beasley added, "And I can assure you are married to some very smart men."

"Oh, you mean 'cocky,' don't you?" replied Kayla, leading to a round of laughs.

Enrique chimed in, "Don't let Jessica sell herself short. I'm sure John will agree how much smarter she made us look in the eyes of the top brass."

Then Jerry Lear opened up. "Oh, Jess may have a high IQ when it comes to war games, but I can assure you she isn't at the top of her class in terms of financial matters."

Beasley playfully wrapped her arm around Jerry and said, "Yeah, Jerry here is one of the few folks in this room who doesn't know a damn thing about the military, but he claims he's a financial genius. So I've given most of my money to him to invest and hope he doesn't lose it all when the next crash hits."

Enrique chimed in. "Well, Jerry, I don't know a thing about finances either. Most of my paycheck goes to Monica, who keeps track of everything."

"So," Jerry asked, looking at Monica, "are you seeking any outside financial investments?"

"Are you kidding? Maintaining two households and paying for braces and college funds barely leaves me with money to buy makeup."

Everyone chuckled a bit, but then Kayla asked, "So you're not up here permanently, Monica?" Beasley glanced at Monica and then Enrique.

"No. Mainly because I'm trying to keep my position in the school system back home, and we didn't want to pull the girls out of high school." No one talked for a couple of seconds, and then Monica said in a sheepish tone, "I guess I'm not the perfect military wife, am I?"

"Honey," Enrique said as he turned to her, "you've been a great military wife. You spent three tours with me stateside and worried yourself to sleep at night during all my overseas tours. Not to mention giving birth to Sofia and Sydney while I was in Iraq and then having to spend so much time raising them on your own."

Monica smiled at Enrique and gave him a quick kiss on the cheek.

Kayla then joined in. "Monica, I can understand completely what you've gone through. I'm a teacher too, and it's been hard packing up over and over again."

After another moment of silence, Beasley then glanced at Monica and Kayla and said, "It was great meeting you both. We'll be seeing you around tonight, but if you don't mind, I want to introduce Jerry to a few other folks here."

Enrique went to the table with the hors d'oeuvres, and as he glanced out the back window, he saw Sofia was already playing footsies with one of the young men by the pool. He smiled to himself and then felt a twinge of remorse. *Sofia's almost a woman now, and I've spent so little time with her.*

****

The catered dinner included ribs and chicken and Chesapeake Bay crab cakes, along with potato salad, a variety of pasta and corn salads, and beans and coleslaw. Then after dinner, Admiral Dennison served as the moderator for a game of Military Pursuit, in which all sorts of historical and other trivia pertinent to the four services was thrown out. There were six teams of three each, with Beasley and Hernandez joining Enrique on one of the teams. There were lots of navy folks, a few marines, and one other army officer—Major General Warren Taylor, with whom Enrique had a short but intriguing conversation earlier in the evening, one that hinted at a later encounter. Oddly, there was only one air force officer—a female major, who accompanied one of the senior navy officers. Enrique's team won going away, with Beasley answering as many questions as the other two combined.

Shortly before the party broke up, Admiral Dennison came over to Enrique. "Colonel, I'm sorry I didn't get more of a chance to talk to you tonight, but I hope you understand. I do want to get to know you a bit more. Do you ever golf?"

"That's not one of my strongest suits, sir."

"Well, start hitting the driving range. I would like you to join me and another officer for a round later this month."

"Even though you're navy, I'll take it as an order, sir." Both the admiral and Enrique smiled, but the exchange made Enrique a little nervous. *I'd better get practicing . . . and soon.*

Around eleven o'clock, when a large part of the gathering started milling around to leave, Admiral Dennison got up to speak a few parting words. Everyone became quiet, and even the teenagers were attentive. "Janet and I are grateful you could join us tonight, and I hope all of you had a great time. But I hope as we head to our nation's birthday party tomorrow that all of you think, if only for a brief moment, what America means to you, what our founding fathers gave us, and what would happen if we lost that."

There was a brief moment of silence until one of the junior officers rang out an "Aye, aye, sir." Then as the cheers and laughter spread around the room, the admiral raised his hand in a playful salute and said to all of them, "Dismissed." Enrique laughed too but was a little disquieted. *Dennison's got charisma. He's a real leader, for sure, but was there more to his message . . . and golf invite?*

****

On the way back to the townhome, the girls lay back in their seats contentedly, actually ruing that they had to leave the party so soon. The games in and out of the pool along with the puerile flirting had all been an unexpected treat, and Sofia had even managed to get the phone number of one of the high school boys, whom she was hoping to text and perhaps go out with. Sydney, meanwhile, had seemed to connect with Hernandez's daughter, Alexis, who was close in age to her, and the two of them had already made plans for a get-together.

Monica's spirits had also been raised, what with her newfound friend Kayla, who shared so much in common with her and with whom she had already made plans to have lunch and go shopping.

Enrique's feelings were decidedly more mixed. On the one hand, it was a fine party, he met a lot of new and interesting officers with a different set of experiences, Monica and the girls seemed to have had great time, and he also seemed to bond with John Hernandez, with whom he had agreed to have lunch later in the month. However, something bothered him about why he was there . . . and who wasn't there. Jessica Beasley had managed to invite both him and Hernandez, who had so much in common, including their rank. He and Hernandez, however, were the only senior officers outside the navy circle of Admiral Dennison, except for General Taylor and Major General Robert Cummings of the U.S. Marines. Conspicuously absent were any senior air force officers. *Why did Beasley feel compelled to invite only the two of us to meet Dennison, and was meeting him and Taylor the real purpose of the meeting?*

The other thing that bothered Enrique was Jessica Beasley herself. Although he had found her intriguing at work, her femininity was muted in the Pentagon, and he could deal with her as an officer. Out of uniform, though, her sexuality was more obvious, and he was confronted with the realization that she was a woman, and a beautiful one at that. He gazed at Monica as she was dozing off on the passenger side. *Enrique, buddy, you have to keep from going there.*

CHAPTER 13

The month of July flew by quickly. After viewing the concert and fireworks on the National Mall the next night, the girls each had a week of summits—Sofia at the National High School Law Conference and Sydney at a junior leadership one. Then it was off to the mountains of West Virginia, where Enrique had rented a cabin for a week at Cacapon State Park in the eastern panhandle near historic Berkeley Springs. There was something for everyone awaiting them there, with horseback riding, hiking, trap shooting, rafting on the Cacapon River, and lots of evening entertainment in the scenic lodge. One day, Enrique drove Monica and the girls south a few hours to see the famous Seneca Rocks, a Tuscarora quartzite formation where Seneca legend had it that a young princess had required her seven potential suitors to accompany her to the summit, only to have the only one to make it to the top slip and nearly fall to his death before she saved and eventually married him. Sofia, probably still thinking of the young man she met at the party, seemed especially intrigued by the legend. Enrique partook of Cacapon's championship golf course on one occasion, hitting the driving range early in the morning and then joining an ad hoc foursome for a round later that morning. He was grateful that, despite his relative inexperience with the game, his natural athleticism enabled him to at least avoid a humiliating outing. *But I'd better keep practicing. It'll be a lot tougher with the admiral.*

The following week Monica took the girls to New York City on the Acela for an overnight. Enrique dropped them off bright and early at Union Station before heading back to the Pentagon.

Later that week, he met Hernandez for lunch at the Pentagon. With similar backgrounds and experiences and career progressions, the two of them continued to hit it off. Both had majored in engineering in college, but unlike Enrique, Hernandez was a second gen, with both sets of grandparents having emigrated from Mexico to Southern California before World War II. Aside from his Iraq tours and his Pentagon and Quantico assignments and his graduate studies, most of Hernandez's stateside time had been spent on the West Coast at Camp Pendleton, where the First Marine Expeditionary Force was based. Like Enrique, Hernandez had also distinguished himself in Iraq, serving in the infantry and earning a Silver Star in addition to several below-zone promotions along the way.

After their initial small talk, Enrique revisited the topic of Dennison's party. "Did Kayla and Alexis have as great a time at the party as Monica and the girls?"

"You bet. I'm glad the wives hit it off, and so I hear Alexis and your Sydney did the same. It's too bad Monica isn't going to be around after the summer."

"Yeah, I'm definitely going to miss her and the girls. After three years in Europe and the Balkans, I feel like I've missed too much of their lives as it is."

"Well, I give Monica credit, not just for pursuing her career, but also for letting you be off by yourself in this town." He paused before choosing his next words deliberately. "I don't want you to take this the wrong way, Colonel—"

"Enrique, please, while we're alone. Or better yet, Kiki, which is my nickname."

"Sure, Kiki. What I was trying to get at is . . . look, I think she's an outstanding young officer and all. But when Kayla first heard Jessica Beasley mention her working with me and all, I could tell her antennae popped up, and she wasn't going to let me anywhere near her."

Enrique smiled. "Wow, I hadn't thought of it that way. Monica didn't seem all that suspicious . . . at least to me."

"C'mon, Kiki, don't tell me you didn't notice her with her tight blouse and shorts?"

Enrique smiled. "Yeah, of course. But damn, I hate to think of her in that way, John. She was such an asset on the tiger team, or maybe I'm just trying to block all that out because Monica *isn't* going to be around." He paused and then smiled again deviously. "Hey, do you think the brass put her there as a test before being selected for O7?"[93]

Hernandez laughed and then grew serious. "You know, you may be on to something. She evidently managed to get us both invited, and I had this vague sense that I was being 'looked over,' so to speak."

"Me too," replied Enrique.

"And near the end of the evening," Hernandez resumed, "Dennison even hinted that he was going to ask me out golfing with him and a couple of other brass."

"You're shittin' me. He did the same with me!" Enrique stared at Hernandez and added, "You know, I don't think they plan to teach us the game . . . so, it might be good for us to start learning it ourselves."

"Yeah, you up for a round next weekend?" Hernandez offered.

"You bet," replied Enrique, hiding his concern.

****

Hernandez and Enrique lined up a golf game for the following Saturday, while Monica and Kayla and the girls all got together to do some shopping at Tyson's Corner before heading back to the Hernandez's rented home in Arlington.

The two colonels decided to try a nearby public golf course, the Hilltop in Alexandria, which boasted beautiful views and challenging holes, many of them excessively so for the two of

---

93 The ranks for general and flag officers are O7 (brigadier general; rear admiral, lower half), 08 (major general; rear admiral, upper half); 09 (lieutenant general; vice admiral), and O10 (general; admiral).

them. Enrique had played a little in high school and off and on since then, but he could barely break one hundred on a good day. He was strong and capable of long drives, and he had reasonably decent short clubs, but he was several lessons and at least a dozen rounds away from a decent handicap. Hernandez was less erratic than Enrique and stronger with his irons, but he was a little shorter off the tee and had more trouble on and near the green. Both men started with a lesson before teaming with another pair for a foursome. The two men laughed about how their best ball probably still wouldn't beat the admiral's, but at least they might avoid embarrassing themselves too much. Of course, neither of them believed their upcoming meeting was about the golf, although they could only speculate on what the true purpose was.

After the round, Enrique and Hernandez quickly showered and drove to join their families for dinner at Hernandez's place. Hernandez grilled some steaks, and Kayla made veggie quiche muffins and a corn and avocado salad. After dinner, the four adults sat outside on the patio while the girls hung out inside, watching a movie. Hernandez was a cigar aficionado and offered one first to the ladies, who laughed him off, and then to Enrique, who gladly lit up. Then as the cicadas started revving up in the woods beyond, their talk turned to the future, with Hernandez opening up first.

"I have nothing against living in Washington, Kiki. There's a lot to do around here. But I'm really pushing hard for a return to Pendleton. I know California's changed a lot these days, but it's still home to me and Kayla."

"I hear you, John." Enrique then turned toward Monica and said, "I promised Monica I'd do the same, putting in for an assignment back in Fort Hood. It'd be nice to finish out my career there, if that's what's in store for me. Of course, we'd probably finally retire somewhere closer to San Antonio."

"Is that where your family is?"

"Yeah, both sets of parents are still there, and Monica has a sister up the road in New Braunfels."

Kayla then joined in. "And what about the rest of your family, Kiki . . . Are they still in the region?"

"No . . . not anymore."

After a few moments of awkward silence, Monica motioned toward Kayla. "C'mon, Kayla, why don't I help you clean up? We can come back out here afterward."

When the two reached the kitchen, Monica explained why Enrique was curt when Kayla asked about his family. "He's lost his two younger brothers, one due to an overdose. The other one, the one he was closest to, was a journalist who investigated the drug trade, hoping to find some answers to the youngest brother's death. His expose didn't sit well with the cartels, and he was murdered last March."

Kayla became upset and turned away. "I'm so sorry for Kiki," she said in a somber voice. Then turning to face Monica, she said, "You won't believe this, but John lost his only brother too . . . in the World Trade Center on September 11. Frank was a stock trader on the ninety-first floor of the first tower and couldn't make it past the fire on the lower floors. John was barely into his senior year at San Diego State when it happened, and that's when he decided to sign up for the marines. It came as a big surprise to me since all the time in college—that's where we met—he had never once expressed an interest in joining the military."

Monica was silent for a few seconds and then replied, "Our husbands are similar in so many ways it's almost eerie. Hopefully, that'll help them make sense of it all, if they can open up to each other."

Kayla nodded and then put her arm around Monica. "Thanks for helping."

****

Since Monica had to be back for pre-semester planning the second week in August, her final week flew by rather quickly. Enrique had promised Monica a nice evening out, but instead of going to the Kennedy Center, Monica suggested a performance of *Madame Butterfly* at the Wolf Trap amphitheater. It was fortunate that Enrique had bought tickets for the Friday before she left because he received a call from Admiral Dennison that Monday, inviting him to the promised golf date for the Saturday after the performance. Immediately after getting off the phone, Enrique texted Hernandez to see if the latter was going to be part of the foursome. When Hernandez replied in the affirmative, Enrique wondered what it all portended. *This isn't going to be just a friendly golf game . . . but what is it? And who's going to be the fourth player?* For a brief moment, he thought it might even be Jessica Beasley but then quickly ruled it out. *No, it's going to be another top officer . . . but from which branch?*

Enrique offered Hernandez a ride, and they both arrived at the River Bend Country Club in Great Falls, just as Admiral Dennison was getting out of his car. Up at the entrance, there was another man waiting with his clubs, whom Enrique recognized from the party as General Cummings.

All four of the men warmed up at the driving range for a half hour or so before their tee time. Admiral Dennison tried to lighten up the situation for the younger officers while being upfront about their invitation. "Gentlemen, we're just going to have a friendly game of golf here today. But I'll be straight with you—in the process, General Cummings and I would like to get to know you two a little better since we've heard that you are two of the finest young officers in our entire military. Don't worry, though, there's nothing riding on this match, except a little pride for the marines."

Hernandez and Enrique looked at each other quizzically, and then Enrique popped the question. "I'm not sure why only marine pride is on the line, Admiral."

Dennison laughed. "Because the Cummings-Hernandez axis is going to defend the honor of the United States Marine Corps in a match against the teal team of Dennison and Ybarra."

They all chuckled, and then Hernandez asked if handicaps would be involved.

"Sure, but the maximum the club can offer is eighteen strokes."

"No problem, sir," added Enrique, "at least if beers are allowed."

"Beers allowed, soldier"—Dennison laughed—"as long as you're buying for everyone!"

During the match, which was full of good-natured banter, Enrique regularly outdrove the other three, but his control was off. He hit mostly roughs, along with a couple of out-of-bounds. One monstrous shot that went awry elicited the only cryptic comment of the day from General Cummings. "You have a helluva drive, Colonel, but something that has the potential to go that far always needs a solid sense of direction."

After the match, Dennison asked if Enrique and Hernandez wanted to join them at the club for drinks and an early dinner, but Enrique begged off. "I hope you don't mind, sir, but my wife is heading back to Texas early Monday morning, and we're hosting John and his wife tonight for a farewell dinner."

"Go for it, Colonel, you need to focus on her for sure. Hopefully, there'll be another round in our future."

Enrique replied, "That'd be great, so long as you and General Cummings weren't too embarrassed by our play."

"Not at all, not at all," Cummings said, almost jovially.

****

On the way back, the two younger men were initially silent. Then Hernandez opened up. "That was some golf game, wasn't it?"

"Yeah, pretty strange."

"Well, I think we did pretty well, all things considered. I can see one advantage of making O7—our golf games should definitely improve."

Enrique smiled. "Yeah, they clearly knew what they were doing out there, but I doubt they've had as much experience as us playing out of sand," he deadpanned.

Hernandez laughed, picking up on the Iraq reference right away. "So what do you think, Kiki . . . is this is a standard ritual for those in possible line for bee-gee?"

Enrique grew pensive. "Actually, I don't think it was about that at all. There's some other reason they're checking us out. I can't put my finger on it though."

"Yeah, it's almost like they're checking us out not because we *might* get promoted but because they *expect* us to get promoted."

Enrique sensed there was something to Hernandez's insight. "You know, Johnnie boy, it's thinking like that that's going to get you your star ahead of me . . . but not before I down the first beer when we get back!"

"Oorah, baby!"

****

Monica had prepared most of the food when Enrique and Hernandez arrived back at the townhome. The two went out back where they shared a couple of Shiner Bocks as Enrique began cooking the fajitas. Inside, Kayla and Monica couldn't relay enough of their military-wife experiences to each other, while Sofia was lording it over Sydney and Alexis in the "cool" department.

Everyone was amazed at how, in only a month's time, the two families had become so close. Enrique and Hernandez became more than close though—the two colonels started trusting each other as if they were the brothers that both had lost. They were joined together not only by a shared past with their similar experiences and honors and losses but also by a growing realization that they might be sharing a common future, whatever that might be.

As the evening wore on, Monica began to sense the promise of a normal and happy future with Enrique again after all the pain and separation in their lives. It had been awkward for her when they had had sex soon after her arrival, but now she felt some of their intimacy had been restored, although there was still a distance between them. She began to regret her decision not to stay with him during the fall and winter, as she now began to worry that another nine-month separation could set everything back again.

As the evening wound down, the four adults again started talking. Kayla opened up about Monica's leaving.

"I'm really going to miss you, Monica. I don't always get as close to other military wives this fast, but it seems as if we've known each other for a really long time."

"Yeah, isn't it amazing? You and me, John and Kiki, the girls—we all seem to hit it off so well. I know we'll stay in touch, and we'll hopefully be seeing each other a few times in the year. The girls and I are hoping to come up for Thanksgiving, if you're planning to be here."

"I think so," John replied. "And don't worry about Kiki here." He winked. "We'll be sure to keep an eye on him."

They all laughed, but Enrique winced a bit inside as he picked up on Hernandez's obvious reference to Jessica Beasley. He quickly turned to Monica and said, "Yeah, but who's going to keep an eye on you, honey?"

"Don't you forget you've got two daughters who don't miss a trick?"

Enrique replied, "Well, maybe so, but good luck finding Sofia on a weekend night!"

Kayla tried to close on an upbeat note. "I'm sure everything will work out okay. If you made it through those Iraq tours—those were the worst for John and me—everything else is easy-peasy."

Monica and Enrique nodded, restraining the same thought. *Except for three years of separation at that damn Camp Bondsteel.*

****

The next day, Monica packed her bags and prepared to leave. Enrique sensed her reluctance but also the independence that had grown inside her during the years of separation. *I wonder what she'd be like—we'd be like—if I hadn't had those long tours away.*

Enrique promised the girls during the final two weeks that he would take them to the coast. He had originally booked a single room with two doubles for two nights at Rehoboth Beach, but then the girls started pestering him to invite Alexis along, so he decided to bite the bullet and secure an additional second room after Alexis had received her parent's permission to join them. *At least Alexis joining on the trip is better than Sofia's new male friend she'd been texting.* Aside from the trip to the beach, Enrique also took a day off to show Sofia around a few of the colleges in the Washington area while he dropped Sydney off with Alexis.

When the girls left, Enrique felt a loneliness again creeping inside him, but at least now he wasn't as far away as in the past, and he had managed to reconnect with his family somewhat over the summer. Moreover, he had acquired a new friend in John Hernandez, with whom he had bonded faster than anyone else in his long military career. Although they hadn't mentioned their deceased brothers to each other, he knew from Monica that Hernandez had lost his, just as he presumed Hernandez had learned the same from Kayla. Sometime soon he would broach the topic with him. *But now I need to find a way to get back to Texas before my daughters—and my marriage—are gone for good.* He vowed that he would submit an assignment preference to Fort Hood the next week. Hopefully, he could find a senior officer slot open there sooner rather than later.

CHAPTER 14

After Sofia and Sydney had left, Enrique quickly got back into the thick of his strategic planning at the Pentagon, continuing to monitor the various commands for General Johnson in addition to receiving another tiger-team assignment, this time involving trouble in the Baltic states.

He had one more lunch with John Hernandez before Labor Day. Hernandez started off by asking about the girls and Monica, and then they discussed getting together for another round of golf. Hernandez had also rented some space on a Potomac River charter in mid-September and invited Enrique to join him and a couple of his marine friends.

"You've been on a boat before, haven't you, Kiki?" Hernandez kidded.

"Yeah, once or twice—in between jumping out of a plane and landing on my Abrams."

They both laughed. That was what it was all about—good-natured ribbing mixed with some work-related observations and gossip and a little sports and political commentary. The one topic they avoided was the one thing most people would think they might open up to each other most about—a shared loss of their brothers. But military field officers who had seen so much death don't dwell on it but compartmentalize, holding back until the right moment to share their feelings.

They did share some of their strategic simulations, with Hernandez most recently participating in a Pacific war games exercise.

"You know, Kiki, I know we can't discuss any of the specifics, but I was a little surprised—actually, more like worried—at the outcome of the Pacific simulation. There's a lot of new red stuff out there—supersonic missiles, supercavitating torpedoes, jamming, stuff like that—that's hard to assess until the shit hits the fan in combat. The navy guys seem pretty concerned about it,[94] but our air force partners strike me as a little too complacent . . . as if we're still facing down Saddam. The world's changed a lot since the '70s in Vietnam, when we had our last serious aerial challenge. There've been several generations of SAMs,[95] but are our fighters all that much better than before? A lot of folks are saying that the F-35 is a piece of junk—way too hard to maintain."[96]

"I don't know, maybe. Yeah, I've heard some of the same shit about the F-35, but you should know better than me—after all, you guys are beginning to train on it. All I know is that the air force is planning to overcome any aircraft shortcomings with a lot of drones and C4I crap,[97] but you and I've learned the hard way what's shit and what shines—hell, we probably wouldn't even

---

94 http://www.military.com/daily-news/2016/02/27/china-military-buildup-in-pacific-could-require-us-response.html.

95 "SAM" stands for surface-to-air missiles, such as the S-300 and S-400 (see also footnote 89), usually designed to down aircraft.

96 The F-35 Joint Strike Fighter is projected to be the mainline fighter of the future for the Unite States Air Force but has been widely criticized for its enormous cost overruns, production delays, under-performance, and high maintenance costs: http://www.foxnews.com/opinion/2015/10/21/sorry-saga-f-35-when-pentagon-wastes-money-all-get-vegas-hangover.html. Indeed, shortly after being declared "combat-ready," the air force grounded over half of the F-35 fleet because of wiring insulation problems: http://www.cnn.com/2016/09/16/politics/us-air-force-grounds-f-35.

97 "C4I" stands for command, control, computers, communications, and intelligence. For the new United States Air Force doctrine on air superiority, see http://www.af.mil/Portals/1/documents/airpower/Air%20Superiority%202030%20Flight%20Plan.pdf.

be talking here if we hadn't had air superiority back in Iraq. Our flyboys better keep that up in the next war, or else all hell's gonna break loose."

"Speaking of all hell breaking loose, you should have seen our friend Jessica Beasley kick-boxing at the gym the other day. She's pretty damn ferocious in her short shorts." Then after a slight pause, he added, "You're heeding my advice about staying away from her, right?"

"What're you, my dad or something? Look, I think I'm pretty good at keeping out of trouble, at least that kind. Maybe you're the one with the hots for her?"

"Fuck no. And even if I did, I wouldn't tell you because it probably would get straight back to Kayla. All I said she was ferocious at kick-boxing—"

Enrique smiled and added, "In her short-shorts."

****

A few days later, Enrique ran across Beasley heading to the corridor 3 food court. As she approached him, she saluted and greeted him with a "Hi, Colonel." Then she said playfully, "I hear you hit a pretty long drive off the tee."

Enrique smiled but was a little taken aback. "So how is it that you know so much about our little golf game, Commander?"

"Oh, you do remember how Admiral Dennison is a good family friend, right? We get together periodically to chat, and in this case, the chat happened to involve you and Colonel Hernandez." She continued perkily, "By the way, speaking of chatting, I have some interesting stuff I'd like to bounce off you, if you don't mind another quick lunch sometime."

Enrique was intrigued, although Hernandez's admonishments about staying away from her made him a little wary. After a pause, he replied, "Sure, how about next Wednesday? There's a nice little Thai restaurant in Pentagon City just off the metro stop. I like to have lunch there 'cuz it's pretty good food and easy to get in if you arrive by eleven fifteen. Are you into Thai?"

"Thai would be great. Why don't we meet outside the Southeast Corner at eleven?"

"Okay, but your stuff has to be good."

Beasley hesitated and then smiled. "I definitely think you'll find it interesting."

****

As they sat down for lunch, Beasley started with some small talk. "So are you planning to keep working on your golf game, Colonel?"

Enrique looked her in the face, almost frowning. "Why do you keep obsessing about my golf game? I'm actually not all that keen on the game, and by the way, when we're off duty like this, please call me Enrique."

"I'm sorry. It's just that it's hard to get out the habit, but I'll call you Enrique from here on out. In fact, En-ri-que," she said, slowly rolling out his name, "what *do* you like to do for sport?"

Enrique's eyes gazed upward for a moment. "Well, this may seem a little out of the ordinary, but I like to ride horses. I was in the cavalry regiment in the Corps of Cadets at A&M, and I always like to ride when I get the chance. I haven't done much in the past several years though."

"Well, isn't that a coincidence? Through middle school, I spent a lot of time on horses. We lived in Vienna at the time, and I took riding lessons a little west of Middleburg. Perhaps you know that it's the heart of horse-breeding country in Virginia." She paused before smiling slightly and adding, "In fact, why don't you join me some Saturday morning for a little riding at the farm where I took lessons? They have a few horses for riding and miles of trails and fields."

Enrique's expression turned pensive. "Look, thanks for the offer, but what about your friend Jerry? I imagine he wouldn't be too thrilled about me heading off with you for a Saturday."

Beasley smiled. "Oh, Jerry won't care . . . He works all day Saturday anyways, seeing clients. I'm surprised you're even thinking that way, Colonel. I mean Enrique. I have lots of male friends, and Jerry understands all this and is pretty cool about it."

"That's good. It's often a problem for military men—and women—dating or marrying people who don't understand the military."

"Actually, Jerry and I hardly ever talk about the military when we're alone, which is one of the things I like about him."

Enrique tried to absorb it all. *What is it about her that makes her so enticing? Is it because she's so damn beautiful and confident, or is it because she's "taken"?*

Enrique let out a slight blush underneath his olive skin. Finally, he said, "Okay, I'm in . . . but it'll have to be the weekend of the tenth. I'm playing golf this weekend with Colonel Hernandez and two weekends later going fishing with him and some of his friends."

"Well, Saturday the tenth it'll be."

Enrique changed the subject. "Okay, Commander—"

"Jessica when we're off-duty, right?"

"Okay then, Jessica, what was it that you *really* wanted to talk to me about?"

She stared at him. "I'm on another strategic planning team."

"And?"

"More like 'but.' It's nothing like your team. It doesn't even involve anything overseas." After a brief pause, she asked, "Does 'JADE HELM' ring a bell?"

"Yeah, that exercise involving special ops a few years back that a lot of conspiracy folks in Texas were all bent out of shape about.[98] What about it?"

---

98 See http://www.nytimes.com/2015/09/17/us/jade-helm-military-exercise-ends-with-little-fanfare-and-less-paranoia.html. Although the fears of locals and others concerning JADE HELM did not materialize, the United States military never explained directly why the exercise was conducted alongside the United States general population and even what the acronym "HELM" referred to. Conspiracy theorists maintain that "HELM" referred to "Homeland Eradication of Local Militants": https://www.youtube.com/watch?v=TbkePjyyZ8o.

"Well, the new stuff our team's planning is like JADE HELM on steroids. It doesn't involve just special ops—it brings in a lot of military, including your Third Corps headquartered at Fort Hood. I have to be very careful that I don't mention any classified stuff, but someone's envisioning a major action here on American soil. Aren't we supposed to leave all that to the guard?"

Enrique gently nodded. "It would seem. I'll check around a bit . . . and see what I can find out. Who do you think's behind it all?"

"It's coming from the top brass for sure. But I don't think it's their own idea. It's a political thing, no doubt, probably coming from POTUS."[99]

"Who's the army's spot on the team? Maybe I know him."

"Or her," she teased. Enrique nodded but barely smiled.

"He's Colonel Terence Matthews out of Fort Belvoir. Have you heard of him?"

Enrique stared at Beasley and then, in a quiet voice, said, "Yeah, I know him. In fact, I once saved his life." Then after a pause, he added, "But that's just between you and me, okay?"

Beasley stared at him briefly and then nodded.

****

Two Saturdays later, Enrique picked Beasley up at her mother's house in Reston, where she was staying during her tour at the Pentagon. Beasley was in jeans and riding boots and a cotton blouse, with her riding helmet in her hand and her hair tied up in a ponytail, almost as if she had come from a photoshoot. It made sense that she would be living at home, saving on housing and spending time with her mother. *But could it also mean that she and Jerry aren't really that serious about each other?*

It was a half-hour ride west on Route 50 to Middleburg, with small towns and lush estates gradually replacing the suburban developments that were increasingly pockmarking the Northern Virginia countryside. The "farm" Beasley mentioned was actually

---

99 "President of the United States."

one of the larger estates, emblematic of the old money that surrounded the historic town. Its expanse covered over five hundred acres, mostly pastures and woodlands set on top of rolling hills. The large stables served a dual purpose—one side was used for breeding operations, mostly equestrian, while the other half was used for older riding horses. Inside its wooden picket fences were an equestrian circle for training and several pens, while several long trails wound up into the hills. Because she was familiar with the stables, Enrique let Beasley choose a couple of older geldings for their ride. Over the wider trails and open fields, the horses mostly trotted and cantered; while on the narrower trails in the woods, they walked. Beasley obviously still rode frequently and had no trouble with her horse, but Enrique's was a little feistier and even reared on one occasion. He was glad his horse wasn't more spirited, given that his riding skills were a little rusty. It was a gorgeous late summer day, with a faint yellow tinge appearing on some of the maples. Beasley led most of the way since she knew the trails, and the two of them rode mostly in silence, broken only by occasional conversation or observations. Enrique was glad that Beasley was lost in her thoughts as well, because he relished hearing only the sound of the hooves touching the ground in synch with the rhythm of the horse's gentle vertical undulations.

After an hour and a half of riding, they spent another hour touring the stables and watching some equestrians train. Afterward, they went off to lunch at the historic Red Fox Inn, a colonial structure that served a variety of sandwiches and crab cakes along with a few southern meat recipes.

After ordering, she was the first to speak. "So what did you think of it all this morning?"

"Well, it's a bit different from Texas—and Kosovo," he deadpanned. After she smiled, he grew more serious. "Actually, it was very peaceful, especially in the woods. A few quiet moments on a horse underscores the insane amount of information and noise and stress and drama that's our so-called normal existence nowadays. When I do get to ride, it's rarely alone, but it was almost as if I was alone at times because you seemed equally immersed."

"You know, that's exactly the experience I love—just the horse and me in solitude. I come out here about once a month, except in the winter. It's one of the reasons why I wouldn't mind staying in DC for a while."

"And the other reasons?"

"Oh, I don't know. Being at the Pentagon now, I get to see the big picture, a glimpse of the future even. And there's no serious supervisory stuff. Most of the people I deal with are fellow officers, like you and Colonel Hernandez."

"And Jerry?"

She smiled. "Now don't go too far into my personal life, Colonel!" she teased. Then she said in a pensive tone, "To be honest, I don't know how I feel about Jerry. I know he's crazy about me, and I really do like him. He lets me have my space, and I appreciate that. Even my mom likes him."

"But there's something lacking, isn't there?"

She turned her head and blushed slightly. "Now you *are* getting too personal. Let's put it this way. I want to get my twenty years in. I'll be sent off to Naval War College after here and then on to either a fleet or stateside tour. I'll be in my early thirties by then, and I imagine Jerry and I will tie the knot, if we're still together." She paused. "The military sure makes it tough on our personal lives, doesn't it?"

"Yes, it does." *But hopefully, it'll be easier on you since you'll be marrying toward the end of your career, when you can already begin the process of settling down.*

Beasley then added, "One thing I really admire about you is the way you stood up for your wife at the admiral's party. She was probably feeling a little insecure at the moment, and you made her feel so special."

"Well, I owed her at least that. Monica's been so supportive of me over the years." He paused before adding, "I'm not going to lie to you though. It's a lot different than in the past. She has to think about her own career as well as the girls. She loves teaching the kids, and God knows we need dedicated teachers like her in this world. I'm hoping to get back to Texas after this assignment—maybe finish out there." Then after a pause, he smiled. "Maybe even buy a few acres of pasture for a horse or two."

"So I take it you'd like to go riding again?"

"Sure, but not until early next month. Remember, I'm going fishing with Colonel Hernandez next week, and then I'm planning a surprise visit to Monica and the girls. Did you know Texas and A&M are playing each other for the first time in almost a decade? I've got two tickets to the game in Austin for Monica and me. Afterward, we'll probably have dinner with some friends."

Beasley stared at him and smiled, "I don't follow college football much, but I can only guess who you'll be rooting for." Then after a pause, she added, "Early October it'll be."

CHAPTER 15

That next week, Enrique was feeling positive about the way things were going. He was looking forward to the fishing trip and then visiting with Monica and the girls. He did start having second thoughts about his "surprise," though, and he decided he would text Sofia about it the day before if she promised to keep his visit a secret from Sydney and her mom.

It turns out that one of Hernandez's friends couldn't make it on the boat that weekend, but the one who did was a fellow marine, Zach Rogers. Rogers, a single amputee, was a recently promoted lieutenant colonel also stationed at the Pentagon and seemingly about the same age as Hernandez and Enrique. Hernandez picked Enrique up at five in the morning, and they arrived at the dock and departed just before sunrise. The boat was smaller than Enrique had expected, and there were only a few other guests on the six-hour trip into the Chesapeake Bay. The boat went south from Herrington Harbor to a few of the best fishing spots along the western shore of the bay. Hernandez had promised that he'd fry anything of a decent size he or anyone else caught. It turns out that all three of them managed to reel in at least one medium-sized rockfish, and Hernandez even caught a twenty-two-inch bluefish. Enrique was surprised at how little remained after cleaning and filleting—barely enough for a single meal for the three of them plus Kayla and Alexis.

Hernandez dropped each of the other two men off at their places before heading back to his house to grill. Enrique took a nice long shower and then caught a little nap before arriving early that evening. Kayla was there to greet him, and she straight off asked about Monica and the girls and hoped that Enrique would send along her greetings to them. Then she confessed that she and Monica were in frequent e-mail contact since her return to Texas and, in fact, were drawing up tentative plans to reunite over Christmas and maybe do some skiing rather than getting together at Thanksgiving. Enrique kidded her about how she and Monica were "going behind their backs," and then he mentioned the surprise visit he was planning the next weekend and warned her not to spill the beans.

The captain of the charter had given Hernandez a delicious recipe for grilling the rockfish, using a mélange of herbs. Kayla had made some coleslaw and boiled some corn to go along with the fish, and the five of them quickly devoured the day's catch. After dinner, the three men went out on the back patio to down beers and engage in some male banter. Hernandez offered Enrique and Rogers cigars but pulled out a cigarette for himself. "Like PTSD, an unfortunate residue of his time in Iraq," he kidded. Although most of the conversation involved discussions of Pentagon workplace politics and intrigue, Rogers and Hernandez alluded to some of the harrowing experiences they had had in Iraq together. Enrique was mostly silent as they reminisced but chuckled when Hernandez teased him that "Of course, I'm sure you never had any exciting experiences over there, Kiki, lounging around in your Abrams fortress all day."

After a little more than an hour, Rogers had to leave for another gathering, and afterward, Hernandez opened up more to Enrique about his relationship with Rogers.

"Zach's a good soldier, Kiki, and we get along great, but it wasn't always that way."

"Why's that?"

"When we were in Fallujah in Fall of '04, Zach was second in command of my platoon. We were cleaning up block by block until one afternoon we get hit by tons of fire coming from all directions. Zach and our gunny—Stan Singletary was his name, a tough black kid from Detroit—both got pinned down on the other side of the street when the fire came." His eyes staring ahead, Hernandez then recounted the action during the firefight. "We're being peppered right and left and covering as best as we can while frantically trying to figure out where the muj[100] are through all the smoke and noise. Goddamn, you could barely think through all that crap! All of a sudden, Zach cries out, 'Stan and me've been hit!' At that point, I'm doing all I can to stay cool and figure things out. Now I'd never been in any shit like this before, but I know we had to get 'em out, and I start thinking like I'm back in engineering school, struggling with a fluids problem. When I signed up, they were all saying an engineer like me should sign up for air and go fly fighters or helos, but I don't know why I kept insisting I wanted to go into infantry—maybe to prove something to myself. In any case, I decided that I'd be the one to go get Zach and Stan. I told everyone else to fire away if only to create enough smoke to cover me."

Hernandez continued on, "But when I got there, I could see Stan was shot in the head and wasn't going to make it. Zach was really bleeding bad through his leg, so I slapped a tourniquet on it and grabbed him over my shoulders and made a run for it. That's when I got hit in the leg myself and fell, but he and I fortunately managed to crawl to cover. The whole time Zach was angry at me because he wanted me to take Stan first, but it wasn't registering that Stan was already a goner. When I got back, the medic started working on both Zach and me, but against my orders, another one of our guys went to get Singletary and got clipped before returning. With me and several others in our platoon out of action, I called in the Apaches, and they started strafing. Not long afterward, the fighting died down."

After a pause, Enrique interjected, "But Zach still had survivor's guilt, didn't he?"

"Yeah, especially since he and Stan were pretty close. Eventually, he came around, and ever since, we've maintained close contact, even when we weren't together. Zach, deep down, still

---

100 "Muj," short for mujahedeen, was a term American soldiers applied to Iraqi insurgents during Operation Iraqi Freedom.

thinks he owes me one, but I tell him not to think that way, that I know he would have done the same for me."

Enrique replied that he had the same experience over in Iraq with a couple of guys who were now colonels like them, not mentioning TJ Matthews or Travis Rackley by name. He described the tanker ambush and the fires in the Bradleys and how he too had to do some quick thinking by ditching some of the equipment. "I did what I was supposed to do, just like you, what any good officer would do. There really wasn't a lot of hesitation when it all happened."

"You know, I don't know if we're going higher or not, but if you or I ever get a star, I hope the younger guys don't look at us as some sort of freaks or something. We just did our jobs, what we were trained to do. That's one of the things I like about the current assignment—it's a lot of paper-pushing for sure, but at least we're among fellow ranks and the generals, and we don't stand out so much."

After a pause, Hernandez added, "Fallujah's when I started seriously smoking these babies"—pointing to the fresh Camel he was about to strike up—"and I've never quite been able to shake them since. You know, Kiki, it never got to me before or during a mission, but after some of the rougher ones, I couldn't stop shaking. The cigs and the whiskey helped calm me down. Kayla got me to stop the drinking mostly because I'd get ugly sometimes, but she didn't care as much about the smoking as long as it wasn't in the house."

Then he asked, "How about you?"

Enrique replied, "To be honest, I never developed much of a smoking or drinking habit over there. It was the opposite with me. I would get all nervous and deal with premonitions *before* the action, but afterward, I'd hit the weights hard until I couldn't feel the nerves anymore."

"Oh, c'mon, Kiki, admit it . . . You didn't get the shakes 'cuz you knew were safe in that steel-plated RV."

"Yeah, like fuck, maroon."

After laughing, both men silently listened to the cicadas as they stared out at the darkened woods behind the back fence, their wartime experiences flickering in each other's consciousness. Then Hernandez remarked on how similar their lives had been despite their different branches of service. Enrique nodded and was almost about bring up the subject of their brothers, but something inside him told him to hold back. *I know he knows, so what good would it do either of us if I did?*

Then Hernandez changed gears. "I received an interesting call from Admiral Dennison yesterday. He invited me over next Sunday to watch the 'Skins and Chargers on TV—maybe he figured I'm still a Chargers fan—and to discuss 'a few other things.' You didn't by chance receive a similar invite, did you?"

"Not yet. But if I did, that would be really strange . . . certainly not a coincidence."

"No. I have a feeling that football's not going to be on his mind, but I just don't know *what* he's really interested in . . . with either you or me."

"I'll let you know as soon as I hear anything."

****

The trip to Killeen the next weekend didn't go as planned. He barely saw Sofia, except while watching her on the volleyball court Saturday morning, and Sydney seemed preoccupied with her friends. Even though Sofia had told Monica at the last minute about the football outing on Saturday, the latter seemed distant at the tailgate party before and during the game and even somewhat at the dinner afterward with their mutual friends.

On the way home to Killeen, Enrique pressed her on her feelings.

"I hope you had a good time today, honey. It was good to have you by my side."

"I did, Kiki . . . Thanks for arranging everything," she said without emotion, looking straight ahead.

"I'm glad . . . because it seemed at times like you weren't having such a good time."

"Oh, I'm just not big into football, Kiki, you know that. . . though it was good to see some of the friends from college again after all these years."

"But we're still good, right?"

Monica waited a few seconds to respond, carefully choosing her words. "I wouldn't go that far, Kiki. I don't know where we—maybe more I—stand anymore."

Enrique asked, "What do you mean? Are you saying you want to get out?"

Again, Monica carefully chose her words. "I don't know what I want, Kiki, honestly. I wish I could generate the same feelings I once had for you . . . but that's not the same as wanting to leave the marriage."

"You're not telling me everything. I *know* there must be someone else."

"Kiki, I've already told you, it's not like that. Killeen is such a small town, and most of the people I know respect you for what you've done. So I haven't really even been pursued, but I'm not sure I would want to get involved with anyone in any case. The girls still need me, the house always has something that needs attention, and I've got my hands full at work and worrying about my parents."

Enrique didn't say anything. Then all of a sudden, Monica started to cry plaintively. "They asked too much of you, Kiki! Why did you have to go back overseas after all these years? Didn't you give enough to them? They get into all these wars over there and have you guys spread out all over the world, but do they ever think what it does to the families over here, let alone all the poor people over there? Why do we need to be in everybody's business anyways!"

Enrique was devastated and even a little angry to think of how she viewed his service, and he now finally realized how much of a toll his overseas tours had taken on her psyche. Then his initial anger at the situation quickly turned toward sympathy for Monica's conflicted views. He began to regret anew that he had ever been stationed at Bondsteel, and then in angst, he suddenly visualized Carlos and his admonitions about its role in protecting the Kosovar cartels.

A few moments later, Enrique turned to Monica and, in a quiet voice, said, "I'm sorry you feel that way, honey. I was hoping the time this summer helped to rekindle some things. I'm not going to tell you *shouldn't* feel that way, but I'll always love you regardless of how you feel toward me."

"As much as I'd like to believe you, Kiki, I think you love something more than me—the army. I bet you're still hoping to make general."

"Not anymore. I've got less than two years for my twenty, and then I can return here for good. Would you accept me?"

Monica was mum for a few seconds. "Maybe, but it won't ever be the same as it could have been. Sofia will be gone off to college, Sydney will be almost gone, and who knows what I'll be doing. We'd share the same roof but not necessarily the same life anymore."

Enrique went another long stretch before replying. "I understand. All I ask is that you think it over and not burn any bridges." Without letting on about his conversation with Kayla, Enrique added that "I'm planning to spend Thanksgiving with the family, and perhaps we can do something fun for Christmas, maybe a ski trip or something." After another pause, he said, "Sometime in the next year, I'll be up for my promotion review. I'll tell them I'm going to pass. Maybe they'll even let me finish up at Fort Hood."

"Whatever you decide is up to you. I'm just not sure we can ever return to the way it once was . . . or could have been."

Neither of them said anything more until they greeted the girls upon arriving at the house.

****

On Monday, Enrique left Killeen early in the morning to drop off the rental car at Austin's Bergstrom Airport for the flight back.

Upon arriving in Washington just short of noon, he drove straight to the Pentagon and put in a half day at his desk. Despite his brief trip, there were already over forty e-mails awaiting him, mostly trivial ones on this matter or that. One of the messages was from Admiral Dennison, requesting that Enrique call him. The number he gave appeared to be a personal cell.

Immediately after arriving back at his townhome after work, Enrique contacted the admiral, who promptly answered, "Thanks for getting back to me so quickly, Colonel. I hope you had a nice trip back home." He briefly wondered how Dennison knew about his trip. *Must have been Jessica.*

Admiral Dennison continued, "You're no doubt wondering what I called you about. Well, it's not about another golf game for now, but how would you like to join me and a couple of others to see the Redskins and Cowboys on TV Sunday two weeks from now. I think the game starts about noon. I'm sure you're a Cowboys fan, right?"

"Well, I used to be more of one until I started moving all over the place and they started losing everywhere." After a pause, he added, "But it sounds like it would be a good gathering. Would Colonel Hernandez be there as well?" Enrique immediately regretted his last question since he realized that Dennison most likely knew that Hernandez had already contacted him about the earlier meeting.

"No, not this time, Colonel. Look, I know you're probably wondering if there's something more, and there may be a little discussion after the game. Mostly, though, it'll just be relaxing and talking with a couple of guys you've already met, like General Cummings."

"Admiral, I'm honored by the invite and would be glad to make it, but I hope I'm not the only one cheering for the Cowboys."

"You might be . . . but we won't hold it against you."

****

The next day, Enrique called John Hernandez and left a message but did not get a response. He waited another day before e-mailing him about the invite. All he got back was a cryptic reply that read, "Be prepared . . . It's not about the football."

Enrique didn't know whom to talk to, except possibly Jessica Beasley. But he wasn't sure how much she would know about all this or even if he could trust her, given her apparently close relationship with Dennison. With his failing marriage, he feared talking or even being near her. Two days later, though, he received an e-mail from her, asking if the riding outing was still on. *Damn, she got to me before I could cancel on her.*

Enrique called Beasley on Thursday and confirmed that he was still up for the riding if the weather cooperated, but the remnants of a tropical storm were moving in, and several inches of rain were expected over the weekend. Rather than canceling altogether, Beasley suggested an alternative plan in case of rain—to go to an indoor shooting range that she frequented in nearby Chantilly. Despite his combat experience and occasional refresher training, Enrique wasn't really into firearms anymore, especially small arms. He had fired the M16 in Iraq, and he also at times carried a Beretta M9, but the sounds and smells of the range inevitably brought up bad memories of overseas, which he could do without. Yet part of him yearned to be with Beasley despite the risks, and so he accepted her invite.

It was pouring on Saturday morning, as predicted, and so they agreed to meet at her shooting range, the Blue Ridge Arsenal, located a few miles from her mother's place. They got there right at its opening, avoiding the large crowd that would show later in the day and increase the wait times. Beasley had brought her Glock semiautomatic 9mm and ammunition with her, but Enrique had to rent an M9. Beasley had a membership—heavily discounted because she was military—and paid for everything except his rentals. Beasley was dressed for the occasion, in a black t-shirt with fatigue pants, and her biceps grew taut against the fitted sleeve when she started firing. Enrique could see she was very proficient, especially after her first round's sheet was retrieved and showed a small dispersal of holes surrounding the target's heart. Enrique then shot a few rounds with much less accuracy before they traded guns. Enrique proved more accurate with the Glock, while Beasley had a little more trouble with the greater recoil on the larger pistol.

After an hour on the range, Enrique's shoulder that was injured in Tal Afar started hurting slightly, so they decided to call it quits and went to lunch at a nearby Tex-Mex restaurant that compared favorably to some of his favorite taquerias in San Antonio. On the way, Enrique congratulated her on her shooting and asked how she became so proficient. "Oh, an old boyfriend took me to the range one day, and I sort of got hooked. I really like the one-on-one challenge and the mental focus required. I'm pretty regular here on Ladies Night each Monday and occasionally on weekends. It's mainly for recreation, but it doesn't hurt to have one around the house just in case."

"Does Jerry ever go with you?"

"Yeah, sometimes." Then she smiled as she said, "But he's pretty hopeless at shooting. I think he must have been cross-eyed or something when he was young!"

Enrique smiled but didn't reply. She then continued, "But I take it you don't do this sort of thing very much."

"No. I guess I had my fill of all that in Iraq. My family isn't into this stuff either."

"Speaking of family, how did it go last weekend?"

Enrique paused. "Not well. But I'd rather not talk about it." Then he added, "Commander—"

"Please, don't make me remind you to call me Jessica when we're out of uniform."

"Okay, Jessica. What I was going to say was how much the military takes of your family life. When I was your age, I never really gave it much thought, but now I realize what I've lost. Enough said."

They didn't say anything again until after they ordered. Then Enrique opened up somewhat cryptically about the invite from Admiral Dennison without specifically mentioning the football game cover. "You're good friends with him. Do you have any idea as to why he might be asking me over?"

"I haven't a clue, though it does seem like he's taken a special interest in you and Colonel Hernandez. I'm not sure why. I certainly don't recall anything like that in the past, although it's been several years since my first Pentagon tour."

"Speaking of Hernandez, evidently he was invited by Dennison last weekend. He was sort of incommunicado about what transpired."

Beasley just shrugged but then opened up on a different tack. "By the way, do you remember that new team I'm on that I told you about a month or so ago?"

"Yeah, the JADE HELM one. What're your guys now planning for us?"

Beasley was careful in choosing her words. "Well, for sure it goes a lot beyond the current JADE HELM exercises.[101] Based on our scenarios, it involves major military actions, like takeovers of airports, interstates, government installations, and the like. I already mentioned how a lot of the Third Corps may be involved, but there may also be marine divisions and even members of the air force."

"Who's the supposed enemy?"

"Supposedly, mostly right-wing militias from the midsection— Texas, Oklahoma, Arkansas, Missouri, some of the Plains states, even Virginia."

"No way. This sounds pretty fishy to me."

"More than that. You know, it's starting to bother me more than a little."

"Yeah, especially since the mainstream media seems to be going along with it all. They downplayed the recent exercise and

---

101 For a similar scenario outlined for army leadership instruction, see Benson, K, and Weber, J. "Full Spectrum Operations in the Homeland: A 'Vision' of the Future." (July 25, 2012) Retrieved from: http://smallwarsjournal.com/jrnl/art/full-spectrum-operations-in-the-homeland-a-%E2%80%9Cvision%E2%80%9D-of-the-future.

made the folks down in Central Texas out to be kooks. Of course, nothing was going to happen then, but by dismissing the locals, they were able to avoid the more important question: *why the hell is our military even doing these exercises?* The local police and National Guard are more than sufficient to handle all this stuff. Why bring in the army and marines? You know, I've been meaning to contact TJ Matthews, since I haven't seen him since he pinned Eagle recently. Maybe he'll give me his take on all this."

"Please don't, Colonel—"

"Enrique, remember?"

She smiled briefly. "Yes, you're right, but as you can imagine it's harder for me as a junior officer to wave off the formal." She paused before continuing, "Anyways, please don't mention it to Matthews. He might get suspicious if he finds out I know you. As you can imagine, most of this stuff is highly classified."

"Okay." He stared at her and realized he didn't want to leave even after the check came. *John Hernandez was spot on in warning me about her. The combination of masculine confidence and feminine beauty is way too dangerous . . . especially with my marriage tanking.*

Finally, just as he was about to get up from the table, she read his thoughts and teased him. "So what's our next outing going to be . . . Enrique?"

"What do you want it to be?"

"Oh, I don't know. How about something different, unique to these parts? Have you ever been sailing?"

"I can't say that I have. I wouldn't know the first thing about it."

"Don't worry, I'll teach you what you need to know. You know, there are still a few good sailing weeks left, where the water's still warm enough and the winds feel good on your face. How about two weeks from now? Jerry's going away for the weekend, supposedly hunting with his family, although he will be drinking beer mostly. We could rent a sailboat out of Annapolis and sail the morning and then drive out to St. Michael's across the bay. We could eat a late lunch there, tour the town—it's a really neat little place. I'll show you the academy before dark, if you've never been there, and we can eat dinner in the Annapolis historic district."

Enrique was already fantasizing about seeing Beasley in her bikini, Before accepting, though, he decided to test her. "And you don't think Jerry will mind?"

"Jerry won't know about it and won't care. What do you think I'm going to do, seduce you?"

Enrique almost started blushing. "C'mon, Jessica, give me more credit than that." *Are you kidding me? No, you're not going to seduce me . . . You already have.*

When she looked away, he said, "Sure, sailing sounds like a great idea, Jessica. I'd love to find out what it's like to be a sailor and midshipman at least once in my life. Of course, not if it's going to rain like today."

"No, not if it's going to rain like today." She smiled. When it's like this, even us navy folks like to head inside to shoot guns . . . or watch football."

The last reference set off renewed alarm bells inside Enrique's head. *I hope she's not referring to Admiral Dennison's invite because that would mean she knows a lot more than she's pretending—and that's a real danger sign.*

CHAPTER 16

The next Sunday, Enrique stopped by the Safeway on his way to Dennison's house to pick up a six-pack of beer. He knew they'd chuckle at him for bringing the beer, but he wanted to send a signal that he regarded it as a social gathering, not a military affair. When Enrique walked in during the middle of the first quarter, it turned out that it was only Dennison and Generals Taylor and Cummings watching the game—the same trio of senior officers that was at Dennison's July Fourth party.

The older men showed only a slight, almost-feigned interest in the game. Taylor, who had played defensive end for Army, did ask Enrique if he had ever played, and the latter briefly described his linebacking career at Balcones High. Dennison seemed to favor the Redskins, but the other men were less partisan. This didn't surprise Enrique because if they came from military families, they inevitably would have spent too little time in a place to develop "sports" roots.

When the Redskins started pulling away midway through the fourth quarter, Dennison got up and started moving in the direction of the study, signaling to the other men and Enrique that it was time to get down to business. Enrique took a position opposite Dennison on the small conference table in the study, while Taylor and Cummings sat at the flanks.

After a brief but pregnant silence, Dennison opened up, not with a statement but with a question. "So, Colonel, why do you think you're here today?"

"I would surmise for the same reason I was at your party in July and Colonel Hernandez and I played golf with you and General Cummings, sir." When he got no response, he added, "I figure it has something to do with the process of becoming a general officer."

Dennison looked at the other two men and then faced Enrique. In a soft voice, he said, "Yes, Colonel, it has something to do with that, but that's not the main reason for your visit. Did Colonel Hernandez tell you anything about *his* visit here two weeks ago?"

"No, not really." Enrique pondered his words and then replied, "All he wrote in his e-mail was that it wasn't just about the football."

"That's all he said?" Cummings asked.

"That's it. He didn't even call back when I left a message."

The three men nodded at one another. "That's good," Dennison said, sighing slightly. "Well, we're going to throw out a lot today that might surprise you, disturb you, even shock you. You might think we're even dangerous. In the end, though, we're hoping you'll see us as just regular military men, concerned for our nation. Above all, stay relaxed, Colonel . . . This isn't even close to an inquisition. In fact, I'm going to start addressing you as Enrique, if you don't mind."

"Actually, if you're going that far, you might as well call me Kiki, sir. That's what all my friends call me when I'm not on duty."

Dennison and the others smiled. "Sure. In the same vein, even if you don't feel comfortable calling us by our nicknames—mine's Jack, by the way—at least don't bother addressing us with 'sir.' Okay?"

When Enrique nodded affirmatively, Dennison said, "Good, let's begin." Then he added, "By the way, I hope you don't mind if I light up while we talk, Kiki." He offered everyone a Cohiba.

"No, not at all." Enrique hesitated briefly before deciding to decline one.

After a few seconds of silence while the men lit up their cigars, Dennison nodded to Taylor, who finally got to the point of the meeting. "I see you signed up in June of 2002, Kiki. Did the events of September 11 influence your decision?"

"Not really. I was already in the Corps of Cadets at A&M, and my dad had served before me. I wanted to join the army from the time I was just a kid."

Taylor then asked, "So have you ever though much about what happened that day . . . how it went down, what our government did or didn't do, why our government didn't prevent it?"

Enrique was a little taken aback. *So this is what this meeting's going to be about? Totally unexpected . . . I'd better be careful here.* "Not a lot recently, no."

"So you're implying you once did think more about it."

"Yes, perhaps."

"Did you ever do any research on it, at least a bit? Surely, you must have had some questions or concerns about what happened on that day?"

"Sure, I'm aware of how the towers—and Building 7—fell." [102]

"And you never had any discussions with any of your fellow soldiers . . . or at least friends and family members?"

"It's not something very many soldiers want to talk about . . . or question. Stuff like that you'd hold close to your vest." Enrique paused. "And my dad was an old-school chief master sergeant— he'd never in a thousand years believe our government had anything to do with 9/11."

"But your brother Carlos wasn't like him, was he? I bet he'd argue these things with you."

The mention of Carlos's name was disquieting. *So they basically know everything about me. Just go along with them . . . and keep your guard up.*

---

102 Although the fall of the larger World Trade Center Towers 1 and 2 due to aircraft strikes has been disputed vigorously by the Truther movement, the fall of Building 7 (which was not hit by an aircraft) has received the most support for being a controlled demolition: http://www.ae911truth. org/news/275-news-media-events-canadian-civil-engineering-researchers-disprove-official-explanation-of-wtc-7-s-destruction.html.

"Yeah, Carlos was into a lot of conspiracy theories . . . especially about September 11."

"Did he ever talk about what happened at the Pentagon?"

"Not as much. But he did mention on at least one occasion that no plane could have hit it."

"Did he say what he thought *did* hit it?"

"I guess he figured it was a missile or something. I can't remember, really."

General Cummings then took over the questioning. "Did you know the original hole in the Pentagon, even after the roof caved in later on, was half the size of a Boeing 757 profile?[103] And that a CNN reporter on the scene right next to the Pentagon claimed that there was absolutely nothing to suggest a plane hit it except for a few small pieces of some nondescript fuselage,[104] which could easily have been planted? And that no serial numbers traceable to any part of the plane were ever found? And that the data from what was claimed to be the flight data recorder were entered only a few hours before it was supposedly found, two days later? Not to mention a host of other anomalies."[105]

General Taylor then chimed in, "But of course, according to the official record, there is no evidence that Flight 77 ever took off... so *how could it have been hijacked and crashed*?"[106]

---

103 See the documentary film *Zero: An Investigation into 9/11* (starting at 29:00): https://www.youtube.com/watch?v=UFx1WaK54Vo.

104 https://www.youtube.com/watch?v=SFz7gLz7CVk; http://911blogger.com/node/15636.

105 One interesting finding was that the flight data recorder showed that the plane was at least 180 feet above ground when it supposedly intersected the Pentagon and traveled along a flight path that matched most eyewitness accounts (see footnote 107) but not the official flight path as determined by the 9/11 Commission: https://truthandshadows.wordpress.com/2010/09/29/flight-77-missed-the-pentagon-flight-data-recorder.

106 See http://www.serendipity.li/wot/aa_flts/aa_flts.htm.

Enrique's mind was racing to comprehend all of what was being thrown his way. After a few seconds, he asked, "But weren't there lots of eyewitnesses?"

"Yeah," Dennison replied, "there were some who claimed to have seen the plane fly overhead, but very few who were in a position to see the actual crash. On the contrary, some of the ones who *were* in a position didn't see a thing. Since some of the witnesses seemed genuine, one surmises there was a plane actually overflying the Pentagon that day, although even the bogus flight data showed it couldn't have hit the Pentagon. But here's the strange part: the route virtually all the closest witnesses said the plane took was way off—over *forty-five degrees* off—the direction of the light pole damage in the approach to the Pentagon."[107]

"But what about the video footage? Didn't some of it show a plane hitting the building?"

Taylor jumped in. "There were a few videotapes from neighboring businesses, all later confiscated, and you're right, there was one security camera footage—out of eighty located around the Pentagon that day[108]—that supposedly showed *something* hitting the building. But the kicker is that the only footage that the government produced was time-stamped *September 12*, with the key frame with the flying object not even close to matching up with the neighboring frames."

---

107 See the Citizen's Investigation Team (CIT) video on http://www.citizeninvestigationteam.com/videos/national-security-alert. This is the perhaps the single best refutation of the government's conclusion that American Airlines Flight 77 hit the Pentagon.

108 See above CIT analysis for a discussion of the confiscation of videotapes from businesses surrounding the alleged crash site. Some later released showed explosions but not planes. Of the eighty or so security cameras on the Pentagon in a position to view the crash of AA77, the only one initially released had missing frames, a wrong date stamp, and an undecipherable blur of an image that looked nothing like a Boeing 757: https://truthandshadows.wordpress.com/2014/06/13/doctored-pentagon-video-proves-911-cover-up-and-inside-job.

"So you're saying the video was all faked?" Enrique retorted.

"Absolutely. And that's not the only thing that was faked that day," Cummings added. "There were supposed phone calls from the planes that couldn't have been made. Indeed, there's no record of them ever having *been made*, and some of the passengers' names were clearly faked.[109] Nor were any of the so-called hijackers on the flight manifest that day. Of course, it wouldn't have mattered even if they had been because the supposed pilot couldn't even fly a Cessna according to his flight instructor, let alone a commercial airliner flying along the ground almost at the speed of sound hitting light poles along the way."[110]

"Okay, so if what you're saying is true, that no plane hit the Pentagon on September 11, I still don't see what any of this has to do with why I'm here today."

The three senior officers grew quiet, and Cummings and Taylor looked down, with Cummings fidgeting slightly. Then Dennison, in a soft and deliberate voice, asked Enrique, "Do you know who died in the Pentagon that day, Kiki?" When Enrique didn't respond, Dennison said with his voice rising a bit, "Soldiers and sailors died that day, Kiki. Fifty-five in all, plus a bunch of military

---

109 For evidence that the passengers on AA Flight 77 and the calls they supposedly made appear to have been faked: https://davidraygriffin.com/articles/was-america-attacked-by-muslims-on-911.

110 https://davidraygriffin.com/articles/was-america-attacked-by-muslims-on-911

contractors.[111] *American* soldiers and sailors! Soldiers and sailors who never got the truth of their sacrifice in a court of law!"[112]

The room grew quiet again before Taylor spoke next, in a quiet voice as well. "There were some fine people killed that day, including Tim Maude, the highest-ranking army officer killed since World War II.[113] Perhaps you've heard his name. I had actually met General Maude on one of my Pentagon tours. He was a good and decent man, by the book, well-liked by those who served with and under him."

"And there was another senior officer who was killed that day, one who was about your age at the time. He was the deputy in charge of naval intelligence, about to be selected early for promotion to rear admiral. I got to know him at the academy, where he graduated at the top of his class . . . *just like his daughter.*" Dennison paused just long enough for his words to have their

---

111 https://en.wikipedia.org/wiki/Casualties_of_the_September_11_attacks.

112 Despite the many lawsuits being filed over the deaths in the September 11 attacks, none have ever reached full trial in a court of law. One of the most noteworthy was that of April Gallop, an army military specialist who was injured in the Pentagon attacks along with her two-month-old infant. She filed a lawsuit in 2008 against high-ranking defense officials, including Vice President Cheney and Secretary Rumsfeld (https://willyloman.wordpress.com/2008/12/21/text-of-the-april-gallop-lawsuit; http://vealetruth.com/2012/11/10/conclusion-of-gallop-v-cheney-affidavit-of-evidence) that was dismissed *with prejudice* for being the product of "cynical delusion and fantasy" (http://www.abajournal.com/news/article/fantastical_9-11_lawsuit_could_lead_to_sanctions_for_lawyer_2nd_circuit_say) despite the fact that Gallop had many scientific and military experts willing to testify on her behalf. The circuit court that dismissed the lawsuit included the cousin of former president George W. Bush, which, even the mainstream cable and Internet news site CNBC decried as an "extraordinary conflict of interest": https://hiddenamerica.wordpress.com/2012/11/18/hidden-april-gallop-911-case-against-cheney-rumsfeld-myers.

113 https://en.wikipedia.org/wiki/Timothy_Maude.

effect. "Captain William Beasley was the best man at my wedding, Colonel, and he was and still remains the finest United States naval officer I have ever met in my life. He died on September 11, 2001, in the west wing of the Pentagon."

Enrique was stunned. His mind started swirling with thoughts. *What's going on here, what are these guys really up to, and what's Jessica doing in the middle of all this?*

Dennison continued on, "Do you think it plausible that a plane full of jet fuel and out to damage our capital would skirt the White House, skirt the Capitol Building, where hundreds of congressmen and senators were working, skirt the secretary of defense and all the top military brass in the north sector of the Pentagon, and avoid killing many hundreds, if not thousands, of people before circling over three hundred degrees to hit a sparsely populated wedge that housed mostly junior officers? And I might add, *a newly renovated wedge,* completed only a month earlier by the *same contractor* that renovated and then cleaned up the debris—or should I say evidence—after the Twin Towers fell and at the same time helped haul off all the debris at the Pentagon."[114]

Enrique remained silent, his gaze still riveted on the admiral. Dennison then leaned toward him and spoke so softly he was barely audible. "Thirty-nine of the military personnel killed in the Pentagon that day were part of Captain Beasley's Office of Naval Intelligence contingent. Only one survived.[115] And do you know what the ONI was tasked with?"

---

114 http://pilotsfor911truth.org/forum/index.php?showtopic=631. The strange case of AMEC is one of many so-called engineering firms that were regularly involved in cleanup after alleged terrorist incidents: https://digwithin.net/2012/01/01/a-small-world. One individual who has controlled the investigations of many terrorist attacks is Dr. Gene Corley, who headed the investigation of the Twin Tower collapses and who has repeatedly been accused of planting evidence: http://pilotsfor911truth.org/forum/lofiversion/index.php?t21357.html.

115 A total of forty-two military and civilian personnel working for the U.S. Navy were killed in the Pentagon on September 11.

Again, Enrique just shook his head as Dennison continued, "The Office of Naval Intelligence is our oldest military intelligence arm and mostly does standard electronic intelligence gathering using cryptologists, drones, and the like. Like other intel groups, it's also been involved in a lot of covert activities since World War II. Because of all this, it has—or had—a trove of documents related to a lot of these secret operations. Among other things, it was monitoring a program called 'Project Hammer,' which used hundreds of billions in illicit funds—most of which involved collateral accounts linked to stolen gold—to sabotage the Soviet Union and then, after its fall, Russia.[116] Bill Beasley was an honorable man and was disturbed at the scale to which certain parts of our government were skirting Congress and, of course, the American people—with all the illicit projects. He had to be careful about what he told me, of course, but in somewhat cryptic language, he referred to what he called a vast 'Deep State'—a cabal—that secretly operated in cahoots with the Federal Reserve and other elements of the banking system, a variety of intelligence agencies, the courts, and the media.[117] He and a few other of what he called the 'white hats' started investigating Project Hammer and some other black ops, but there were evidently some leaks from his

---

116 See Guy Razer for a detailed research on Project Hammer and its relationship to the events of September 11: www.scribd.com/doc/4866520/ Collateral-Damage-911-Covert-Ops-Funding-Targeted. See E. P. Heidner and Deanna Spingola for two additional accounts of Hammer and other shadowy financial dealings surrounding the events of September 11: http://www.israelshamir.net/Contributors/Collateral_Damage_Part_II_26122008.pdf; http://arcticcompass.blogspot.com/2010/02/ vvvvvvvvvvvvv.html.

117 https://wikispooks.com/wiki/Deep_state.

office that began to rattle some of the conspirators.[118] I know he was worried about what could happen, but I don't think even he expected that the ONI itself would have ever been attacked—*in the heart of the Pentagon.*"

"So you're implying the Pentagon attack was an inside job, carried out by explosives?"

"We're not implying it," Taylor replied forcefully. "We're presenting it to you as fact. The hole on the west wing, before the roof caved in long after the explosion, was way too small for a plane to have entered, especially at an angle. The pillars were pushed outward, not inward, and there was the smell of cordite everywhere but no evidence of the massive fireball that would have occurred if a plane loaded with over sixty tons of jet fuel had hit. Hell, there were papers and computers left unscathed in the area immediately adjacent to the hole. Does that seem likely if jet fuel had ignited everywhere?"[119]

There was an awkward silence for a few seconds before Dennison finally got to the point of the meeting. "Even if the mainstream media will never allow the truth of 9/11 to be aired,[120] a lot of us in the military already know it, And we know the reality of the shadow government, the Deep State if you will, whose sociopaths have been getting us into all the wars overseas . . . the wars you were part of, Colonel."

---

118 "White hats" refer to the hat worn by sailors in the United States Navy but also those in the military opposing the Deep State. Two of the most controversial individuals allegedly tied to the Office of Naval Intelligence and who have allegedly revealed details of September 11 events and other covert operations are Demart Vreeland (http://www.prisonplanet. com/vreeland_interview.html) and Gunther Russbacher (http://www. rumormillnews.com/secretlife.htm).

119 http://www.twf.org/News/Y2005/0307-Pentagon.html; http:// www.thepowerhour.com/911_analysis/pentagon-911.htm; http://www. citizeninvestigationteam.com/videos/national-security-alert op. cit.

120 http://stateofthenation2012.com/?p=7293.

"Then if you know all of it, why aren't you doing something about it? You don't need me to avenge Beasley's and the others' deaths. I still don't know what you want from me."

The three older men looked at one another, and then Cummings broached the issue. "We *are* doing something about it, Colonel. When the crucial battle unfolds between us and the 'black hats' now ruining the republic—and that day is definitely coming—the three of us and the much larger group of officers and enlisted who are aligned with us are hoping you'll be on our side."

Enrique was incredulous. *Are you kidding me? These guys are plotting some sort of coup against the rest of the government and military! What if this is all a setup?* "I'm sorry," he said somewhat testily, "but I'm having trouble comprehending all this. Even if what you say is true, you're telling me you're going to engage in treason because of some stuff that happened two decades ago?"

Dennison waited for a few seconds before responding. "It seems that you may be confused about the meaning of 'treason,' Kiki. Do you remember the oath you took when you joined the army? What did it say?"

"That I will support and defend the Constitution of the United States against all enemies, foreign or domestic. More or less."[121]

---

121 All officers in the military, regardless of branch, must take the following oath: "I, _____ (SSAN), having been appointed an officer in the Army of the United States, as indicated above in the grade of _____ do solemnly swear (or affirm) that I will support and defend the Constitution of the United States against all enemies, foreign or domestic, that I will bear true faith and allegiance to the same; that I take this obligation freely, without any mental reservations or purpose of evasion; and that I will well and faithfully discharge the duties of the office upon which I am about to enter; So help me God." The enlisted oath, but not the officer oath, also contains the words "obey the orders of the President of the United States." The officer oath to the Constitution is the basis for the name of the organization of current and retired military known as the Oath Keepers: https://www.oathkeepers.org.

"That's right. Does it say anything about obeying the president of the United States?"

"That's implied under the Constitution."

"As long as the president acts in accordance with the Constitution, correct?" Dennison paused, continuing to stare at Enrique, who remained impassive. "But what if the president doesn't act constitutionally?"

Enrique pondered the question before answering. "That can only be decided by the supreme court, Admiral."

"But what if there *isn't time* for the supreme court to weigh in?" Cummings interjected.

"Offhand, I can't imagine a scenario like that."

General Taylor then relayed something that surprised Enrique. "Colonel, do you remember how in August of 2013, we were all set to bomb Syria over the sarin gas attack? Everyone in the administration was blaming it all on Assad, but we now know it was actually carried out by rebel groups under the aegis of Turkey—one of our 'allies.'[122] Do you remember when Secretary Kerry announced we were poised to strike Syria, and then less than a day later, Obama backed down and agreed to accept congressional authorization?[123] Do you know *why* that sudden change in tack occurred?"

---

122 Despite Obama administration protestations that the sarin gas attack on August 2013 that killed anywhere from 150 to over 1,400 civilians (the latter being the widely discredited number originally put forth by the United States government), it has been maintained that the sarin actually was provided to Western-backed rebels in Syria by Turkey (and possibly Saudi Arabia), under the auspices of the United States: http://www.lrb.co.uk/v35/n24/seymour-m-hersh/whose-sarin; http://nsnbc.me/2013/10/07/top-us-and-saudi-officials-responsible-for-chemical-weapons-in-syria.

123 The Obama administration's dramatic about-face on the planned bombing of Syria over the alleged sarin attack by Syrian forces was very strange: https://www.theguardian.com/world/2013/aug/31/syrian-air-strikes-obama-congress.

When Enrique didn't reply, Taylor answered his own rhetorical question. "It came about because senior naval intelligence officers couldn't back up the sarin claims and some key admirals, recognizing the mutual defense treaties between Russia and Iran and Syria, knew that even a limited bombing campaign by the United States could very likely trigger a larger war, especially with most of Russia's Black Sea fleet off the coast of Syria. They refused to go along without authorization of Congress, which, as you know, is the only entity under our Constitution with the power to declare war. Of course, Congress chickened out when the e-mails and phone calls came in massively against the planned bombing."[124]

Dennison then interjected, "What you may not know is that this wasn't the only time that our military has refused a presidential order, and it's not going to be the last time either. Did anyone ever mention JADE HELM and its future iterations to you?"

Enrique spoke carefully since he didn't want to get Beasley in trouble for releasing top-secret information. "Yes, I am aware of it and some things that could happen along those lines in the future."

"Well, I can assure you that we already know everything that's being planned by the cabal, sometime in the next five years, and it's going to involve a total sabotage of our Constitution. There's going to be imposition of martial law, a whole lot of other dangerous actions. *Unless we in the military take action.*"

---

124 It has been alleged by Pulitzer prize-winning author Seymour Hersh and others that senior military leaders refused to order the bombing without congressional approval: http://www.lrb.co.uk/v36/n08/seymour-m-hersh/the-red-line-and-the-rat-line; http://www.dcclothesline.com/2013/09/04/u-s-soldiers-in-open-rebellion-against-obamas-war-in-syria; http://www.politico.com/magazine/story/2013/11/obama-vs-the-generals-099379. Certainly, action against Syria was also very unpopular among the general public (http://www.cnn.com/2013/09/09/politics/syria-poll-main), and Congress never even voted on whether to launch air strikes or not after a massive public outcry, with phone calls running over 500 to 1 against: http://www.wnd.com/2013/09/calls-to-congress-244-to-1-against-syria-war.

Enrique was feeling frustrated. "I understand your concerns, Admiral, but I'm just not sure why you singled out me and Colonel Hernandez for your team."

Dennison's voice again became soft. "Because it's *not* just about avenging Captain Beasley and General Maude and all the others who died in the Pentagon that day, Kiki. What about all the men under your command who died in Iraq . . . under false pretenses? What about all the millions killed directly or indirectly by our involvements in places like Southeast Asia, Central America, and Afghanistan, where our shadowy military alliances with drug dealers has resulted in a torrent of heroin, cocaine, and other toxins raging into the heart of every city and community in America?"

So this is what it's all about. They're trying to make me feel guilty about Bennie and Carlos so I'll join up with them. I wonder if they did the same to John about his brother.

Dennison must have again read Enrique's thoughts because before he could respond, the admiral asked, "Did you know Colonel Hernandez also lost a brother, Kiki? His brother died in Tower One on September 11? But that's not the only reason why we've met with each of you."

Taylor then spoke up. "You and Colonel Hernandez are in our sights because we've followed your careers and know that both of you are going to receive your stars—and soon. There are some others we're following, but you and he rank at the top of the crop of the future generals. You're both smart, you've proven yourselves in combat, and from what we've heard, you have several officers right behind you who would be loyal as hell."

"Who told you all of this? Jessica Beasley?"

Dennison smiled. "Don't fixate on Jessica, Kiki. I'm very good friends with her and her mother, but it's not about her. You still haven't grasped the significance of all that we have been telling you . . . or you don't really believe it."

"I don't know what to believe anymore. A lot of what you're saying echoes what my brother used to argue, but I dismissed it because I thought it smacked of anti-military conspiracy crap. Now though, I'm hearing the same from three of the highest-ranking officers in our military."

The senior officers stared intently at Enrique, who was struggling with what he was being asked to do. "There're a lot of implications in all this. I'm going to talk it over with some folks—"

"Please don't, Colonel," Cummings quickly interjected. "It's fine to do all the research you can about this, but this decision has to be yours and yours alone. We've asked the same of Colonel Hernandez and everyone else we've met with. That's why he probably seemed a little cool to you over the past couple of weeks. In the end, this is an intensely personal decision that you, and you alone, have to make. You don't have to decide right now, but sooner or later we're going to need an answer from you."

"I understand, but it would help if you could give me a better glimpse of your group. No disrespect, but even though you are all flag and general officers, you're still only three out of hundreds. Even if what you're saying is true, I don't think I can put my whole career on the line for a hopeless cause."

Dennison looked at the two generals, who nodded. "Would it help if we meet again with someone who could show you we're for real?" When Enrique nodded in the affirmative, Dennison added, "In the meantime, I would do a little research of your own, examining some of the various 'Truther' accounts. Would you be willing to meet with us again within the next month or so?"

"Yes, but there's another problem." Enrique took a deep breath before acknowledging his discussions with Monica the previous weekend. "Last weekend, I promised my wife that I wouldn't stand for promotion. Four overseas tours and a bunch of stateside tours have been rough on the family. My older daughter will soon be off to college, and my younger isn't far behind."

Dennison's response was surprisingly sympathetic. "Yes, that's the way it is with the military, especially these days, with our troops spread all over the globe. We've all been through the same quandary you're facing. But if it's any consolation, we believe that, if you decide to join us, your selection for general will be quick, and most of your time after that will be at Fort Hood . . . although you probably will have one more stateside tour outside of Texas before the big moment arrives."

Dennison then reiterated what they had discussed. "The ball's in your court, Kiki. If you agree to join, we'll get things rolling from our end. If you don't, that's fine with us. You'll still probably make general if you want it, and we'll wish the best of success to you." Then after a brief pause, he looked directly at Enrique and said, "If you want to meet again, you know my number."

Enrique was still overwhelmed by what had transpired in the space of little more than an hour. The one man he really wished he could talk to about all this was the one man they expressly *didn't* want him to talk to—John Hernandez. After a few seconds, he finally mustered up the courage to ask one remaining question that was lingering in his mind.

"Okay, Admiral, but answer me one question. Aren't you gentlemen worried what would happen if you were ever found out?"

Dennison smiled at the others, who smiled back, and then turned to Enrique. "I don't know what you mean, Colonel. Who's concerned about a few senior military men who just get together now and then to smoke cigars and watch the Redskins on TV?"

CHAPTER 17

For the next week, Enrique slept fitfully, tossing and turning during the night and even uncharacteristically napping on a couple of afternoons. As far as his predicament was concerned, he didn't know where to begin. Certainly, he wasn't going to alarm Monica since he still didn't know where this would all lead. He did book a flight to Austin over Thanksgiving, when he planned to let her know of his decision, but he then realized that there could be a change of plans with John Hernandez and his family. *If Monica hears I'm planning to stay on, she won't be doing anything with me— or them—over the holidays.*

He bemoaned the fact that he and Hernandez would be largely out of touch professionally for the next several months—at least until both of them had made their decisions. It wasn't just that he needed his advice; because of Bondsteel, he hadn't found any other close fellow officers to commiserate and relax with in years, let alone confide in.

He then thought about Jessica Beasley and what she was doing in the middle of all this. *I hope she isn't conspiring with Dennison and the others. Didn't John warn me about her? Of course, it didn't prevent him from getting snared in this whole net either.* He then realized that he was supposed to go sailing with her the next weekend. It could be awkward if he cancelled outright, and the outing could prove to be a way to get some more info from her, although with her intel skills, she'd probably get more from him than the other way around. *What a damn mess all this has become!*

He tried to analyze the motives of the three senior officers. It was clear that Dennison and even Taylor were affected at a gut level by what happened. He couldn't figure why Cummings would be with them, but maybe he was brought in to make fellow marine Hernandez feel more comfortable. He tried to assess how many others were aligned with Dennison's group—*He's obviously the leader of it, from what I can tell*—or whether this might still be some sort of test. He had never heard of anything like this being thrown at general officer candidates, but he was well aware that there had been a bunch of generals fired by Obama, and maybe they were tightening up the selection process, probing for hidden flaws in the candidates.[125]

Of course, all that they said could have been true, which meant he really needed to start doing some research on his own. He was well aware of a lot of the 9/11 conspiracy theories, but he had always been too invested in his career and too trustful of his nation's leaders to pay much attention to them. He started by reading a couple of books by David Ray Griffin,[126] watched a couple of full-length documentaries on 9/11, and pored over the Citizen's Investigation Team analysis of the Pentagon attack, which vigorously claimed on the basis of interview and other data that no plane had hit the Pentagon.[127] He also read some of the strange opinions of those *inside* the Truther movement that

125 President Barack Obama purged or fired, for various reasons, more than two hundred general and flag officers from 2011to 2016 (http://stateofthenation2012.com/?p=43850) and caused deep animosity within the military: http://www.politico.com/magazine/story/2013/11/obama-vs-the-generals-099379, op. cit.

126 Theologian David Ray Griffin has written over a half-dozen books on the subject of the government's role in the September 11 attacks, most notably *The New Pearl Harbor: Disturbing Questions about the Bush Administration and 9/11* (Interlink, 2004) and *9/11 Ten Years Later: When State Crimes against Democracy Succeed* (2012), op. cit. (see footnote 18)

127 http://www.citizeninvestigationteam.com/videos/national-security-alert, op. cit.

actually seemed to support the government's case.[128] And while the government's case had been impugned virtually in its entirety, Enrique was also aware of the old mantra that "absence of evidence is not evidence of absence." Of course, the "absence of evidence" in this case was largely attributable to the fact that the entire site had never been properly treated and investigated as a crime scene to begin with. While the decisive smoking gun proving the Deep State's involvement in the actual explosions themselves remained elusive, there was undeniably a lot of official smoke being blown around from all directions, starting with the doctored videotapes of the supposed crash and the fake calls from American Airlines 77 and the ridiculously fake information about the passengers being bandied about. The most curious was the case of Dora Menchaca, whose obituary had been prepared days in advance and whose handwritten note in the wreckage miraculously survived the fireball that supposedly vaporized most of the plane and bodies.[129] The hijackers themselves were even less believable—why did so many of them turn up alive, especially when they weren't on the flight manifest to begin with?[130] Of course, the plane itself was a huge enigma for, as Taylor noted, the damn thing hadn't even been listed as taking off. A tire and a nosewheel were supposedly found in the inner C ring, but none of the parts had any serial numbers that could prove they came from the Boeing 757 that

---

128 For example, see http://stj911.org/legge/Legge Chandler NOC Refutation.html.

129 Dora Menchaca's obituary was time-stamped three days before September 11: http://letsrollforums.com//flight-77-fraud-dora-t22428.html; see http://archive.vcstar.com/news/cason-local-sept-11-victim-left-behind-life-of-great-notes-ep-375054548-352799141.html for a discussion of how her handwritten note to her family on Marriott stationary miraculously survived the near-vaporization of the American Airlines Boeing 757.

130 https://davidraygriffin.com/articles/was-america-attacked-by-muslims-on-911, op. cit.

supposedly crashed.[131] So could they have been planted just like the engine found on the street near the World Trade Center that came from the wrong aircraft?[132] It would have been very easy for the government to dispel any doubts if it had a single serial number or uncontested flight data recorder output or video recording. *Why, in the end, couldn't the government provide any of those?*

He understood that there were discrepancies in the eyewitness accounts and that a fair number of individuals, some seemingly unbiased, did report a plane going overhead and even, in some cases, hitting the building. However, no one believed eyewitness testimony was sacrosanct anymore. Some individuals could have ended up erroneously linking together a decoy plane flying overhead with the explosion at the Pentagon, and there may have been military or contractor plants linked to the Deep State who were outright lying about the plane hit.[133] The thing that struck him most about the eyewitness testimony from those directly underneath the aircraft as it approached the Pentagon—from individuals who seemed to have little connection to the military— was that the observed flight path in almost all cases differed from the more southerly direction of the row of light poles that had allegedly been bent on impact with the underside of the fuselage.[134] *What if the pole damage was actually created by people who were told the "wrong" flight path in advance?*

What Enrique began to sense was that the Pentagon was the key to unlocking the rationale for September 11. Even if one distrusted the government's theory and believed the twin towers were brought down by controlled demolitions, there were plenty of reasons why someone would want the towers pulled, starting with simple greed. After all, the World Trade Center was a big

---

131 http://pilotsfor911truth.org/forum/index.php?showtopic=11066.

132 www.rense.com/general63/wtcc.htm.

133 See David Ray Griffin, 2012, op. cit., chapter 7.

134 http://www.citizeninvestigationteam.com/videos/national-security-alert, op. cit.

money loser and would have cost billions to fix all the asbestos inside it and a vast amount more to tear it down and dispose of the debris safely.[135] Larry Silverstein, its owner, propitiously leveraged a little over one hundred million dollars down to produce an insurance payout of over four billion, and he didn't have to pay a dime for either tower's demolition.[136] Of course, a much bigger financial payoff than the buildings' collapses resulted from the ensuing catapulting of the United States into a bunch of Middle Eastern wars, which in the end made hundreds of billions for various defense contractors and their banker friends. The Pentagon situation was much different, though. Bombing a poorly populated wing of it far removed from the offices of the top uniformed and civilian leadership of the United States military didn't have anywhere near the shock value of attacking the White House or Capitol or even the headquarters of the Pentagon, which would have been much easier targets. The sheer implausibility of it all begged the question—why did the perpetuators choose that area, unless there was something extremely important going on inside? Enrique thought more about Dennison's team and their argument, and now it sunk in why the government also seemed especially determined to infiltrate the Truther movement and prevent a consensus from emerging on what actually happened at the Pentagon that day. If it became clear to all that the Office of Naval Intelligence was targeted, that would blow up the shadow government from its very core and expose not only Project Hammer but also a vast number of the cabal's other illicit dealings.

What was being asked of him, though, was not simply to agree with white-hat arguments. It was something much wilder, something he had never dreamed of: *to commit to possible action against a democratically elected government of the United States.* All because of a false flag that happened almost two decades earlier

---

135 http://killtown.blogspot.com/2006/01/real-reason-wtc-was-targeted. html.

136 https://www.corbettreport.com/episode-308-911-trillions -follow-the-money.

and another even more ominous false flag that *might* occur several years down the road. The word "treason" didn't form at his lips, but it reverberated in his brain. His thoughts went to his dad and what he could ever say to him to justify such an action. Enrique knew that Pops didn't have time for all the nuances of modern military law—things were black and white in his book, and countermanding an order from the president of the United States would fall in the former category. Supporting the Constitution over the president was unthinkable. In Pop's world, it wasn't the military's job to decide those issues. Of course, his dad was enlisted, and the enlisted oath included obeying the orders of the commander-in-chief.

Enrique was torn by his impending decision, but he was determined he wasn't going to be a patsy in any feckless coup d'état. *I'm going to call Dennison and his team's bluff. They're going to have to show me more of their cards . . . or else they can count me out.*

****

For that week and the next, Enrique worked mostly on briefings by the chief of staff before congressional committees trying to hammer out the final details of the Defense Authorization Bill, which was already six weeks into the fiscal year without passage. It seemed that each year, the congressional funding was ever more delayed, regardless of who was in power.

At midweek, just when he was mulling over whether to call Beasley to cancel, he received a text from her, reminding him of the outing they had planned. Since the weather for that weekend again seemed ominous, she suggested they could just go out for a day trip to Annapolis and have dinner there as a backup plan. He thought about his visit to Annapolis many years before with Monica and the girls during his first Pentagon stint, and despite his misgivings about Beasley, he didn't really mind visiting the well-preserved colonial heart of it again. His hometown of San Antonio also had lots of history, but it was of a different sort, more Spanish colonial and less directly tied to the larger American experience. He had come to love the northeast, with its historical resonances and four seasons and varied landscapes and lush greenery. Given the chance, he could easily retire there, but that was pretty much out of the question, what with Pops becoming sicker by the day with his diabetes and his mother already showing signs of impending dementia and he being the only child left. Nor did Monica and the girls seem ready to leave Texas, especially with her family in San Antonio, although damned if was going to retire for good in Killeen—maybe Austin or San Antonio or somewhere else near to the Hill Country, any place where there was less crime and more energy. *God knows why I am even thinking about retirement, what with all this stuff swirling about?*

Enrique accepted Beasley' suggestion, in part because he still wanted to gain some information from her about her relationship with Dennison and what all of this was about. As Saturday approached, however, a norther had moved in, and it was raining hard and cold, even more so than the day at the shooting range three weeks earlier. When Beasley called to confirm their plans, she suggested another day at the range, but Enrique wasn't especially interested. Instead, he suggested they go to dinner that night at an Italian restaurant in Georgetown that a colleague had recently raved about. Beasley accepted and agreed to meet him there.

Enrique arrived early. The rain had let up, but it was still cool and damp outside. He saw Beasley approach in her dark blue Mustang and then get out as she handed the keys to the valet. She looked very smart in her thigh-length leather coat and stylish boots, but what Enrique noticed most when they entered the restaurant was how much more feminine her appearance was than previously. She wore a white cashmere sweater with a gold necklace and small pearl earrings with a gold set. Whereas her hair had always been in a bun at work or in a ponytail when they had gone riding or shooting, now its dark auburn strands flowed to her shoulders in gentle waves, accentuating her hazel eyes. She had been merely intriguing or even beguiling in the other venues, but now in her evening attire she appeared downright alluring.

The dinner conversation was mostly about current events and workplace stuff. Enrique asked about JADE HELM, but Beasley mentioned that her team hadn't even met since the last time they had talked, although it was slated to do so in the coming week. She probed a little about his family, even asking at one point whether either of his daughters might ever join the military. Enrique chuckled at that one and admitted he couldn't ever imagine Sofia or Sydney in uniform, especially after probably hearing Monica complain more than a few times about the overseas deployments and all the family strife they caused. Enrique, in turn, tried to find out more about Jerry Lear, such as how they met (at a party hosted by one her fellow navy officers) and what they had in common (sailing and skiing and an occasional concert or two). Enrique got the distinct impression that Beasley was pulling the strings in the relationship, even to the point of deluding Lear into believing *he* was in charge.

After dinner, Enrique was conflicted over wanting much more of Beasley or letting her go. Should he, or even *could* he, resist her any longer simply to preserve his vows in a marriage that no longer seemed even to have a future? He tested Beasley by mentioning that the evening was still young and that he knew a nice bar with music where they could talk a bit more . . . or that she was welcome to come back to his place and have a nightcap there. He was surprised when she agreed to the latter, to—in her laughing words—"see all his old army photos." She followed him across the Key Bridge and onto the George Washington Parkway into Alexandria and his quaint faux-colonial two-bedroom townhome overlooking the Potomac.

When they arrived, Enrique offered her a malted beverage, and then they went to the balcony and took in the view of the Washington Monument, slightly shrouded in mist. She looked ravishing in the dim light, her hair slightly furled in the wind. Her enticing fragrance further excited him, and part of him ached to embrace and kiss her right then. Instead, though, he motioned her inside where he put on some soft jazz music.

As they sat down on the couch, Enrique opened up by asking Beasley "So tell me why you're here?"

Beasley replied coyly, "Because you asked me. Why *did* you invite me in?"

"Probably because I shouldn't have. Not good for a married senior officer to invite a very attractive junior officer of the opposite sex into his apartment on a Saturday night."

"C'mon, don't be so old-fashioned, Enrique. After all, nowadays people might get just as suspicious if I were a *same*-sexed junior officer."

Enrique smiled but still felt uncomfortable. "You know, one of the things I find so enticing—perhaps even dangerous—about you is that you always seem to be in control, not just of yourself but of . . . events."

"Boy, aren't you being the cryptic one."

"Take Jerry, for example. I'm sure he's an intelligent guy and all, but I don't think he has a clue that you've got him exactly where you want him."

"Would you please stop asking about Jerry? Our relationship is really none of your business, and I resent your insinuation that I'm some sort of master temptress. People ultimately get into situations and relationships of their own free will. Do you really think I seduced you against your will into asking me here tonight? Because if you do, I can leave right now."

"No, please don't. I'm sorry for bringing up Jerry, and yes, I invited you here out of my own free will." He paused and tried to calm down, but he couldn't stop his fidgeting. He looked up at her and was about to say something, but then she read his mind.

She drew closer to him and put her hand on his and said, "For a man who's faced the ultimate danger more than once, you seem almost terrified of me, Enrique. Please tell me why you're holding back? I understand if you feel you're betraying your wife."

"It's more than that." Enrique paused for a moment. "It's also because I have a sneaky suspicion that you're in the middle of all this stuff with the admiral," he blurted out. "It almost seems that you know where all this is leading . . . but I'm worried about whether I can trust you in the end."

Beasley removed her hand from his and showed her irritation. "There you go again, accusing me of being a siren who's going to make you do something dangerous. I really don't know what I expected tonight, but it wasn't this," she said testily.

Enrique hated himself for being so abrupt, and he hated that he was about to ask the next question, one that had been bothering him ever since his meeting with Dennison and the generals. "But, Jessica, why didn't you tell me that your father died in the Pentagon on September 11? Dennison seems almost obsessed with his death, and surely all this stuff he wants John Hernandez and me to get into has something to do with that. Tell me you haven't been working with him to get us involved."

"It's not like that at all," Beasley replied curtly. "If he's obsessed with my father's death, it's about him, not me. He came to me when he knew I was working with you and Hernandez, but all I did was relay his information."

Then Enrique witnessed something he never thought he would see: the beautiful, self-assured young naval officer sitting next to him started to well up. In a soft voice, staring straight ahead as if transfixed, she said, "I don't know what Admiral Dennison's up to. You've got to believe me, I really don't. But I can tell you that the admiral is a good man." After a brief pause, she continued, "That day, my mom and I were into some petty argument before I left for school, and my dad came to give me a hug as he always tried to do when he was home. He said, 'You know, sweetie, it's too beautiful a day outside to start it off with some little argument that you and your mom probably won't even remember when I come home, so Daddy's little girl better smile by the time I leave the driveway, okay?'" Fighting off tears, she turned to Enrique and said, "And those were his last words."

"I'm really sorry, Jessica."

She continued to stare ahead, struggling to hold back her tears, almost oblivious to his words. "And that morning, all of us students left school early, and my mom told me to pray for Daddy because the building he was in was attacked by a plane. The rest of the day and the ensuing ones were all a blur, what with reporters and funerals and all, but all I knew was that my daddy wasn't coming home, as he always did after one of his sea tours. I quickly went into a huge tailspin, going from an energetic little girl to a depressed mess for months. My mom took me to see a psychologist, and it helped a little, but I was still lost. Then she asked Admiral Dennison, who was my dad's best friend, if he might be able to do something for me, perhaps restore a little of my dad by visiting me." Beasley's mood lightened slightly as she added, "One of the reasons I love horseback riding so much was because as the warm weather returned, Admiral Dennison took me riding on Sundays, sometimes just him and me, sometimes with his own kids. We would ride at different places, often at the farm in Middleburg that we went to. When we were alone, he'd tell me stories about my dad and keep him alive for me and always told me to be strong like he would have wanted me to be. I gradually started to regain my footing and my will to follow in Daddy's footsteps."

Then she turned to Enrique. "Maybe that's part of why I've wanted to be with you all these months. You not only look a lot like my dad—he was dark-haired and dark-eyed, too—but your strength and decency remind me of him, not like he would be today but the way he was on the day he left my life." Turning away to cover her face, her tears flowing, she added in a quiet voice, "So yes, I'm sorry I misled you because somewhere deep in my psyche I misled myself into hoping I could bring my dad back and hold him once more."

Enrique could barely hold back the tears himself as he drew closer to her and hugged her around the shoulders as she leaned into his. After a few moments, he said to her in a soothing voice, "I understand, Jessica, I really do. Not only did I lose two brothers along the way, but I feel I've lost my own family through all the years overseas and even in the States without them. Perhaps I was looking for some of the same things in you."

Then for several minutes, the two officers just sat on the sofa, looking out the window, holding each other's hand, realizing how much they had misjudged each other. He was no longer the strong, handsome war hero who had captivated her, but a version of the father she had lost that day as a little girl. And she was no longer a ravishing young naval officer, but an older version of the daughters he had never gotten to know enough as they were growing up.

After several more minutes, he said to her, "Come, dry those tears, Commander." After she started smiling a little again, almost sheepishly, and finished her drink and was about to leave, she said to him, "Enrique, I don't know what the admiral has in mind for you, and I really don't want to. But whatever it is, you should take it very seriously. He's a good man and a good officer, and for what he did for me, I would even say he's a *great* man."

Enrique nodded but responded with slightly different message. "I'll take your advice into account, Jessica, if you let me give you some of my own."

"Sure, but not about my personal life."

"Sorry, it is. Be a good solider—or sailor, I should say—and honor your commitment . . . but don't ever let the military consume you. If you and Jerry hit it off, and he's as crazy about you as you indicate, don't give up your chance for a family. I know you have some more fleet time, but eventually you can swing it so you're stateside or you can finish out in the reserves. It may have helped my career, but I now regret that last tour in Kosovo. It was too much, too late, and it ruined my last chance to have a strong marriage and family life."

She nodded and then smiled and whispered "Hooyah!" before kissing him on his cheek and picking up her coat and quietly exiting.

****

They saw each other a few times more for lunch and at the gym after that night, but it was mostly small talk. They no longer needed to talk about their relationship because they now deeply understood each other, without even uttering a word. They went out riding once more at the farm in Middleburg, and in late April, on a warm day with a gentle breeze, he finally accompanied her on the promised trip to Annapolis and St. Michael's. This time, though, Jerry and another friend were in tow, downing a couple of six-packs along the way. Enrique knew it was still important to her to show him where she had lived at the academy and where she had first learned to sail.

Both were also at Admiral Dennison's July Fourth party that next summer, but this time Enrique went by himself. In late July, she was already off to the Naval Command and Staff College in Newport, Rhode Island, on her way for later promotion at the young age of thirty-four to naval commander. They maintained only sporadic contact for several years thereafter, but their paths would later cross, albeit somewhat remotely, in the most momentous event in modern American history.

CHAPTER 18

With his relationship with Beasley cleared up, Enrique finally came to grips with the momentous choice he was facing. He decided the next week to call Dennison to set up another meeting. He wasn't going to decide anything rashly because he wanted to talk it over with Monica when he visited Killeen at Thanksgiving. He knew Monica would be upset if he decided to stay on and receive his brigadier general promotion, but he wasn't expecting her to welcome him back with enthusiasm in any case.

Dennison invited him over two weeks later, on another Sunday. Though the football season was still in full swing, Dennison didn't even bother to mention the game as a pretext. He insinuated that there would be at least one, possibly two, more officers in attendance and that there would be little doubt left as to the credibility of his team.

Enrique resumed his efforts to help pass the Defense authorization bill, accompanying the chief of staff and other top army officials on multiple shuttles to congressional committees. Despite a bipartisan commitment to maintain funding levels for the army, it was stretched thin and thwarted in its modernization efforts by political and industrial interests. Nowhere was this more pronounced than in the contentious fight to stop production of the Abrams tank, which had saved Enrique's life in Iraq but which the army had concluded no longer needed to be manufactured because of its declining force structure.[137]

Much as he tried to put it out of his mind, Enrique couldn't shake the implications of what Dennison and his group had proffered. His sleep became even more restless, and he started downing several beers a night to block the anxiety over his impending decision. He knew he needed someone to talk to, but whom? He couldn't talk to John Hernandez, his brother Carlos was dead, Jessica Beasley would represent too much of a breach, and Monica? *She wouldn't understand, even if she were still close to me.*

Two weeks before Thanksgiving, on a cold, blustery gray afternoon, he ventured to the admiral's house once more, this time with much more trepidation. Upon entering the house, he was again greeted by Dennison and Generals Taylor and Cummings. Toward the back of the room also stood one of the most well-known army officers in recent history, whose dark olive skin and graying hair had peppered the media for almost three decades. Enrique was shocked at the famous general's presence—*So this is their "ace," or at least one of them*—and at the same time unnerved by the realization that this whole thing went well beyond Dennison and couldn't be brushed aside anymore.

As before, the men wandered into the study to continue their discussions from the previous month. Cigars and drinks were passed around, and Dennison again took the lead in the discussions. He asked if Enrique had done any more research on his own and if he had any more questions for the group. Enrique waited a few seconds before replying, "Yeah, I have a whole bagful of questions, not so much about your account of what happened that day but more along the lines of what's the end game of your whole plan and how many high-ranking officers are actually with you?"

Dennison quickly addressed the second question. "I don't want to give out our whole organizational chart. In fact, I don't even

---

137 http://www.military.com/daily-news/2016/02/11/ohio-wins-again-in-armys-budget-for-more-m1-abrams-tanks.html.

know our exact numbers. I can assure you, though, we're the tip of the iceberg and are positioned at a lot of levels."

"If you're so big, why hadn't I heard even a whisper about you? How did you go about recruiting everyone under the radar? You can't keep a secret this big under wraps."

It was the famous general's turn to speak up. "It's hard for civilians to keep a secret, Colonel, but not the military . . . once we're aware of the consequences. Tell me, would you have ever done anything in combat to place your fellow soldiers in danger?"

Enrique looked down and replied, "No."

The elderly officer continued, "I can't speak for the admiral and the generals, but I can tell you how I got involved. I understand you did a little research on what happened on September 11. Did you ever listen to Albert Stubblevine's account?"

"Yes, I've recently seen a video of him talking about how the hole in the Pentagon was blasted from within." [138]

"But it wasn't what he said—others had said the same—but *that* he said it. And said it *publicly*. Do you realize the courage it takes for a retired major general in the United States Army to publicly accuse the highest-ranking officials of the United States government of mass murder? It's one thing for former top government scientists or political figures to dispute the official account of what happened on September 11—but *a top general?*"[139] After a brief pause to let his words sink in, he added, "In doing so, he was able to be the conduit for countless other officers who felt the same way and had questions about a lot of other things as well."

---

138 http://consciouslifenews.com/911-prove-airplane-hit-pentagon-major-general-albert-stubblebine/1145271.

139 There are actually many different Truther organizations, including Scholars for 9/11 Truth, Military Officers for 9/11 Truth, Pilots for 9/11 Truth, and the largest and most well known, Architects and Engineers for 9/11 Truth: http://www.ae911truth.org. Over three thousand architects, engineers, scientists, and other individuals have signed its petition to reopen the investigation into the destruction of the World Trade Center Towers.

"But weren't you a key player in the administration at the time, General?"

"I was. But after talking with General Stubblevine, who then referred me on to John and Warren and Bob here, I now realize what I should have known—and done—back then."

Dennison then interjected that he too was galvanized by first hearing Stubblevine's views on the Pentagon attack. "As you know, I lost a good friend and fellow officer in Bill Beasley and was looking for answers. His arguments made a lot of sense to me, although it was hard for me as a loyal career officer to believe that the leaders of our government could have had anything to do with 9/11. As you can now attest, the dissonance was tremendous. I personally spoke to the general, and he counseled me that there were many others who had the same doubts that I did and, after getting their permission, gave me some of their names. One of the first was General Taylor; General Cummings came on board later. More than anyone else, I started delving into the 9/11 Truther literature, carefully hiding my tracks. I became the unofficial leader of what has now become a very large group of senior officers, but our network is under the radar because we all understand what we're up against. There's still no paper or electronic trail."

Enrique sat quietly, facing each of the men in turn as he tried to absorb it all. Then he raised a question that went back to the very first encounter with Dennison. "You claim to have a large number of officers allied with you, Admiral, but why aren't there any air force leaders in your group? I noticed that from the beginning, at your July Fourth party. Whatever you're trying to pull off—and I'm still not sure what it is—is going to need the support of the air force."

The four men all looked at one other slightly uneasily before General Taylor spoke up. "As you know, Colonel, there weren't any airmen killed in the Pentagon on September 11."

"And?"

"And," Dennison interjected, "the simple fact is that we can't trust all of our air force generals." His words sliced through the tension in the room, but the aftermath opened up some very deep and obvious wounds. "Kiki, this may sound harsh, but there was collusion between NORAD generals and the perpetrators of September 11. Their testimony was shown on repeated occasions to be contradictory as to why fighter aircraft were not activated that day, flinging blame in all sorts of directions.[140] The reason for their misstatements is obvious—no fighter aircraft were activated simply because *there were no planes attacking us* on September 11. There were commercial planes involved in the major hijacking drills taking place that day such as Vigilant Guardian, but the normal chain of command had been usurped so that our fighters couldn't be activated in response to any FAA requests. [141] So our top air force generals either had to admit under oath that there were no planes, which would have blown the entire 'official story' out of the water, or they had to lie." He paused slightly to let his words sink in before adding in a somber voice, "It's easy to castigate them, Kiki, but in a way I can sympathize with them. After all, it was to them

---

140 There were glaring inconsistencies over the course of several years in the testimony of high-ranking United States Air Force generals such as Ralph Eberhart and Richard Myers concerning why the air force did not scramble fighters to intercept the "hijacked" airliners: see https://www.corbettreport. com/911-suspects-ralph-eberhart and http://www.911truth.org/senator-dayton-norad-lied-about-911. Ultimately, the blame was placed on the Federal Aviation Administration for delayed notification of the hijackings.

141 For a discussion of the war games and their role in the events of September 11, see http://911proof.com/9.html and https://hcgroups. wordpress.com/2009/06/14/two-days-before-911-military-exercise-simulated-suicide-hijack-targeting-new-york. It is important to note that the ability of local commanders to act on FAA orders was rescinded in Joint Chiefs of Staff directive CJCSI 3610.01, dated June 1, 2001, and rescinded on September 12, 2001: http://www.rense.com/general50/fdd.htm. The directive required that approval to intercept hostile aircraft be transferred to the secretary of defense, but on the morning of September 11, then DoD secretary Donald Rumsfeld allegedly went about his normal business: http://www. historycommons.org/timeline.jsp?timeline=complete_911_timeline&day_of_9/11=donaldRumsfeld&printerfriendly=true.

just a set of exercises. No one was killed because of any planes...but their careers and possibly more would have been destroyed if they had admitted the truth."

Enrique listened intently and then started to gently shake his head. "What about that saying 'United we stand, divided we fall'? Shouldn't you at least make an effort to test whether some air force officers could be brought on board?"

"There are a lot of air force officers who know the truth about September 11, Colonel, some that know about us," General Taylor replied. "But there are a lot of guys in the air force and even the other services who wouldn't be sympathetic to us either. We decided not to risk bringing them into the inner circle . . . so at least for now it's going to have to be 'divided we stand.'"

Enrique remained silent, not knowing what to add, but his stomach was churning, and he knew he had to make a decision.

Dennison tried to allay his angst. "Kiki, none of us has taken this task on lightly. All of us have had serious reservations. We're not trying to replay the events of September 11. If there are any more investigations or whatnot, the impetus will have to come from the families of the victims. What we're more concerned about is the larger picture, about future events that could seriously threaten the freedoms embedded in our Constitution."

"You're talking about JADE HELM... and its extensions, right?"

"Yeah, that's right," Cummings replied. "Those 'extensions' are not going to be merely pissass repeats of the original one, which involved a few marine and other special ops forces in Texas and Utah and a couple of other states. Those were merely fodder for the radical fringe, which went way overboard with it. The corporate media then had a field day making fun of the locals who were spewing out all sorts of doomsday predictions. When nothing came of the exercises, the public received a healthy inoculation against any future JADE HELM hysteria, which is what the Deep State wanted. We believe the real JADE HELM will be infinitely more dangerous."

"In what way?" Enrique asked.

Cummings leaned forward a bit. "There will be regular military forces deployed against a major secessionist hotspot—presumably a city that then gains the backing of the governor of a big state like Texas. Our sources indicate they're planning a big role for the Third Corps in carrying out the suppression in Texas, but it's envisioned that the 'rebellion' will then spread to other parts of the country. This will allow the president to declare martial law across most of the country and allow for mass arrest and internment, in sites already identified. The whole exercise is designed to wipe out, among other things, most of the Truther movement and its allies in the alternative media. A lot of legitimate Truther movements are already being painted as hate and terror organizations[142] and have been infiltrated."

"And how do you know this is all going to happen?"

Taylor quickly responded, "There are scenarios being developed that will soon be used in training.[143] You can find some of them on the web, although not precisely the scenario that General Cummings just described. We have even more specific inside information coming from some of the planners. We know how it's going to begin—leading political figures in key states are already being groomed for election as are some of the shills in the media that will stoke the conspiracy fires. I don't know if you realize it, Colonel, but major false flag operations—and this will be by far the biggest in our history, dwarfing what happened on September 11—take years to prepare."

Enrique became emboldened. "So Commander Beasley provided all this information to you, didn't she?"

Dennison showed his impatience. "No, our sources don't include her. Some of them, in fact, lie deep in the middle of their

---

142 See http://www.usnews.com/news/articles/2016-09-12/what-is-the-alt-right. The pejorative "alt-right" label has been pinned on even widely read Internet sites such as *Breitbart News* and *Infowars*. Even mainstream Truther groups such as We Are Change are forced to repudiate the label of hate group on their website: http://wearechange.org/about.

143 See footnote 101.

organization. Look, as I've told you before, you're too hung up on Jessica and her relationship to me, Kiki. What I did for her was out of compassion for her and respect for her father, but she's not in any way involved with our group nor would I ever ask her to be involved. What this *is* about is you and whether you are prepared to join us."

"You mean me and Colonel Hernandez, don't you?"

"Yes, and several others," Dennison replied. "As I mentioned last time, we flagged the two of you because your superb military records make you sure bets to get your stars. If something goes down in the next five years, you could be O8s or even O9s and commanding some major forces." Then glancing at Taylor and Cummings, Dennison added, "And if all goes as planned, we also may have one or more of us sitting at the joint chiefs' table."

"How are you so sure?"

No one spoke for a few seconds, and then the famous general spoke up. "Colonel Ybarra, you wanted these men to show that there was much more to this group than themselves. I can assure of that much. There is an important hidden struggle going on in the military, and there are powerful officers in the background trying to make these things happen."

Enrique stared at the general and then bowed his head in agitation, his thoughts still swirling about.

Dennison tried to assuage him. "Kiki, I know exactly what you're thinking. There's no precedent for any of this. And you're right—there isn't any. Despite our oath, the Constitution doesn't include any provisions for the military taking over even *temporarily* to save the republic. Moreover, all fictional coups by the American military have been portrayed negatively in the popular media.[144] So why would anyone ever consider getting involved in this stuff?"

Enrique knew it was the decisive rhetorical question and that now was the moment of truth for him commit to Dennison's group or not. Nothing came out of his mouth for what seemed to be an eternity but in reality was only seconds, and the words that he finally uttered almost seemed to emanate from somewhere deep inside his psyche. In a slow cadence, Enrique stared at each of the generals as he said, "Because people who could kill thousands of people could just as easily kill or imprison hundreds of thousands or even millions and end up controlling the entire society. *And then there would be no republic left to defend.*"

Upon hearing his words, the generals looked at one another while remaining expressionless. Then Admiral Dennison stood up, and the others followed. The admiral walked over to Enrique and looked him in the eye and smiled slightly and shook his hand and said "We were hoping we could count on you, Colonel." The other generals, each in turn, shook his hand. His emotions spent, Enrique closed his eyes to hide the slight welling of his eyes.

The generals returned to their seats, and Dennison spoke again. "Kiki, what this means in the concrete is that you will receive another below-the-zone promotion by the end of next year . . . not that you mightn't have in any case. Assuming you remain in good standing, you will receive another promotion within three years. You will not hear from us again directly for several more years. We're almost certain that, within five years, the scenario we described will unfold, and the signs will be apparent to you at least

---

144 The two most famous novels/movies about attempted military coups— Sinclair Lewis's *It Can't Happen Here* (Doubleday, Doran and Company, 1935) and Fletcher Knebel's and Charles Bailey's *Seven Days in May* (Harper & Row, 1962)—portrayed the coups in a negative light. Notwithstanding, a 2015 online survey taken about Americans' attitudes toward a military coup has shown that 43 percent would support one if a civilian government was violating the Constitution: https://today.yougov.com/news/2015/09/09/could-coup-happen-in-united-states.

several months in advance. When the moment is right, specific instructions will be given to you, which we trust you will follow. We caution you again not to discuss any of this, even with Colonel Hernandez."

"Who's made his decision too?" asked Enrique.

Dennison smiled. "Events in the coming months will make it plain to you what his decision was."

"What about my wife? Can I tell her?"

"Tell her only that she may soon be the wife of a general officer."

Yes, she will, Enrique thought. *If she doesn't divorce me first.*

CHAPTER 19

Enrique flew to Austin the Tuesday before Thanksgiving and was picked up in the late afternoon by Monica at Bergstrom International. They had a nice dinner at a Cajun restaurant in Round Rock on their way to Killeen, where Monica updated Enrique on some of Sofia's and Sydney's doings. Monica seemed more relaxed than last time, enjoying the weeklong vacation that most of the Texas schools enjoyed. Their plan was to spend Thanksgiving at her parent's house in San Antonio, with Enrique's parents and a few other family members in attendance. Enrique made it a point to withhold his decision to stay in the army from her until later, so there wouldn't be any fireworks before the holiday.

It had been a long time since Enrique last saw his parents—over six months previously at Carlos's funeral—and they seemed to be fading faster than even he had realized, both mentally and physically. In addition to their various physical ailments, the loss of their two younger sons created an aura of sadness that enveloped them both. They barely talked at dinner, even to Enrique, and Sofia and Sydney didn't seem to pay a lot of attention to them. Afterward, Enrique retired to his parents' home with the girls, who spent most of the time watching television and texting. Enrique noticed how musty and dated much of the décor seemed in his old house, as if his parents had stopped living and retired to a museum. The room that Carlos and Bennie once shared and where Sofia and Sydney were sleeping for the night was the worst, full of old photos and trophies and knickknacks and pretty much left as it was when the boys were teenagers. His old room, used when infrequent guests stayed overnight, was a little better in that it had received a brighter coat of paint and a new mattress and box springs. He was saddened to realize his once-youthful parents rarely ventured out of the house, his dad to an occasional veteran's gathering and his mom to her biweekly masses. Family gatherings where nieces and nephews might be roaming about were especially painful for them to attend, with too many reminders of the absences of their own three boys. Enrique tried to conjure up memories of his once-vibrant family life, with Pops throwing the ball to him and Carlos in the backyard and the spicy aroma of his mother's chiles rellenos wafting from the kitchen window, signaling dinner was on its way. The images were fleeting, though, as the darker reality of the present kept intruding.

The next morning, Enrique sat down with his father and mentioned that he had something important to tell him but that he had to keep it a secret from everyone, including his mother. He told him that it was likely he would pin his first star on within a year and that it was a credit to Pops, who had instilled in him what it meant to be a military officer. His father was overcome with emotion and hugged Enrique for several seconds. He then confided to Enrique that the loss of his brothers had taken its toll on his mother, who often seemed more and more in her own world these days and was speaking much of the time in her native Spanish. He told Enrique that she might smile if he could at least tell her that "Maria, your Kiki will soon make us very *orgulloso.*"

Monica, who had stayed the night with her parents to help clean up, came by for an early lunch at Enrique's parents' home, along with Bennie's last girlfriend, Mercedes, and Bennie's only child, Jasmine, now almost three. After lunch on Friday, Enrique and Monica and the girls all headed back to Killeen, stopping briefly in San Marcos to show the girls Monica's old apartment—where, she hinted that she and Enrique first made love—and then in Austin. There they toured around the University of Texas campus—one of about a half-dozen Sofia was considering—and had dinner near campus at Freedmen's, one of the top barbecue places in the city.

When they arrived back at their house in Killeen, Monica seemed in good spirits and receptive. They shared a bottle of chardonnay, and afterward, she and Enrique had sex for the first time in months. Immediately after their lovemaking, he started growing anxious about what—and when—he would tell her about the decision. He decided to wait until the next morning over a cup of strong coffee and pastries, which he would personally bring to Monica in bed. When the pastries arrived, she grew immediately suspicious.

"Why, thank you, Kiki," Monica cooed as she sipped the coffee. "But why are you being so nice to me? I hope you're not feeling too guilty these days."

"C'mon, you wouldn't have thought that way a few years back!"

"That's because I'm no longer the same woman I was back then."

Enrique nodded.

"I hope it's not about that Jessica Beasley girl, is it?"

"You haven't been talking about her with Kayla, have you?"

Monica smiled. "What does it matter? A woman knows when something's up. I wasn't wearing blinders at that party on July Fourth, you know."

Enrique was peeved but also worried. "No, it's not about *Commander* Beasley."

"Okay, then . . . what is it?"

Enrique paused to choose his words carefully, "Monica, I've heard through the grapevine that I'll probably become selected for general officer by the end of the summer."

"So? You're not going to accept . . . *or are you?*"

Enrique looked down and away.

Monica's face reddened and her voice rose. "You gave me your word, Kiki! What the hell are you doing this for? Don't you realize what that would mean? You'd have another three years after that, half of which would probably be spent away. Don't you care about your family!"

"You know I care about you and the girls, hon. It's just that something's come up I can't really tell you about . . . It's super-sensitive. It could be really important to our country."

Monica was livid. "Important to our country . . . *Bullshit!*" she shrieked. "How about what's 'important to your family'? By the time you'd retire, even Sydney would be gone from home. Then what?"

"Look, I know you're angry, and I don't blame you, but someday it'll all make sense."

"No, Kiki, what makes sense is that you love the army a lot more than you fucking love me." Enrique was taken aback at the force of Monica's expletive, which she almost never used. Monica paused before adding, "What's really pissed me off is that you played with my emotions again before telling me all this shit."

"I'm sorry. I just didn't want to tell you earlier, so it didn't ruin our Thanksgiving."

"Well, maybe it didn't ruin Thanksgiving, but don't expect me to come up to Washington over Christmas. And don't expect to sleep in our bed again anymore, at least not when I'm here."

"C'mon, Monica, we're only talking about one more night and a few visits. There's a good chance my next assignment will be at Fort Hood, and then I can spend a lot more time down here."

"Before going off again to some god-awful place and leaving us alone again? Can't you see through all of this? Look at what Bondsteel did. It ruined our relationship. For what? Did you ever read your brother's story on all that? And you're going to throw away our final chance just for another damn promotion?"

Monica's words stung Enrique even though he had expected them. "Look, I understand about Bondsteel, but the reasons why I'm doing this are very different—and much more important—than my promotion."

"Like what?" she fumed.

Enrique pondered his words. "Like something that could prove decisive for our freedoms as Americans someday. I wish I could tell you more, but I'm pledged to secrecy, even to you, Monica."

"See, that's the problem, Enrique," she said irately. "I don't trust you anymore, and it's clear you don't have any trust in me either. So why should I share my bed with you?" After a brief pause, she added, "We can put a sofa bed in the study. You can use that when, *or if,* you ever come back here."

Enrique realized how Dennison and the others had underestimated Monica's reaction. *How can I even be promoted without a wife in support?*

Then Enrique said, "I'll ask you again, Monica . . . Do you want a divorce or not?"

Monica thought for a few seconds and then replied softly, "No, not at this time. Let Sofia at least finish school. I'll even put on a good charade when it comes to your ceremonies and functions." Then she added sarcastically, "I wouldn't want anyone to think I was being a bad military wife, especially to a war hero."

"You didn't have to go there, Monica."

She looked down and said somewhat glumly, "You're right, Kiki, I shouldn't have gone there. *But I'm very angry.*" Then she started to cry. "I'm sorry, but I just don't want to go through all this anymore. I've never told you before—I didn't want to worry you—but I've been seeing a therapist and been on antidepressants ever since you were stationed in Bondsteel. Some days are more of a struggle than others."

Enrique went over to put his hands on her shoulders from behind and then got up and turned around to leave, pausing at the door to say, "I'm sorry, Monica." He truly meant it . . . although he wasn't sorry enough to back off his commitment to Admiral Dennison and his white hats.

****

Enrique spent the rest of the Saturday afternoon watching A&M play its last regular season game against Louisiana State, and he treated the girls to a dinner and a movie that night. He slept in the sofa bed that night, and he and Monica barely spoke the rest of his time in Killeen. Enrique made bacon and egg jalapeno tacos for breakfast, but afterward Monica asked Sofia if she could take her dad to Austin for the return flight since "another one of her migraines" had hit her.

That Christmas, Monica stayed behind as the girls flew to Washington to join Enrique and John Hernandez and his family for Christmas dinner and the ensuing planned ski trip to Canaan Valley in West Virginia. Monica had lied to Kayla about her absence, telling her that her parents weren't doing very well and needed her help over the holidays.

The new powder on the trails at Canaan Valley made the skiing excellent, and outwardly, everyone seemed to have a good time. No one mentioned Monica's absence, however, nor did Hernandez and Enrique speak even once about the momentous decisions they had made and would have to live with.

CHAPTER 20

After the girls left, a loneliness enveloped Enrique that was darker than he had ever experienced before. Even at Bondsteel, where he had been without his own family, he commanded several thousand men and was constantly interacting with them, even on weekends. Now he was mostly working with officers who had their own lives and families to tend to, and his major social functions were mostly limited to those hosted by the chief of staff. He managed to have dinner with TJ Matthews once in Alexandria, but they didn't talk much about their Iraq time and neither mentioned JADE HELM. At least his work was steady, with the budgetary cycle just getting under way and sequestrations and other cuts putting pressure on funding priorities and making his job more challenging.

Aside from a trip to Texas for spring break in March, where he drove the girls and a couple of their friends (sans Monica) to Port Aransas for a four-day stay, he hung around the DC metro area mostly. To soak up his free time, he started spending long hours in the gym, mostly lifting weights. He also started reading extensively, which, being more of an action-oriented than telic personality, he had never done much before. He read mostly historical fiction, and he especially became enamored with the works of James Clavell and the Australian novelist Richard Flanagan.

In late May, he received an invitation to a party in Hernandez's honor to celebrate the latter's selection to brigadier general. Enrique wasn't surprised that Hernandez was moving up, but his selection was way quicker than normal, and that meant only one thing—Dennison and Cummings and the rest had pushed hard for it because Hernandez had accepted the invite to be on their team. Enrique mused that Hernandez would thereby become the youngest general officer in modern United States military history despite the fact that everyone around him always said that *he* would someday grab that distinction.[145] He knew his own promotion board was near, so it probably wouldn't be long until he was hosting his own party—with or without Monica.

There were dozens of people at Hernandez's promotion party in early June, held at his and Kayla's house. Enrique recognized only a few of the guests, mostly marine officers and their wives, including Zach Rogers, and he noticed the absence of Dennison's team and Jessica Beasley. Hernandez was downing a few beers, but Enrique knew the former engineering student was too controlled to get sloshed at his party. Kayla, of course, asked about Monica and the girls and was told that it still hadn't been worked out as to when they were coming up. Kayla indicated she hoped it would be soon since she and John were headed to Camp Pendleton before the end of the summer. Kayla was excited since it would mean she would be closer to home, and Alexis could at least finish her last three years in one high school. *I wonder what the secret is for Kayla, why she seemingly accepts all the moving and disruptions that Monica grew tired of.*

Hernandez himself didn't talk much with Enrique at the party. At one point, though, he got close to Enrique and whispered, "Met with your board yet?"

Enrique replied, "Yeah, about three weeks ago."

Hernandez smiled. "Then I presume your turn is coming . . . and soon."

"Yeah, but it doesn't matter. You beat me to it, asshole!"

---

145 While the fictional promotions of Hernandez and Ybarra may be considered unusually rapid, several other prominent post-World War II U.S. Army officers were promoted to brigadier general before the age of forty-five, including Barry McCafferty, James Okayama, Jr., and Norman Schwarzkopf.

"That's what marines always do, tankboy. *Semper fi!*"

They both smiled, and Enrique gave Hernandez a brief but firm hug before the latter resumed his commiserating with the other guests.

****

As Hernandez surmised, Enrique was selected by the end of the month—again, an unusually short turnaround time after his board date but one to be expected if high-ranking officers were pulling the strings. Enrique's party was set for early August, and just as she had promised, Monica agreed to come to the nation's capital to be at his side, although she only stayed the weekend. Sydney was already in town, having arrived for a leadership conference in July before spending a couple of weeks hanging out with Alexis, while Sofia, who was working at a Starbucks in Killeen, arrived just before the ceremony. Enrique's party was a little smaller than Hernandez's, but at least the latter and his family were able to attend just before Hernandez was shipped off to Pendleton the next week. Enrique toyed with the idea of inviting Dennison and Taylor, but he knew they would decline, so he didn't bother in the end.

Enriquez and Hernandez engaged in a little more banter this time, especially after most of the guests left and their families were by themselves. Kayla mentioned that Monica must be really happy that Enrique would be back at Fort Hood for his next assignment, which Kayla had just found out about earlier in the day, and Monica tried to put on a brace face. "Yes, it will be good for all of us, Kayla. I'm sure Enrique will enjoy Sofia's final year of high school and seeing her graduate. It will be even better if you and John and Alexis can manage to visit us sometime."

As the evening drew to a close, Hernandez pulled Enrique aside and whispered to him. "I don't how much we'll see of each other in the coming years, but you're like a brother to me, Kiki. I don't know what's in store or whether we made the right decision or not, but I'll tell you this—I'll be damn proud to hang next to you if all this shit goes haywire."

Enrique smiled and nodded and then grew serious. "Trust in Dennison, my friend. Our friend Jessica knows him well and told me once that she thinks he's one of the greatest men she ever met."

****

Enrique returned to Killeen and the Third Corps early that September. Although he had been home several times since he began his most recent Pentagon stint, he had not really spent any significant time at Fort Hood since he was last stationed there over five years earlier. The first thing he noticed was how much less activity there was on the massive base than before. Since the end of large-scale American operations in the Middle East, Fort Hood had borne its share of the large cuts to the regular army, losing half of its active-duty forces. His new official title was deputy commander for readiness, although he wouldn't formally enter into that position until he pinned on his star in mid-January of the following year. In his new role, he was responsible for ensuring that all procedures, particularly regarding safety, were executed properly. His staff used a variety of metrics to keep track of the status of each unit, from platoons all the way to battalions. Enrique's job wasn't glamorous or strategic, and it came with all the usual messy personnel issues to boot. However, it was necessary to maintain a certain morale and discipline in the division, even in peacetime, given that large segments of the First Cavalry, tanks and all, could be flown in a matter of weeks in huge C-5 planes to anywhere in the world where there might be trouble.

His home life wasn't glamorous, either, especially since Monica was still offish toward him. Sofia was frisking about with her senior year activities and newly found boyfriend, and Sydney was also deep into her own high school academics and activities, principally volleyball. Monica started speaking to him a little more, but he continued to sleep on the sofa bed in the study, at least when guests weren't visiting. As in the previous year, the entire family went to San Antonio for Thanksgiving, and at least once a month Enrique returned there on his own to check up on his parents.

He reconnected briefly with TJ Matthews and Travis Rackley, the two men who owed their lives to him during the Iraq conflict and who had both been promoted to colonel in previous posts. Rackley was at Fort Hood only until the beginning of the New Year, when he was slated to take over Enrique's old spot at the Pentagon. Matthews, meanwhile, arrived at Fort Hood later that spring to serve as chief of staff for the Third Corps. Seeing his old Aggie friend Rackley especially helped lift Enrique's spirits, and they enjoyed several weekends together in the fall, fly-fishing in the Llano and Colorado Rivers west of Marble Falls in the Hill Country.

One Friday in late winter, on a trip back to San Antonio for the weekend, Enrique stopped by to give a talk at his old high school. Balcones Heights had heard about one of their own becoming a United States Army general—the first ever for the sixty-year-old school—and invited him to give a special talk before the student body. Enrique was surprised at how much the campus had changed, with major expansions and upgrades everywhere. He found it a little strange to be walking the halls again, and he was slightly taken aback when he saw large photos of both him and Carlos on the "wall of fame" near the principal's office. He had a few prepared remarks but by now had become such a polished speaker after years of briefings and lectures to his fellow soldiers and civilians that he spoke extemporaneously. As the students sat with unusually rapt attention, he started reminiscing about his high school years and then regaled them with some of his wartime experiences and finally turned to the nature of being a soldier in life, not just in uniform.

"As I look around this auditorium, I see lots of things that have changed at Balcones Heights—mostly for the better—even though I see there still aren't enough parking spaces!" Laughter ensued. "I still see some teachers here who once taught me, like Mr. Hanson and Mrs. Hinojosa, and I see hundreds of students who look a lot like those I went to school with, sitting in chairs that resemble the ones I used to sit in in this same auditorium. The thing that has changed the most here is the person standing before you. I am no longer the same young man I was at age eighteen, after being in combat and facing the personal struggles that each and every one of you will face in life. You may think you do, but you don't really know what life is about at age eighteen, and to be honest, I have yet to figure out all its mysteries, even in my early forties. To a great extent, being a member of the United States Army has made me who I am, and I have never doubted that this is what I was meant to do in life. But it is my deepest conviction that no one should join the military lightly—just because it may seem exciting or an opportunity to prove yourself or because others in your family joined. There is an enormous moral burden when one takes the life of another and when one carries out policies that can affect other nations, whether for good or bad. The most important thing anyone can do before joining the military is to study history, to gather lots of information from all sorts of different sources, to find out all you can about *who* you're fighting and *why* you're fighting. I personally don't think a seventeen-year-old high school student can make those decisions. I was twenty-two when I joined the army, fresh out of college at A&M, and I can honestly say even then I didn't know as much as I should have about why I joined.

"Whether you become a soldier, the wife or husband of a soldier, or a teacher or a doctor or policeman or anything else, I can say that the time will come when you have to make some really tough moral decisions and cannot hide behind the organization you belong to or something or someone else. I understand, as a father of two high school students myself, that as young adults, you should be enjoying life and chasing dreams. But I can speak with experience and conviction that all of you gathered here today will have to be ready someday for moments in your personal lives and in our nation's history that will stretch your soul to its very breaking point."

The Balcones Heights students were surprised at the words of Brigadier General (USA) Enrique Ybarra even if they could only partly fathom its cryptic message. Some of the teachers and administrators who had served in the military themselves were more than surprised at the frankness with which he spoke. And, had there been any reporters in the room publicizing his message, his words would have gotten him into some serious hot water with the military brass and probably torpedoed any future stars from being pinned on his epaulets.

****

The Ybarras threw a big party in early June to celebrate their daughter Sofia's graduation from Killeen High. Pops and Maria came up from San Antonio, as did Monica's parents and a few other relatives from her side. Sofia had been accepted into a number of prestigious public and private universities, including Dartmouth, Georgetown, and Stanford, but she decided to stay nearby and attend the University of Texas at Austin. Enrique wasn't too concerned about which university she attended from a financial standpoint since her tuition would be paid for by his GI bill allotment, and he had actually hoped she might choose one of the eastern schools since he had grown attached to that part of the country. He knew he would now take some ribbing from some of his diehard Aggie friends about her becoming a rival Longhorn. Sofia, of course, liked the fact that she could get away from home but would be close enough to return on occasional weekends for a little R & R and clothes laundering and her mother's zesty enchiladas.

As the summer days dwindled, Enrique knew his relative tranquility in Killeen was coming to an end. Sure enough, in late September, he received the papers for his next assignment—commander of the First Infantry Division at Fort Riley, Kansas. Though modern infantry units had aviation and cavalry brigades replete with Apaches and Abrams and Bradleys, Enrique hadn't come up through the infantry ranks. He had served with them over the years and was familiar with their missions, but he knew they had a different tradition and mind-set than the cavalry's. The First Division was a critical component of the Third Corps, so Enrique recognized that commanding it was a critical stepping stone to eventually commanding the latter. *I'll have to give Hernandez a call about this one. Maybe he'll give me some good advice after he yucks it up over how tough it'll be for me to handle a whole division of "ground-pounders."*

PART III

CHAPTER 21

Enrique managed to get his Fort Riley assignment postponed until after the holidays, so on a cold early January morning in Killeen, with the temperature dipping into the low teens, he headed due north on Interstate 35 for the eight-hour trip to Kansas. He had had varying degrees of anticipation before each of his previous assignments, as if something new were going to unfold, but his emotion on the road this time was sadness more than anything else—sadness that he would leave a depressed, estranged wife behind, sadness for a teenage daughter who would spend most of her remaining high school years at home without him, sadness for being so far away from his aging parents when there were no other siblings to look after them. As he reached the gates of the base, though, his military persona took over, and the adrenaline started flowing again.

Fort Riley was an historic fort, built originally in the 1850s to protect the frontier against the Native Americans resisting the settling of the West and later to protect the railroads as they followed. It became famous for, among other things, its cavalry school and its mounted cavalry unit, the last iteration of which was disbanded at the fort in 1946.[146] It had housed the all-black "buffalo" soldier cavalry regiments in the late nineteenth and early twentieth centuries along with such notables as General George Custer, who was once court-martialed for leaving the post to see his wife. That irony was not lost on Enrique, nor was the further

---

146 https://en.wikipedia.org/wiki/Fort_Riley.

irony that, with a large Native American gene pool in him from his mother's side, he was now stationed at his third army installation—Fort Leavenworth, the Carlisle Barracks, and Fort Riley—that had a hand in wiping out Native American resistance and/or indoctrinating them in the ways of the white man.

The First Infantry Division also had a famous history, although it didn't move to Fort Riley until 1955. It was led by George Patton in World War I, bore the brunt of the D-Day attack at Omaha Beach in June of 1944, and sustained huge casualties in its five years in Vietnam.[147] Hence, its official nickname—the "Big Red," after its large red numeral on its shoulder insignia—also came to be referred to as the "Big Dead." Most recently, part of its headquarters was transferred to the Middle East, but that stint ended just before Enrique began his posting at Fort Riley.

Commanding the First Division would ordinarily have been assigned to a major general, but the army was downsizing, and so the slot went to Enrique as a one star. He had numerous duties, mostly overseeing finances and readiness. Training was a top priority, especially since this year the Big Red would be participating in full-scale simulations at the National Training Center at Fort Irwin, California. In preparation, small-scale exercises involving live-fire and communications would be carried out at the gunnery range on base. Enrique had pored over a lot of financial projections while at the Pentagon and Fort Hood, but now he could see with greater clarity how the financial realities he had once dealt with more abstractly were having sobering consequences for the First Division, with funding cuts hampering maintenance and equipment purchases. Contrary to what civilians might think about the powers of a general, he was as much the messenger as the executive at his level. He could propose this or that, but funding decisions made in Washington would ultimately set the course. He felt frustrated after being told on more than one occasion that such-and-such new training had to be implemented or such-and-such new procedures had to be followed, and by the way, he

---

147 https://en.wikipedia.org/wiki/1st_Infantry_Division_(United_States).

wasn't getting all the funds he had requested. In short, his job was listening to everyone's wish lists but, in the end, rallying his troops to do more with less.

Most of his days were taken up with financial and other briefings, ceremonial duties, and travel—to Washington DC and occasionally to Fort Hood, where he could spend at least a little time with Sydney. Early on, during the short days of January and February, Enrique felt more loneliness than he had ever before, even toward the end of his second Pentagon tour. Then he started to do what he knew best—mix with the troops, at base-wide events, occasionally at lunch, and even a few times at the gym—all acceptable fraternizing that helped both his and the troops' morale. He would engage in some of their fitness challenges, doing more pushups and other calisthenics than most of the new enlistees. He would ask pointed questions, and he would listen. Occasionally, he would dispense some of the wisdom he had gathered along the way. On a couple of occasions, he would even lead the Commander's Guards, a volunteer mounted color guard that participated in various ceremonial functions, both on and off the base. As his time lengthened, his moniker as the "soldier's general" continued to spread anew, even beyond the confines of the garrison.

Since Sydney had been wanting to go out and visit Alexis in California, Enrique decided to drive to San Antonio for his leave that summer and then on to Camp Pendleton, where he would deposit Sydney with John and Kayla Hernandez. Sydney didn't talk much along the way out, but she took in the scenery of the desert more than Enrique had expected, even putting her smartphone down altogether when they detoured through Northern Arizona and partook of the red rock canyons of Sedona and the majestic vistas of the Grand Canyon. The plan was for Sydney to stay for two weeks with Alexis and then fly back to Austin. This complemented Alexis's own trip to Killeen over spring break, when Monica took the girls to San Antonio for a few days to do some sightseeing.

Enrique and Sydney arrived at the Hernandez's two-story stucco house on base early on a Saturday afternoon, and he stayed only for dinner before leaving the next day. While Hernandez grilled some beef fajitas to complement Kayla's rice and beans, the two men started talking about their new posts, the adjustments of becoming general officers, and, of course, what was going to transpire in the future.

Enrique asked first about Hernandez's plans. "So where do you think your next assignment will be, Johnboy?"

"Almost certainly, it'll be LeJeune—heading up the Second Expeditionary Force." After a pause, he added, "I'm slated to be here another year more or less as XO and then promoted to major general, which will allow me to lead the Second. How about you?"

"I'm guessing it'll be back to Killeen. It's not uncommon to follow the First Infantry with a command of the First Cavalry."

"Which would require being promoted as well, right?"

"Yeah, for sure, so that means we'll both be two-stars by forty-five . . . Can you believe it? Is there a precedent for that?"

"Not in recent memory . . . and not for two in the same year." Then Hernandez stared at Enrique and said, "You know, we've both received our medals and all, but I feel a little bad for some of the guys I served with who were just as capable. You and I both know that Dennison and those guys have been pulling strings for us. They had us on their radar for longer than we ever imagined . . . and are counting on us."

"Maybe so," Enrique replied. Then after staring away for a few seconds, Enrique turned to Hernandez and said, "It won't be long before we'll be in the spotlight . . . or will we?"

Hernandez smiled nervously but didn't reply. So Enrique then decided to press him on the issue. "So why'd you do it, John?"

Hernandez stared off into the distant hills and then vexed a smile. "At first, I couldn't believe what I was hearing from Dennison and the others as they laid out their case. But when Dennison asked whether I joined up to avenge my brother's death and then if I felt I had completed the job, it got to me. I've never met anyone like him, you know, in or out of the service . . . I can't quite pin it down what makes him so damn compelling. It was almost like he had me in some sort of trance, but in the end, something inside me told me to fight alongside that man."

Enrique replied, "I had the same strange experience with him, and he brought up my brother too, the one killed by the cartels. Maybe it was a little harder for me because my dad was career army, but in the end, I went all in, not knowing what you had decided until later."

Hernandez turned back to Enrique and said, "It's been almost three years since we first met with them, Kiki. Dennison told me it was going down within five years. Did he tell you the same?"

Enrique smiled. "Yeah, he did. But either he was wrong or we're wrong about our next assignments. In a couple of years, if you're leading the Second Expeditionary and I'm heading up the First Cavalry, that doesn't put us in much of a position to carry out anything major."

Hernandez concurred, "Unless there're a lot more generals on his team besides us."

"You mean like dozens?" Enrique asked. When Hernandez didn't respond, Enrique added, "That would mean a lot of golf games, wouldn't it?"

Hernandez chuckled as he flipped the flank meat over. Then he said wryly, "Maybe that's why Dennison and Cummings were so damn good that day!"

Enrique laughingly replied, "Roger that."

****

After breakfast, Enrique said goodbye to Kayla and the girls and toured with Hernandez around the base, with the latter stopping every now and then to show him a closer look at things. By ten o'clock, Enrique was headed to Los Angeles, where he hung out a bit in Santa Monica and drove around Rodeo Drive and Bellaire and the Hollywood Hills areas. For all his travels around the world, he surprisingly had never visited the City of Angels before. That evening, he did something he had always dreamed of since when he was a kid in San Antonio, when he used to go to watch the San Antonio Dodgers' double-A minor league baseball team, affiliated at that time with the National League team of the same name. He bought a third-base box seat ticket to watch the Dodgers play the Pittsburgh Pirates at Dodger Stadium in Chavez Ravine, wearing a newly minted Dodger cap he purchased just before game time.

The next day, he was on his way to Las Vegas, taking a slight detour to visit Fort Irwin in the scorching heat of the Mojave Desert, the site of the upcoming war games for the First Infantry. He donned his fatigues and boots to meet with the commander of the army's National Training Center and to get a tour of the facility. Then he was on to Vegas, where he spent two nights, mostly at the gaming tables playing Texas Hold'em, at which he had some skill from his many poker gatherings with fellow officers over the years. He relished the fact that no one in Vegas knew or cared who or what he was or, even more gratifyingly, needed him. It was a total liberation he hadn't experienced since his school days . . . if then.

After heading east and exploring the grandeur of Zion and Bryce Canyons and the Arches National Park in Southern Utah for a couple of days, Enrique eventually intersected Interstate 70 and followed it as it sliced eastward through the Colorado Rockies. He decided to stay in Aspen rather than Denver, spending two nights there and arranging a daylong fly-fishing trip on the Roaring Fork River. He then traveled all the way back to Fort Riley the next day, arriving in the early evening. As he sped eastward on Interstate 70, he listened intently to various talk radio shows. He was starting to pay more attention to the political news than before, on the lookout for any discernible signs that the false flag scenario outlined by Admiral Dennison in his smoke-filled study that dreary Sunday afternoon was slowly coming to fruition. As he passed the exit to Denver International Airport a few miles east of Aurora, Enrique still had no idea that two years later, he would be leading the equivalent of a full battalion to surround, huddled inside its labyrinth of tunnels, the president of the United States.

CHAPTER 22

As far as election cycles go, 2022 was an off-year one in which the Republicans were expected to do well. Unknown to the general public, three of the GOP gubernatorial candidates had been groomed for years by the shadowy Bilderberger cabal—the true Deep State—that was in control of most of the financial, media, intelligence, and federal law-enforcement agencies.[148] Robert Joseph "BJ" Duvall of Texas, James "Big Jim" Thompson of Virginia, and David Fitzpatrick of Pennsylvania had all agreed that, in exchange for their political rises, they someday would appear to openly flout the authority of the president of the United States. They did so with the full understanding that they would never be prosecuted for their transgressions and would be allowed to take part in lucrative business deals after their terms expired as a reward for helping out the Deep State cabal carry out its most audacious plan ever.

On the surface, Duvall, Thompson, and Fitzpatrick were all prototypical Tea Party conservatives,[149] demanding the protection of Second Amendment rights and less federal government interference in the affairs of the states. Duvall was slated to be a shoo-in, but Thompson and Fitzpatrick were campaigning in swing states and facing tighter races. Nevertheless, they were getting massive and anonymous political action funding and benefiting

---

148 See Estulin, 2009, op. cit.

149 The Tea Party is a loose confederation of populists, libertarians, and conservatives founded in 2009 that claim 10 percent of the U.S. population as supporters: https://en.wikipedia.org/wiki/Tea_Party_movement.

from a series of bizarre sexual and financial scandals involving their opponents. Although most of the mainstream media nominally disapproved of Thompson's and Fitzpatrick's strong stands on gun protections, it also endlessly covered the scandals of their opponents in every salacious detail. What seemed to the outside observer as merely an insatiable grab for higher media ratings was actually a well-orchestrated effort by the Bilderberger-controlled media to torpedo the electoral chances of the more moderate Democratic opponents.

The purpose of all this, known only to a small cadre of the Deep State inner circle, was to create enough of an apparent rebellion to justify the imposition of martial law. Widespread martial law had been implemented only once in the United States—by Lincoln during the Civil War—and it was deemed draconian even by some of the Bilderberger leaders. Lincoln's use of martial law was controversial then and was still being debated by historians,[150] and its use during and after the Civil War had been one of the factors that prompted the passage of the Posse Comitatus Act of 1878.[151] Although the law was somewhat murky, supporters believe it prohibited the use of the United States military for domestic purposes, although subsequent court decisions had upheld the use of limited military actions, such as the use of federal troops in 1954 to desegregate the schools in Little Rock, Arkansas.

The Deep State that had ruled the United States since even before World War I had been drawing up its nefarious plan for over a decade. The vexing problem for them was that they were losing their grip over the media, which they knew was crucial

---

150 While most historians give Lincoln a pass despite misgivings over his widespread suspension of civil liberties and imposition of martial law in certain states (http://www.usnews.com/news/history/articles/2009/02/10/revoking-civil-liberties-lincolns-constitutional-dilemma), some Lincoln scholars are much more critical of his actions in this and other areas: e.g., Thomas DiLorenzo, *The Real Lincoln: A New Look at Abraham Lincoln, His Agenda, and an Unnecessary War* (Crown Publishing Group, 2003).

151 https://en.wikipedia.org/wiki/Posse_Comitatus_Act.

for shaping American opinion and dominating the American political landscape. The consolidation of the mainstream media into basically six corporate-owned entities,[152] along with the close collaboration between it and the security and intelligence agencies,[153] was instrumental in allowing the Bilderbergers to control the foreign policy agenda of the United States. They had then used this clout to corral the financial and political assets of the entire world to help bring about, in their words, a "New World Order." One war after another, mainly in the energy-rich Middle East, was promoted by the media and designed to project the cabal's worldwide influence.[154] There was pushback as well, however, as more and more Americans started to believe the numerous "terrorist attacks" over the years—especially those on September 11—were actually false flag events that were being preposterously portrayed by the mainstream media in order to galvanize the American public into supporting all the foreign interventions. The enormous cost of the American and NATO forays into Afghanistan, Iraq, Libya, and Syria, all of which ended up in failure and chaos, was also becoming apparent. Tens of millions of people in the Middle East and North Africa had been uprooted, and previously stable nations were now sending millions of refugees, many of whom were Islamic fanatics, into

---

152 http://www.businessinsider.com/these-6-corporations-control-90-of-the-media-in-america-2012-6.

153 Collusion between the major Western intelligence agencies and media date back to the early post-WWII era. One of the most long-standing and extensive examples of this was Operation Mockingbird: http://www.carlbernstein.com/magazine_cia_and_media.php. For a more current update of the link between the intelligence agencies and the media and entertainment industry, see Nick Schou's *Spooked: How the CIA Manipulates the Media and Hoodwinks Hollywood* (Hot Books, 2016).

154 See F. William Engdahl's *A Century of War: Anglo-American Oil Politics and the New World Order* (Progressive Press, 2012). For an illustration of how leading media outlets push for war, see https://www.democraticunderground.com/10024653443.

the very bowels of Europe, triggering further political instability in nations that were once solidly under control of the Bilderberger empire.[155] It was also becoming clear that Americans were bearing most of the costs of these interventions: several trillions of dollars of upfront and delayed costs and the pain and suffering of hundreds of thousands of American veterans of those wars, from death and dismemberment and traumatic brain injury to the psychic scars of post-traumatic stress disorder.[156]

The main headache for the Bilderberger cabal was the very thing it helped create—the Internet. The cabal was initially enamored at the possibility of the Internet to influence and monitor Americans and others around the world, and it had infiltrated so many prominent Internet companies and social media outlets,[157] such as Amazon, Google, Wikipedia, and Facebook, that Silicon Valley became a major Bilderberger hub.[158] Even though Western governments still controlled much of the machinery of the web, the vast expansion of the Internet was accompanied by the creation of an entire "alternative media," which incessantly decried the claims of the corporate media as hoaxes and lies. From Infowars to WikiLeaks to RT News, Veteran's Today, and Breitbart News, more and more Americans started getting their news and

---

155 http://www.cnn.com/2016/06/20/world/unhcr-displaced-peoples-report; https://news.vice.com/article/the-year-europe-buckled-under-the-biggest-refugee-crisis-since-world-war-ii.

156 http://www.facethefactsusa.org/facts/the-true-price-of-war-in-human-terms.

157 For evidence of the connection of Western governmental links to major Internet companies, such as Facebook, Google, and Amazon, see globalresearch.ca/nsa-and-facebook-work-together/5439110; https://wikileaks.org/google-is-not-what-it-seems; http://www.wnd.com/2017/06/jeff-bezos-amazon-washington-post-and-the-cia/#F0jLmCcOyYBDYAkY.99.

158 See https://pando.com/2015/06/12/silicon-valley-and-the-ingestible-bilderberg-id-chips for a discussion of the large contingent of prominent Silicon Valley entrepreneurs at recent Bilderberger meetings.

information from sources outside the Deep State's control,[159] as trust in the mainstream media fell precipitously.[160] Indeed, mainstream coverage of every terror event or mass shooting was almost invariably followed by suspicions in the alternative media about "what really happened" and the uncovering of coincidental mass drills, crisis actors, photoshopped images, and the like.[161] Eventually, most Americans turned away from supporting the cabal's wars and started resisting calls for more gun control and other restrictions on civil liberties.

The Deep State wasn't about to let its dream for controlling the United States and the world slip away. It had to find a way to shut down major portions of the alternative media and to scare the rest into submission. Earlier attempts to use the dominance of Google and Facebook and Twitter to thwart the power of what were deemed "fake news" on alternative media sites had failed,[162] and more extreme measures were needed. For the American people

---

159 See http://www.thelastamericanvagabond.com/expanded-knowledge/websites for a list of prominent alternative news sites.

160 Recent national polls show that as little as 6 percent (http://bigstory.ap.org/article/35c595900e0a4ffd99fbdc48a336a6d8/poll-vast-majority-americans-dont-trust-news-media) to 18 percent (http://www.journalism.org/2016/07/07/trust-and-accuracy) to 32 percent (http://www.gallup.com/poll/195542/americans-trust-mass-media-sinks-new-low.aspx) of Americans have substantial trust in the media.

161 For examples, see https://jonrappoport.wordpress.com/category/911-massacre. The Federal Emergency Management Agency employs crisis actors (https://cdp.dhs.gov/news-media/article/role-players-offer-real-world-training-experience), a part of the drills that allegedly accompany major false flag operations, and there are actual companies that provide such resources: http://crisiscast.com.

162 See http://www.ibtimes.com/trump-supporters-consider-google-facebook-boycott-amid-claims-fake-news-battle-2447153 for a discussion of the ad boycotts implemented by dominant Internet media sites against alternative news sites, both on the left and right.

to support a large-scale imposition of martial law, nothing less than a major rebellion in the land had to be created. The Bilderbergers knew they could readily incite and fuel the rebellion by their plants in the alternative media, their plants in major militia groups across the nation, their overtly hostile but secretly aligned governors and other establishment political figures, and, if needed, their old staple—political assassination. Everything had to be in place, though, from the plants to the governors to the media. No one in the Deep State, however, worried or even bothered to think of the American military—it was assumed that it would simply follow the president's orders during the entire staged crisis.

Driving along Interstate 70 past Denver, Brigadier General Enrique Ybarra still had only an inkling of what was shaping up to be the greatest false flag in history, already well along in its execution. But at Camp Smith in Hawaii, as he was in the last months of his tenure as head of the United States Armed Forces Pacific Command and on his way to joining and later heading up the Joint Chiefs of Staff, Admiral John Dennison was on top of everything that was unfolding. He and his fellow white hats had their own secret plan and team in place to "help save the republic," which, above all else, was counting on the two young generals John Hernandez and Enrique Ybarra to carry the day.

CHAPTER 23

Just as Enrique and Hernandez had surmised, both men were off to their new positions by mid-autumn of the following year. Hernandez once again beat Enrique by a few months at his promotion to major general. As additionally predicted, Hernandez's selection coincided with orders to assume command of the Second Expeditionary Force, while Enrique received his selection notice just before his orders to return to Fort Hood as commander of the First Cavalry Division, Third Corps.

Enrique returned to a chillier home than he had left two years earlier. Sydney had already left home to attend Texas A&M, and Monica was even more standoffish in her interactions with him. She seemed more preoccupied with her parents, whom she now tried to visit at least once a month, and she appeared no less depressed than before. Enrique received a brief Christmas card in the mail from Hernandez, which informed him that Kayla was not going east this time, preferring to stay in their new home north of San Diego and keep close tabs on Alexis, who was attending her first year at his old alma mater, San Diego State. He added a "congratulations" on Enrique's promotion and closed with the cryptic words "Less than a year to go. You ready?"

In his own mind, Enrique couldn't answer that question. *Ready for what?* Then as if his mind had been tapped, a brief note with no return address arrived at the house. It read, "Start paying a lot of attention to Duvall, Thompson, Fitzpatrick, and the government's media campaign against the militias. Watch for Williams to start igniting." Enrique knew the note had come from Dennison and figured it presaged the final struggle that he had alluded to at their second meeting. He recognized the admiral's reference to "Williams" meant "Ronnie Williams," the host of *Patriot-News*, one of the more radical of the alternative news sites. Enrique found it hard to believe that Williams was shilling for the Deep State all along while posing as a right-wing Truther. *But why else would Dennison have mentioned him?*

After studying recent news reports, all Enrique could discern was that there were increasing efforts by leading political figures, including the president, to paint domestic terrorism and the widespread availability of guns as serious threats to American security and democracy. In return, some leading bloggers on conspiracy sites were spewing out ever-more incendiary statements, arguing for active resistance against any future government military exercises. A hotbed of activity was a swath of Texas ranging from Waco and Dallas in the east to Midland and Odessa on the west and Amarillo on the north. Enrique could see all the tinder being assembled, but he still wondered what would ignite the demand for a mass imposition of martial law. Things seemed a lot calmer still in Pennsylvania and Virginia despite the elections of Fitzpatrick and Thompson to the governor's seats in those states.

By the summer, though, things were starting to get dicier, as Williams's network was becoming ever more blustery in drumming up fears of an impending government crackdown on the Second Amendment. Then something remarkable occurred: a seemingly insignificant small strip of land less than two thousand acres in size along the Red River in North Texas became the potential flashpoint for the political inferno that Dennison had predicted. The land was originally under the riverbed when it was assigned to the federal government in 1923, when the Texas-Oklahoma border was litigated, but it later ended up on the Texas side when the river shifted.[163] It had been leased by the state to various ranchers for decades without controversy, but new horizontal drilling and

---

163 http://www.politifact.com/texas/statements/2015/jul/17/glenn-hegar/glenn-hegar-says-texas-owns-its-public-lands-uncle.

fracking technologies dramatically escalated the value of the mineral rights underneath the strip, which sat on the northern tip of the Barnett shale.[164] When representatives of the Federal Bureau of Land Management tried to reassess the property in view of its new energy potential, landowners in the area refused them entry, and the state attorney general under pressure from Governor Duvall sided with them. Rather than work quietly with state officials on a solution, though, the president of the United States dug in her heels and threatened to send in federal marshals to gain entry. That's when Ronnie Williams started up a drumbeat of conspiracy rants, in the process rallying a motley collection of libertarians, Tea Party activists, Truthers, Texas secessionists, Minutemen and various other militias, along with a few politically active biker clubs, to head to the Red River to block access to the marshals. Hundreds at a time rotated in and out on stakeouts and started organizing into different divisions, armed with everything from pistols to assault weapons. The situation became too big for law enforcement to handle, and the president became irate, insisting that Governor Duvall order the Texas National Guard to remove the armed protesters. When Duvall refused, the president declared she would federalize the Texas National Guard, but Duvall refused to accede to the order. Large segments of the American public, already polarized, were now galvanized into action, and libertarian and Tea Party groups called for a massive nationwide march on Washington in solidarity with their Red River "patriots."

To outside observers, the "Red River Standoff" was another one of those quirky moments that seemingly popped up randomly and yet ended up changing the course of history on a national or global scale—such as Major Joshua Chamberlain's bayonet charge at Little Round Top after his Twentieth Maine Regiment had run out of ammunition that arguably saved the battle of Gettysburg for the Army of the Potomac and enabled the Union's victory in the American Civil War,[165] or the wrong turn and stall of Archduke

---

164 https://en.wikipedia.org/wiki/Barnett_Shale.

165 https://en.wikipedia.org/wiki/Little_Round_Top.

Ferdinand's car on Franz Josef Street in Sarajevo that allowed for his assassination by Gavrilo Princip and provided the spark for World War I.[166]

Rather than a random event, though, the Red River Standoff and the events that followed were, in reality, carefully orchestrated political theater, whose script was supposed to be known to only to a small cabal of Deep State officials and their Bilderberger masters. Little did they know that Dennison's white hats, having infiltrated and stalked the cabal for over a decade, knew of every last detail of the plan. Even Enrique marveled at how the events started unraveling exactly as Dennison had hinted, with the drama now shifting to the Washington metro area, where the president was facing the prospect of hundreds of thousands of protesters, including some heavily armed militias, converging on the capital from around the nation.

The president met with the Joint Force commanders tasked with defending the capital district, but outside of aerial assets—which no one wanted to deploy against the American populace—there were only scattered regiments available in the immediate vicinity. Most of these were composed of military police or soldiers assigned to ceremonial and training duties or specialized noncombatant military agencies.[167] Joint Force Command decided to gather several hundred military police from Forts Meade, Myers, and Belvoir—supplemented with local police units—to confront the initial wave of protesters. However, the roadblocks set up along the Leesburg Pike and Route 50 to intercept two large caravans of protesters coming from Winchester were overrun, and several military police were taken hostage. Gunfire erupted, with blame assigned to different sides for its outset; eventually, twelve policemen and about two dozen protesters were killed or seriously injured. The president was outwardly livid as she went

---

166 http://byronreese.com/one-wrong-turn-and-a-hundred-million-people-die.

167 https://en.wikipedia.org/wiki/Joint_Force_Headquarters_National_Capital_Region.

on national television to order the hundreds of thousands of other protesters converging on the nation's capital to turn around or face military reprisal. In reality, though, she knew that Washington DC—headquarters to the most powerful military force on the planet—was less able to defend itself with regular military units in its immediate vicinity than at any time since the Civil War. While the city had assembled an impressive air defense system designed to prevent hostile aircraft from entering its airspace in the wake of September 11, no one apparently had counted on a land attack by a large armed domestic rebellion. The president, therefore, hinted in her national television address that she would call on Governor Jim Thompson of Virginia to intervene with elements of his state's national guard.

As with BJ Duvall in Texas, though, Jim Thompson "surprisingly" refused to answer the president's call. He accused the president of "overreacting" and "preventing the exercise of free speech," and he offered to help negotiate a cease-fire and a peaceful end to the conflict. In the meantime, the hostilities on the western outskirts of the capital had further galvanized the "patriot" community nationwide, and caravans were being organized from every state in the continental United States plus Alaska. Tens of thousands were within a day or two of coming up from the south, but what the president seemed most concerned about was a caravan of over one thousand protesters from mostly upper Midwestern states that was snaking its way along Interstate 70 and would soon cross the Pennsylvania border and thereafter converge with over twenty thousand protesters coming from New York, Pennsylvania, and other northeastern and mid-Atlantic states. In a widely publicized conversation, the president demanded that Pennsylvania governor David Fitzpatrick call up the Pennsylvania National Guard to block the caravan in Western Pennsylvania before it could join up with the others. But Fitzpatrick, too, was noncommittal, which led the president to dispatch the secretary of Homeland Security to meet personally with Fitzpatrick in Harrisburg. Despite an armed security contingent accompanying the secretary, a lone protester managed to surprise him after he had just arrived in the Keystone State's capital and lob a grenade, killing him and his two guards instantly. The mainstream corporate media went ballistic, working feverishly to turn public opinion against the protesters, who were garnering wide popular support in the country partly because of the faltering economy that had left tens of millions of Americans angry at the federal government. It blamed the assassination on the protesters, even though more than a few powerful individuals both inside and outside the government knew that the assassination was not a spontaneous event but one that had been planned long in advance and carried out by a patsy who would end up being assassinated herself within hours.

The president now had the green light to make her bold move, one that had been prepared for by years of steadily escalating JADE HELM-type military exercises and enhanced surveillance measures, to which the American public had grown immune. On a dramatic television appearance from the Oval Office, the president laid out her case for the imposition of "limited" martial law in the country. She pointed to the constitutional crisis involving the political standoff with the governors of three states, the recent deaths of federal law enforcement and military personnel, and the impending convergence on the nation's capital of hundreds of thousands of protesters led by armed and dangerous militia members. The president further stated that, while she had no problems with average Americans who wanted to exercise their constitutionally guaranteed rights of assembly and speech, the armed militias and the media arsonists who were inciting them had come to represent a "clear and present danger" to the republic. She then concluded by stating that the situation now called for extraordinary action:

"At the advice of the Joint Chiefs of Staff and under the aegis of Northern Command,[168] which is responsible for the defense of the homeland, I have ordered the following two major military actions. First, to keep all armed militias and supporters from entering the

---

168 The Joint Force Headquarters National Capital Region is under the control of United States Northern Command (USNORTHCOM) located at Peterson Air Force Base, Colorado Springs.

District of Columbia, I have ordered units of the United States Marine Second Expeditionary Force based in Camp Lejeune, under the command of Major General John Hernandez, to immediately redeploy in defense of the nation's capital. The Second Expeditionary Force has been ordered to use all means at its disposal—including aviation, artillery, and police actions—to dislodge and disarm all militia members attempting to enter the Washington capital district. I have also ordered elements of the Third Army Corps, based in Fort Hood under the command of Lieutenant General Wesley Covington, to dislodge the armed militias blocking access to federal lands near Wichita Falls, Texas. The Third Corps has also been ordered to eliminate any armed resistance that gets in its way. I realize that my imposition of martial law has no precedent except for the actions by President Abraham Lincoln as he attempted to restore order to the Union during the Civil War. By most historical accounts, Lincoln is considered our greatest president for having taken all measures necessary to save the republic. I am confident that history will judge my actions in a similar way once order has been restored and our democracy is no longer threatened."

The largest American television audience in history was stunned by the president's words, but Major General Enrique Ybarra, watching from his home in Killeen, was less stunned than anxious. His friend John Hernandez was in the middle of something that could end up destroying him, and he was even more worried about what Dennison had up his sleeves for him. He suspected that Dennison and his colleagues had gone along with the president because they were going to use the martial law and movement of troops against her in the crisis. He was much less sure of his own role, however. *What can I possibly do now, given that I don't even control the Third Corps?*

That answer came very quickly, in the form of an anonymous text on his cell phone. The text read, "Turn prez orders into massive deploy; secure all TX mil airprts within wk; order 4ID to stndwn; take 2nd brigade and head to Denver. Prez will be waiting." Enrique understood the first part of it and its serious implications but not the cryptic last sentence—"Prez will be waiting." *What the hell was that all about?*

CHAPTER 24

As the protesters grew restless waiting outside the capital, two units of the Second Expeditionary, in addition to several of its support battalions, took most of the next week to deploy. Hernandez did manage to send a few advanced regiments that were already preparing for deployment overseas off to Washington within days of the president's address. His plan was to have his troops form a perimeter around the city with a variety of checkpoints, effectively cordoning the city off so that none of the protester caravans would be able to pass, while otherwise minimizing disruption to the traffic flow to and from the city. He also ordered several dozen major governmental installations in the city, including the White House, to be protected with small contingents of marines. It was quickly arranged for most of his soldiers to camp out on military bases in the area, but the logistics of transporting and feeding over twenty thousand soldiers on short notice was no small challenge.

Meanwhile, at Fort Hood, feverish preparations were under way to move several regiments of the First Cavalry's Division up to the Red River. Since he was only weeks shy of his retirement from the army, General Covington shifted most of the responsibility for the deployment onto Enrique's shoulders. Enrique quickly conceived a plan that made the First Cavalry's Second Combat Brigade Team (the Blackjack)—now headed by his good friend Travis Rackley—the spearhead for achieving Dennison's objectives. He proposed the use of two additional battalions from the First Combat Brigade, but Covington and his other deputies felt that only one team would be needed. In the end, four full regiments were allotted, and then Enrique quickly started drawing up his plan to split them up so as to cover all military airports, from Barksdale in Louisiana to Laughlin Air Force Base on the Mexican border to Sheppard and Dyess Air Force Bases in North Texas. When Rackley saw the plan, he gave his old friend a quizzical look.

"Kiki, this doesn't make any sense. Why are you sending my third and fourth squadrons to Del Rio and Barksdale when we're supposed to be converging on North Texas? And why are you holding back on the fifth and ninth regiments?"

Enrique looked Rackley square on and said in a low voice. "Travis, you've simply got to trust me on this one."

Rackley returned his stare, with added suspicion. "Something's up, Kiki." Then as Enrique remained silent, he said, "You've got to let me in on it, man."

Enrique looked away. "Travis, I know we've been through a lot, but I'm sorry, I can't . . . for your sake, not mine."

"Enrique, tell me you're not going rogue on me."

Enrique took a deep sigh and looked away. "Yes and no. I'm getting my orders from higher-ups, but there's much more to all this than even I know." Then looking straight at Travis, he said somberly, "I'm putting everything on the line for this, which is why I don't want to get you involved. Right now, you're safe because you're just following orders."

Rackley was clearly miffed. "This isn't like you, Kiki. You were always a by-the-book officer. What the hell's happened to you?"

Enrique looked away again and clenched his fist but said nothing. *What's happened is a lot of disillusionment, the loss of two brothers, a tanked marriage . . . and then a fortuitous encounter with a guy named John Dennison, which, in the end, wasn't fortuitous at all.*

"Okay, Kiki, you're not going to let me in, so let me tell you what I'm going to do." Rackley sighed before adding tersely, "I'm going to follow your damn orders to a T, not because I think you're anything this side of insane but because you pulled my fucking ass out of that burning M2 in Abu Ghraib. But if you ever want me to do anything shit-brained like this again, you're gonna have to fill me in all the way."

Enrique replied, "Understood, Colonel."

Enrique stared at the door for a few moments after Rackley saluted and left. Then he quickly resumed plans for taking the equivalent of a whole battalion out of the Second Combat Brigade plus a bunch of extra tankers and maintenance vehicles and preparing for the march of his life.

****

One day after the bulk of Hernandez's Second Expeditionary had cordoned off most of the capital, the president summoned the new chairman of the Joint Chiefs of Staff, Admiral John Dennison, to the Oval Office. Her initial demeanor was congratulatory.

"Admiral, I'm very pleased that your troops have moved so rapidly on all this. I hope General Hernandez receives a commendation for his superior leadership."

"Thank you, Madam President. Yes, the Second Expeditionary really ran with it. The general's efforts will not go unrecognized."

Then the president's tone grew more serious. "So when's the next step going to be taken? What's your plan for disarming and arresting the militias and all those folks in the media inciting them?"

Dennison stared impassively at the president. "We see no need for such an action at this time."

The president's face reddened. "But they're breaking the law and threatening the capital, Admiral!"

Dennison remained calm as he replied, "The vast majority of them haven't broken any law, and the few who have are going nowhere at this time. The Midwest caravan has stopped at Frederick and the southern one at Chantilly. There's no need to foment any more violence. Most of the hundreds of thousands of protesters are loyal Americans who are a little stirred up and will go home in the next few weeks."

The president then exploded. "I can't believe what I'm hearing from you. You're under my orders to disarm the militias, and if you can't carry out those orders, I'll damn well fire you and replace you with General Cummings as chairman of the Joint Chiefs!"

Dennison remained silent and then motioned to the door. In walked General—now Commandant—Robert Cummings and Major General John Hernandez. At first, the president seemed perplexed, but then she grew ashen as the admiral introduced Hernandez.

"Madam President, I would like you to meet Major General Hernandez. He won the Silver Star in Iraq and became the youngest general in the United States military since World War II. By the way, his brother died in World Trade Center Two on September 11 . . . the same day that my best friend and the best man at my wedding and the first in our class at Annapolis died in the bomb that went off in the southwest corner of the Pentagon. Although you probably never heard of him, Commander William James Beasley was the finest United States naval officer I ever met."

The president slumped in her chair as Dennison continued with his reproach. "You and your sociopath buddies may have thought you pulled a fast one over the American people on September 11, but we in the military knew the truth and got wind of your even more nefarious plans to strip the American people of their defenses. We've been monitoring your every move for over a decade." Pulling out his smartphone, he then called up some documents and said, "If you don't believe me, why don't you read some of the transcripts of your secretly recorded conversations through the years?"

The president couldn't believe what she was hearing and was too shocked to bring herself to speak, so Dennison continued on, "Madam President, you indicated you were about to fire me, but in reality, the person who's going to be fired is you. You have twenty-four hours to leave the White House or you'll be arrested—by the United States military, since, by the way, we're now under martial law."

Finally, the president was able to muster a feeble response. "You can't do this, Admiral," she said in a worried voice. "The Constitution says I'm the commander-in-chief, not you."

"But our military oath is to the Constitution, not you. And if you and your friends are going to flush it and its freedoms down the toilet, then it's our duty to refuse your orders."

"And who are you to say what's constitutional or not?"

When Dennison didn't reply, the president's nerve returned. "Admiral, you're making a serious mistake. I've got the entire Third Corps in the heartland along with the air force and a whole lot else. You and your gang here are never going to get away with this. Now get the hell out of this office!" she screamed.

Dennison held his tongue before motioning for Cummings and Hernandez to leave with him. As he was leaving, he mused, *The president will be very surprised when she finds out what the Third Corps has in store for her.*

CHAPTER 25

The president knew she was cornered. She thought about another national television address but rejected that idea because Hernandez's troops had surrounded the White House and probably wouldn't allow any news media in. *The bastards are using my own crackdown against me to pen me in!* She was also unnerved by Dennison's veiled blackmail threat to release the transcripts and worried about what else he had on her that could be made public. In the end, she decided to play along and force them to make the next move. *Yes, I'll leave the White House, but dammit if I'm going to resign.* She decided to invoke the contingency plans that had long been in place for top government officials to temporarily vacate Washington in the case of an emergency. She summoned *Marine One*, which took her to Andrews Air Force Base, where she boarded *Air Force One* to Denver International Airport.

Denver International, situated at the foothills of the Rockies, had long been one of the leading trigger points for conspiracy theorists' fulminations over the years. By any account, it was one of the strangest airports ever built, replete with cryptic messages, frightening artwork, and masonic and other symbols—not to mention swastika runways.[169] It also had massive over-budgets, massive delays, and just plain overall massiveness, with its fifty-three square miles, seven underground floors (the bottom of which was totally sealed off to the public), huge tunneling and

---

169 http://postgradproblems.com/conspiracy-thursday-denver-international-airport.

underground bunkers, thousands of miles of fiber optics, and fueling systems capable of pumping thousands of gallons of jet fuel per minute. There was a consensus in the conspiracy world that the airport—twenty-five miles from the center of Denver and surrounded by the former chemical munitions facility known as the Rocky Mountain arsenal to its west and farmland to its east and allegedly connected by tunnels to other nearby underground military facilities such as Cheyenne Mountain—was in reality the hub of a vast underground complex capable of hosting the United States government in a sustained crisis or disaster.[170]

When the president arrived at Denver and was whisked down into the seventh underground level along with most of her top cabinet secretaries, she and the secretary of defense immediately assessed the military situation. Dennison and his group had caught them completely off-guard, and they clearly had a lot of strength in the East. But the president figured she still controlled most of the military, including the air force and the army. Indeed, the army's Third Corps, including both of its infantry divisions, constituted over a fifth of the active-duty army and over half of its combat capability. Then there were all the reserve and guard units, although it wasn't clear exactly how many she could command given the political firestorm engulfing the nation.

The president was worried most about two things: first, she didn't know how deep Dennison's plot went and who else in the top command he had managed to pick off; second, she knew she had to act fast, as the admiral in his role as chairman of the Joint Chiefs had already gone on television to announce the Second Expeditionary Force's success in cordoning off the capital and the president's assumption of command from a secret location. She knew she had to go live to the nation again, but first she had to make sure the army and air force were still on her side. There were strange reports that the First Cavalry was taking over military airports in Louisiana and Texas, and she needed to confer with

---

170 http://www.whiteoutpress.com/articles/2014/q3/leak-says-denver-secret-underground-us-capitol.

Warren Taylor about the status of the army in all this. She ordered the secretary of defense to call General Taylor immediately after Dennison's speech, and she was glad to hear the general's voice at the other end of the phone as it picked up.

"General, thanks for taking my call," said the secretary. "If you don't mind, I've got the president on speaker. We don't know how or why it happened, but Admiral Dennison seems to have gone haywire and taken some of the marines with him—Cummings and that young General Hernandez, for sure. We need your advice on how we can use the army to counterattack."

The other end was silent for a moment. "Well, we already have the First Cavalry taking on the militias along the Red River, so the best bet is to march the First Infantry eastward."

The secretary then asked, "Have you been in touch with General Covington at Third Corps?"

"Yeah, Covington's involved, but he's real short, less than two weeks from I've heard."

"So are you going to order him to move his First Infantry to DC in the next few days?"

Again, there was a pause at the other end. "I can certainly do so, but I think we've got something more pressing to deal with. You need to look at the news channels—right now!"

The president did just that, and she began to witness one of the strangest live streams ever on American television. News helicopters showed a long line of Abrams tanks and Bradley fighting vehicles leaving Fort Hood and moving north on Texas State Highway 36. All the tanks had their tops open, and soldiers in their helmets were smiling and waving at onlookers along the way. In the lead tank was none other than Major General Enrique Ybarra. The president's jaw dropped as she saw the images of the general waving to the public, and then her face grew red.

"Goddammit, General!" the president yelled into the speaker phone. "What the hell's going on down there in Texas? I need you to get in touch with Covington *A-S-A-P* so he can rein in his troops. All we needed him to do was head to the Red River and arrest those goddamned conspiracy nuts, and instead, he's got a bunch of rogue generals ridin' their damn tanks all over the state!"

"Understood. I'll be glad to talk to him."

"And, General, I need you to get the First Infantry on to DC as soon as they can get their butts in gear. I want them to wipe the shit out of Dennison and his traitor buddies!"

"Copy that, ma'am."

****

Despite the late-summer Texas heat, Enrique Ybarra could feel the breeze as his tank plowed along at thirty miles per hour. He knew he could make it at least to Santa Fe before anyone could stop him. Then facing the Fourth Infantry under Brigadier General TJ Matthews, the moment of truth would come.

He had worked feverishly, staying up late at nights, making sure the First Battalion was readying itself for its march into destiny. He knew his troops would respond. He was a legend to them, and they trusted in him completely. He had taken the Fifth and Eighth Cavalry regiments out of Rackley's Second Combat Brigade Team, along with parts of several support regiments and the Rolling Thunder artillery battalion. He prepared for a two-week deployment, knowing that any confrontation wouldn't last beyond that. All told, he had over one hundred Abrams and Bradleys along with a similar number of armored personnel carriers, carrying a total of nearly five thousand troops. He regretted that his little venture was costing taxpayers over thirty thousand dollars per mile, but he knew it was a small price to pay when weighed against the cost to the American people if Dennison's coup failed.

He left in midmorning and made it to Abilene by early afternoon. He had tried to embrace Monica that morning, but she wasn't in the mood. With events happening as fast as they were, all he could do was text her and Sofia and Sydney once he was under way. He wrote that he was leading some cavalry regiments into West Texas and that they would see him on the news but not to worry. He finished with the same words—"Luv u"—to all three of them.

By the time he reached Abilene, the news of his armored thrust into West Texas had gone viral, and people flocked by the thousands along Interstate 20 to view the remarkable site of over one hundred Abrams and Bradleys and other vehicles traversing the West Texas plains. As the convoy passed by one city and town after another—Sweetwater, Big Spring, Midland, Odessa, Monahans, and, finally, Pecos—Enrique had the "Army Goes Rolling Along" and some stirring Sousa marches and even the old cavalry song "The Yellow Rose of Texas" blaring from loudspeakers near the front. Folks in West Texas didn't know what to make of what all was going on. They had a general dislike of the federal government, but they also took pride in the United States Army, in which many of them had served. People of all ages and ethnic groups stood watching at major locales, some silently, some cheering and waving American flags, long into the night. Most bystanders were simply curious and were wondering if Enrique's convoy must be part of the martial law imposition. No one outside of Dennison and a few of his closest allies knew for sure where he was headed or what his purpose was.

But as Enrique and his legions passed Pecos and turned northwest along United States Route 285 headed into New Mexico, the president started getting worried. *By god, that bastard is coming for me . . . I can't believe he would be so stupid!* In her feverish mind, she then started to mount a series of defenses that she knew would thwart Ybarra's convoy and lead to the crushing of Dennison's entire coup attempt.

Bystanders who had waited through the night in Carlsbad, New Mexico, to watch as Enrique's convoy passed through knew nothing of the president's last-ditch efforts. One of those bystanders was a driller at a Permian Basin oil field near Hobbes, New Mexico, who had driven almost an hour to Carlsbad with his wife and family in tow. About three in the morning, with little Carlos asleep at his feet and Sabrina at his side holding their newborn baby, the Albanian immigrant Davud Haxhi—in reality, Danio

Chiapetto—watched as Enrique's lead tank passed by. Of all the spectators that night, Danio was the only one who knew that the general standing and waving in the lead tank was the brother of the man who ended up saving his life, both literally and figuratively, but at the price of his own. *Buona fortuna amico mio.*

CHAPTER 26

From her bunker inside Denver International, the president knew she had to do something, and fast. The first order of business was to reconnect with Taylor and find out what new orders had been given. Then she had to prepare the air force for a strike on Ybarra and his men so his convoy would be stopped dead in its tracks. If all else failed, she could still play her last card, using the Fourth Infantry out of Fort Carson to block Ybarra's movement and gain her the time needed to rally the country behind her.

The president now recognized how the cuts in the military she had supported—along with the continued massive deployment of troops overseas, which she also promoted—left her so vulnerable at home. Of the total active-duty ground forces in the military, the army had 460,000 and the marines had another 180,000.[171] Almost 100,000 army troops were overseas, though, and a lot of the ones in the continental United States were devoted to specialized or support roles. There were less than 250,000 troops in ground combat divisions stateside, but over 50,000 were on the West Coast and directly or indirectly controlled by the United States Pacific Command. If Dennison and his gang could usurp both the Second Expeditionary Force *and* the First Cavalry Division, they would have a commanding share of the military's overall domestic combat capability. Even as she was strategizing her next moves, she had a sinking feeling that she was surrounded and in serious trouble.

---

171 See http://www.globalsecurity.org/military/agency/end-strength.htm for projected 2017 troop levels.

She further pondered how she had underestimated—in fact, never even thought about—how easy it would be to carry off a military coup, with most of the combat troops on American soil confined to a handful of divisions. She further blamed herself for misreading Dennison and his generals. She never really had a feel for the military or, for that matter, men in general. She had never gotten along with her harsh and domineering father while growing up, she loathed her two brothers for always belittling her when she was young, and her marriage to her husband was a sham. She had never played sports and didn't understand why men found them so important and energizing. In fact, she had taken the military for granted. In her mind, Dennison and Cummings were simply trained to take orders, and she was destined to give them. Other than the fact that she thought older white males like them were always trying to block women from getting ahead in the world, she couldn't care less how they thought and acted when she wasn't around.

Her mind went back to that fateful meeting when she and her husband first met the Bilderberger men who would ultimately determine the course of his and her political lives. It was at the university, where her husband had attracted their interest because of his folksy intellectual charm and hint of a corruptible ambition that the cabal realized could propel him to become a major political figure someday. Little did she know that she and her husband were about to make a deal with the devil, that they would have to perform many a nasty deed on their end over the years, from looking the other way during CIA drug-running to sponsoring the overthrow of recalcitrant foreign leaders. She had her own agenda, and in her mind, the "other stuff" was more than offset by the good she was going to accomplish by her rise to the top of the political world—namely, to enhance the status of women at home and worldwide. This latest action she had to perform for the cabal—implementing martial law against the militias—was actually one she relished. In her eyes, the right-wing militiamen were nothing but misogynistic, racist brutes who stood in the way of her political vision for America. *All the better if a whole of lot of the right-wing lunatic media fringe were taken out as well.*

A quick text from the secretary of defense took her out of her ruminations and forced her to confront the situation at hand. The president placed a call to General Taylor, but strangely he was of out of communication. She then connected with General Covington and tried to get some answers, along with quick action. This time, when Covington got on the line, the president herself did the talking.

"General, this is the president. I'm flabbergasted at the situation down there in Texas. You've got a couple of outlaw generals running wild, all the way from Louisiana to New Mexico, shutting down airports and doing everything but what I ordered."

"I understand your concerns, Madam President."

"Yes, of course, you understand, General," she said sarcastically. "My question is, *what are you doing about it?* Have you mobilized the First Infantry to go east yet, and have you called your sidekicks Rackley and Ybarra back from their prancing about all over the southwest?"

"I'm sorry, Madam President, my orders are to have the First stand down and let General Ybarra and his troops accomplish their missions."

The president's eyes were bulging in rage. "And who the fuck gave you those orders, General?" she shrieked.

"My orders came straight from General Taylor."

The president's mind started exploding. *So Taylor's on Dennison's goddamned team too. How can this all be happening!* The president tried to control her rage and, in a few seconds, calmed down enough to reply to Covington.

"Well, General, you may have been taking orders from General Taylor, but now you're taking orders from me. And I want the First mobilized immediately and Ybarra and his legion to return to base!"

There was silence on the other end of the line until Covington replied in a firm voice, "I'm sorry, but I can't do that, Madam President. My superior is General Taylor, and the Third Corps takes its orders only from him."

The president's end abruptly went dead.

****

The president next turned to General Michael Posvar, chief of staff of the United States Air Force. He had deliberately been kept in the dark by Dennison, and now he felt not only loyalty to the commander-in-chief but also a sense of betrayal by the other chiefs. When the president requested his help, he immediately drew up a plan to go after Enrique's troops first and then follow it up with an attack on Hernandez's Second Expeditionary units.

With most of the nearby airfields disabled by Rackley's troops, Posvar decided to deploy bombers out of Cannon Air Force Base in Clovis, New Mexico, and two squadrons of fighters from Davis-Monthan Air Force Base in Tucson. He knew the First Cavalry had some limited anti-aircraft capability but not against the fast movers, and he figured a couple of quick strikes could prevent the convoy from reaching Santa Fe and force it into a retreat.

Back in Washington, Admiral Dennison had already anticipated by several moves the president's orders and Posvar's response. He had his submarine captains off the East and West Coasts on alert, with plans already drawn up for a cruise missile attack on the very bases from which the air force attack would be launched. The USS *Blackfish Two*, submerged in one hundred and fifty meters of water less than ten kilometers off the Southern California coast, was assigned the duty of carrying out the preemptive attack on the two air force bases.

Commander Jessica Beasley, finishing up her third tour of the Pentagon, was in the control room of the joint task force that Dennison had hastily assembled to coordinate the attack. She was now the wife of Jerry Lear and the mother of one-year-old William James Lear and soon to be an instructor in Fundamentals of Naval Intelligence at Annapolis. Shortly after the orders from General Posvar were handed on down to the bomber and fighter wings, Beasley relayed the orders from Dennison for the *Blackfish Two* to fire its missiles.

Captain Billingsley of the *Blackfish Two* was hesitant. "This could be viewed as treason, Commander, and I'm not sure I could ever kill another fellow American deliberately, no matter the circumstances."

"You're not being asked to kill anyone, Captain. All that's involved is shooting a bunch of missiles at a couple of runways. We're not planning for anyone to get hurt . . . maybe a few aircraft damaged or destroyed, that's it. What you're doing is sending a message, not a deathblow."

The captain remained adamant. "Tell Admiral Dennison that I'm not sure I can go through with this. At the very least, I need a direct order from him."

Beasley was frustrated. "C'mon, Captain, we're running out of time." As her moments with Enrique flickered rapidly in her mind, she implored Billingsley to attack. "In a matter of hours at most, one of our finest generals with two Silver Stars pinned to him is going to be cut down by a bunch of five-hundred-pounders rained from the sky. Are you willing to let that happen?"

When Billingsley returned her plea with silence, Admiral Dennison's face suddenly appeared on a new screen. "Excuse me, Captain, Admiral Dennison here. I understand your reluctance, but extraordinary circumstances call for extraordinary leadership. You've got everything in place—*now do it!*"

With that last plea from Dennison, Billingsley finally mustered an "Aye, aye, sir." Within minutes, two dozen of his cruise missiles had struck their targets, producing huge craters in the runways of Cannon and Davis-Monthan Air Bases and destroying a few nearby aircraft but avoiding any serious casualties. The missile attacks only shut down air operations at those bases temporarily, but their main purpose was to send a message, which came through loud and clear to a stunned General Posvar: *Stand down, General . . . or you'll lose a lot more of your assets to a foe you can't see.*[172]

****

The president was already in the midst of playing her last card when the news from Davis-Monthan and Cannon came through. Though desperate, she felt confident that she could get the commander of the Fourth Infantry Division, Brigadier General Terence Jackson Matthews, to deploy to the New Mexico border and stop Ybarra's troops dead in their tracks. True, Ybarra evidently carried a lot of the First Cavalry's firepower with him, but it could be stopped by a well-armed infantry division with firepower of its own, including anti-tank missiles.

The reason she was confident was that Matthews's father, Loren, was a member of the Deep State cabal's inner circle. After leaving the military, Matthews Senior became the chief operating officer of the nation's second-largest defense contractor as well as a leading member of the Council on Foreign Relations[173] and a key adviser to several Democratic presidents. She had socialized

---

172 The military branches are known to differ in their political opinions, and it has been speculated that they might respond in a similar manner as has been fictionalized here in response to a perceived threat to the Constitution: http://www.thecommonsenseshow. com/2015/05/24/prominent-lt-general-tells-dave-hodges-of-the-coming-civil-war. Scenarios involving branches of the military fighting against one another have also been envisioned, and there is a certain plausibility that the relative invulnerability of sea-based firepower may be important in the short run: https://www.quora.com/ What-is-the-most-powerful-branch-of-the-United-States-military.

173 The Council on Foreign Relations is considered the "intellectual arm" of the Bilderberger group in the United States, and membership in it is almost a requirement to attain a top-level cabinet appointment in the U.S. government. See James Perloff, *The Shadows of Power: The Council on Foreign Relations and the American Decline* (Western Islands, 1988).

frequently with him and even remembered vaguely seeing TJ as a young man. She would ask Loren to help convince his son that he needed to step up and heroically defend the republic against an unconstitutional and unprecedented military coup and that if he didn't, the consequences would be disastrous for the future prospects of American democracy, turning the United States into a North American version of a banana republic, where military coups were like a revolving door.

The president knew that if Matthews could hold the line, she'd have enough time to rally her supporters. Though hated by a large segment of the American public, she was an iconic figure to others, serving as the first woman president and preaching women's rights and tolerance at home and firmness abroad. It didn't matter that most of the foreign ventures that her Bilderberger masters had ordered her to support over the years resulted in the replacement of mostly secular regimes by Islamic republics in which the status of women suffered badly, nor that her power brokers might be rich male bankers and industrialists and their mostly male friends in the media and intelligence circles. Her ground support came from women and minorities, for she was the master of identity politics, playing the different ethnic and gender communities off against the "white male establishment." She knew that if the Fourth Infantry could hold its ground, she could go live on national television and rally her troops, pointing to Dennison, Cummings, and Taylor as epitomes of the reactionary, undemocratic, racist extremism that was growing in America and that she was determined to stamp out. She would, of course, neglect to mention that the two famed young generals spearheading the charge against her were both Mexican-Americans.

What the president hadn't counted on was that TJ Matthews had a complicated, even troubled, relationship with his overbearing father and was not about to kowtow to him in a situation where his superior officer had ordered his troops to stand down. Nor had she reckoned that, almost two decades earlier, TJ Matthews had been rescued under withering sniper fire from his burning Bradley Fighting Vehicle in Tal Afar, Nineveh Province, by the very man who was leading his troops up from Santa Fe to her bunker at Denver International. Most importantly, she hadn't realized that Major General Enrique Ybarra had already had a long and cordial conversation with the leader of the Fourth Infantry two hours earlier.

When Enrique entered Colorado Springs meeting no resistance from Fort Carson and the Fourth Infantry, the president knew it was over, not just for her but for the entire Deep State that had controlled the American government since World War II. She hastily called John Dennison to negotiate the terms of her surrender. She was relieved when the admiral told her that an arrest by General Ybarra was not imminent and that all she and her vice president and top cabinet officials needed to do at this point was to offer their resignations and make it seem as though she was doing so because of a "failure to perform her responsibilities as commander-in-chief in an effective and principled manner." Dennison's ultimate gambit paid off—not only had he pulled off the only military coup in the history of the United States flawlessly and bloodlessly, but the majority of Americans never even realized that presidential authority had ever been usurped.

CHAPTER 27

With the president and vice president gone, along with the secretaries of state, defense, and treasury, the speaker of the House of Representatives was the next in line in the presidential succession. Eric McKinney, representing the Third Congressional District of Oklahoma, had laid low during the martial law but now was about to give the speech of his life to a confused and worried American public. His task before him was fourfold: to announce the lifting of martial law; to thank the military for its bravery and restraint during the martial law, in which no loss of life had occurred; to reassure the American public that the "great American experience with democracy" had survived yet another crisis of governance and that the republic would continue to stand strong in the coming days; and, finally, to hint that the American people would witness a new openness and transparency in their federal government in the coming months. He promised the protesters gathered in Texas and outside Washington that the government would no longer pursue its land claim along the Red River—the dispute that had ignited the entire crisis—and that the hundreds of thousands of protesters outside the capital would be granted a one-day permit the coming weekend for a peaceful rally on the national mall to air their views as long as they didn't bring their arms with them since open-carry was illegal in the city. He then trusted that all of them would return to their cities and towns and farms afterward so the life of the nation's capital could return to normal.

Although the protesters did, in fact, disperse after the rally, the political life of Washington underwent a veritable revolution. Eric McKinney was, besides being a prominent Republican politician, a closet Truther who had relished for decades the opportunity to see justice done for the victims of the Oklahoma City bombings and the World Trade Center and what he believed were various other false flag events on American soil—most of which had led to the increasing restriction of civil liberties.[174] As Congress voted for an extended recess to allow the political tensions to cool, McKinney managed by executive action to create and fund various "truth and reconciliation" commissions—all streamed live to the American people—and ordered the release of millions of sensitive documents related to the government's role in some of the most controversial and notorious of these events. At first, few realized how consequential the commissions would be, but when McKinney's new handpicked attorney general threatened to open some of the past events as legal matters and that anyone not testifying completely and truthfully in front of the commissions would be subsequently prosecuted for treasonous crimes that had no statute of limitation, the trickle of individuals who testified before the commissions soon turned into a torrent. None of those testifying

---

174 Some of the most prominent false flag attacks that have been exposed are Operation Gladio (https://wikispooks.com/wiki/Operation_Gladio) and Operation Northwoods (http://911review.com/precedent/century/northwoods.html). The alleged purpose of false flags is to frighten the public and to turn it against a real or imagined enemy and to allow governments to curtail civil liberties. For example, two of the most widely alleged false flags of the last twenty-five years on American soil were followed by legislation curtailing civil liberties: 1) the bombing of the Alfred P. Murrah Building in Oklahoma City in 1995 (http://freemindfilms.com/films/anoblelie) was followed by the Antiterrorism and Effective Death Penalty Act of 1996 (http://www.nytimes.com/1995/04/21/us/terror-oklahoma-congress-anti-terrorism-bill-blast-turns-snail-into-race-horse.html); and 2) The attack on September 11 was quickly followed authorization of the USA PATRIOT Act (https://en.wikipedia.org/wiki/Patriot_Act).

knew what documents or other evidence the government held in its possession, so almost all told the truth of their involvements, even at the cost of their reputations. In the end, thousands of politicians, former cabinet secretaries, law enforcement personnel, intelligence and military officers, financiers, leading media figures, and even prominent scientists admitted to participating in the actual events or the cover-ups of false flags ranging from Oklahoma City to September 11 to the anthrax attacks and even smaller affairs such as the Boston Marathon bombings. The American people watched the death throes of the Deep State with a combination of fascination and revulsion until they couldn't stand any more sordid accounts of the cabal's high crimes and misdemeanors. What most stunned the public was how many individuals in the media and scientific and other professions were secretly working for the Deep State over the decades to maintain the monstrous deceptions associated with the false flags. Almost all the prominent media and scientific collaborators lost their jobs, including the uncloaked government shill Ronnie Williams of *Patriot-News*. Several dozen congressmen and senators even ended up testifying, and all of them later resigned or declined to run in the upcoming elections. Eventually, calls were made to do away with the commissions and for the government, now armed with the massive testimony of thousands of conspirators, to void the immunity agreements and prosecute some of the worst offenders. President McKinney remained adamant that getting out the entire truth was the sweetest vengeance for victims and that justice for those who perpetuated the heinous acts would occur when they "met their maker". Many in the Deep State ranks did just that, and quickly, preferring to take their own lives rather than face the ignominy of testifying before the commissions or living with the testimony they were forced to provide. Although the suicide rate for the entire nation registered only a modest blip in the actuarial statistics that year, a noticeable spike occurred in the rate for wealthy, powerful white males in the northeast.

The truth about the false flags leading to the recent imposition of martial law also was brought forth during the commission's testimony. The ex-president and her vice president did not end up testifying themselves in public but did submit written responses to questions posed by individual Truth and Reconciliation commission members. Technically, the president and vice president were free from prosecution and could move about freely, but the secret agreement with Dennison stipulated that they would never be allowed to participate in public discourse again—essentially a "political house arrest." The restriction was basically moot in that the president and vice president were so hated by most of the nation now that, had they attempted to reenter political life, no one could guarantee their safety.

In contrast, the story of how Admiral Dennison and his group of generals "helped save the republic" became enshrined in legend, leading President McKinney to award an unprecedented joint Medal of Honor to all the generals involved. With the presidential elections approaching, there were loud calls for Dennison to run for president, especially since he had announced his retirement shortly after the lifting of martial law. Dennison, who decided to run as an independent, had the support of key political figures from both the Republican and Democratic parties and was considered pretty much of a shoo-in. At the very least, he had the vote of one key voter in Texas, who knew firsthand about Dennison's bravery, strategic vision, moral clarity, and unsurpassed leadership. *Yes,* Enrique thought, *Jessica was right: Dennison is a great man . . . and I can always say I had the honor of being at his side when the republic was on the line.*

There were also calls for John Hernandez and Enrique to run for office. Hernandez actually took the bait, declaring himself a candidate for governor of California on the Republican ticket shortly after retiring. After decades of electoral frustration, the Republican establishment was salivating at his chances of winning the governorship and breaking the stranglehold of the Democrats in Sacramento. After all, who could vote against a native Californian of Mexican-American ancestry, a Medal of Honor winner, and war hero who led the Second Marine Expeditionary Force in resolutely defending the United States against a usurping

Democratic president? It turned out that a slight majority of the Golden State electorate could and did vote against him, which shocked the Republicans into the final realization that there was virtually nothing under the sun that would keep the majority of Californians from abandoning the Democratic Party ranks.

Enrique texted Hernandez after his electoral loss, joshing, "Despite the hosing, I still love ya, man!"

To which Hernandez replied, "FU, Gomer . . . See if you can piss any better!"

Enrique hadn't seen his marine brother since the Medal of Honor ceremony the previous year, and they rarely talked on the phone. They hardly needed to anymore—a few periodic quips and razzing were enough to remind each other of the deep bond that was forged by their shared tragedies and sacrifices and their dramatic moment in history.

After finishing his army commitment, Enrique was also approached by politicians to run for governor in Texas, especially by Democrats, who were almost as hapless in the Lone Star State as the Republicans were in California. But Enrique never took up Hernandez's challenge, preferring to stay at home and occasionally make speeches and work on his memoirs. He vowed he wasn't ever going to leave Monica again but instead would wait it out until she started warming up to him. He could see she was slowly coming around, as her once-acrimonious interactions started to mellow; and occasionally, they would even share a laugh together. He also knew that she was impressed with the role he had played during the martial law, although she wasn't effusive in her praise. Although she still wasn't sleeping with him, he at least had moved from the couch to one of the girls' beds. Then something came along that peeked his interest: his alma mater was looking for a new president, and Enrique decided to apply even though he didn't have all that much of an academic pedigree. Enrique was totally surprised when he was offered the presidency of the Texas A&M system, only the second Hispanic-American to ever be offered the position, even though Enrique had seen too much of the world and learned from too many people of all backgrounds to even feel Mexican-American anymore.

That evening, he gingerly walked into the bedroom to announce the news to her. "Monica," he said, "I know I broke my word to you, and I wasn't always there when you needed me. But I'm never going to leave you again, unless . . ."

"Unless what?" she replied suspiciously.

"Unless you're okay with it."

"Don't beat around the bush, Kiki. Okay with what?"

Enrique took a deep breath. "A few months ago, I applied to A&M . . . Maybe you heard they were looking for a new president. I really didn't think they'd get back to me, but I just received an offer from them today." He paused. "I told them I'd think it over. But I'm not going to take it unless you agree to come with me."

Monica looked away, as if in thought. "There you go again, Kiki." Then she smiled and said, "Dammit, how did you know that I always wanted to be the wife of a college president?"

Enrique was taken aback by her words and especially when Monica got up from the bed and put her arms around him. Though he rarely showed his emotions, Enrique released years of emotional turmoil and separation and sequestered grief over the loss of his brothers as he broke down and cried on her shoulders, while clutching her tightly. His catharsis revealed the deep gratitude he now felt for her forgiveness and restoration of love.

Then Monica started to well up. "Kiki, I never should have lost faith in you. What you did for our girls and all the others by standing up for the country was magnificent. Don't worry about what's happened in the past. I'll always be proud to be your wife."

Then she smiled and added in a very coy voice, "Besides, what girl wouldn't want to tag along with a guy who looked so handsome gallivanting all over West Texas with his head popped out of that big tank!"

Enrique couldn't contain his laugh, and for the first time in many years, he and Monica made love.